WITCH QUEEN BOOK ONE

THE DARKEST NIGHT

A.D. STARRLING

COPYRIGHT

CHAPTER ONE

THE DEAD MAN WORE RED SHOES. THEY WERE BRAND-new, wholecut, Italian-leather Oxfords and looked to be worth about half her paycheck. Hana Mae Jin studied the gory bloodstains dulling the expensive material.

There's not enough hydrogen peroxide in the world to get rid of those.

She removed the items from the dead man's feet and placed them in a labeled bag on the steel countertop to her left. The man's clothes followed. Soon, he was a cold, stiff body lying on the autopsy table, head propped up by a plastic block and naked but for the yellow I.D. tag on his toe.

Alexei 'Colin' Antonovich had died from a single bullet wound to the head. The police report accompanying the corpse indicated he was a member of *Oniks*, a Russian crime gang that started operating in New York a year ago. *Oniks*'s rapidly growing influence in the city's underworld meant they were now in conflict with the more established gangs in Brooklyn and Queens, a fact NYPD and the forensic pathology centers working under the aegis of the Office of the Chief Medical Examiner were all too aware of from the mounting body count this summer. As far as the cops knew, *Oniks* was operating independently of the most powerful Russian crime syndicate in New York, a fact both law enforcement and city officials found puzzling.

The gang's specialty was protection rackets and loan-shark operations. The detectives in charge of Antonovich's murder case had reconstructed his movements from Brooklyn to Queens late last night from his phone GPS. The working theory was that Antonovich had been lured to an alleyway in Ozone Park by rival gang members or a would-be victim before meeting his untimely death. His body was discovered under a subway overpass close to the 88th Boyd Ave station at 4 a.m. by someone out for an early morning run.

Bar the bullet wound to his head, Antonovich bore no signs of physical injury. His attackers had stripped him of his wallet and the gun that had been registered to his name, but left his clothes and shoes intact. Considering Antonovich's suit cost almost as much as his Oxfords, Mae could only presume his killers didn't fancy wearing a dead man's outfit.

She glanced at the digital clock on the wall to her left and grimaced at the time. It was already past 7 p.m.

Rose is gonna be pissed if I miss our dinner date again.

She sent a quick text to her best friend, left her phone on the worktop at the end of the room, and returned to the autopsy table. She adjusted her splash shield before picking up a scalpel from the instrument tray to her right.

This was her tenth postmortem of the day.

She should have clocked out an hour ago, but had agreed to stay behind and finish this one last job. With three mortuary assistants and two pathologists on sick leave across the forensic autopsy centers that served the city, the labs at Grandview General Hospital had been swamped as of late. Everyone had done overtime this month, including Steve Hodge, the director of pathology services.

With the detectives investigating Antonovich's murder having impressed upon Hodge the urgency of obtaining a full autopsy report on the Russian mobster, Mae hadn't begrudged her boss his decision when he'd assigned her the case that morning. Hodge was also working overtime in the lab next door and would likely be there well after she left.

A trickle of sweat danced down Mae's back as she stretched out the kinks in her neck. The unusually oppressive heat that had lingered over the city these past couple of weeks made for unpleasant working conditions, even in the air-conditioned rooms in the basement of the hospital. She promised herself a cold shower as soon as she finished, started the digital voice recorder and transcription software on the mobile computer station, and made the first incision.

Skin and flesh gave way smoothly under her blade. It didn't take her long to extract and process the thoracic and abdominal organs, her movements swift and efficient from thousands of hours of practice, her voice the only sound breaking the silence as she dictated her findings. She'd left the dead man's innards in their respective blocks on the adjacent metal table, separated his scalp from his skull, and just reached for the electric saw to cut into the bone when she heard the outer door to the lab open. A tall, pretty blonde with clear gray eyes came through the inner door a moment later.

Kathryn Rose Blake's gold sneakers squeaked to a halt on the linoleum floor. Her eyebrows drew together as she looked from Mae to the saw and the body on the autopsy table. The third-year surgical resident propped her hands on her hips and tapped out an impatient beat with her left foot, the pink-sapphire bracelet Mae had given her as a birthday gift glittering at her wrist.

"Our reservation is in twenty minutes, Mae."

Mae sighed. "I know. Did you get my message?"

"Why do you think I'm here?" Rose grumbled. "You realize you canceled on me last time too, right?"

"Yeah, sorry about that."

Rose's frown deepened. "You don't sound the least bit remorseful. May I remind you that I missed out on getting laid because you bailed on me?"

Mae rolled her eyes hard. "I wish you'd stop organizing our dinner dates in places where you want to pick up guys. It's unhygienic."

"This from a woman about to carve out a dead man's brain." Rose shrugged. "I don't see the problem. Two birds, one stone. We're both busy and don't have time for a relationship. And, FYI, you could really do with letting off some steam the old-fashioned way. A vibrator may be a girl's best friend, but yours is gonna explode from overuse."

"Please leave Bob out of this conversation," Mae muttered as she applied the saw to Antonovich's skull. The blade came to life with a smooth whir. "I thought you had a hot date with Tom the ob-gyn last week?"

"I did." Rose made a face. "Turns out Tom doesn't push my buttons in the bedroom."

Mae paused, surgical saw aloft and surprise pasted across her face behind her splash shield. "But he's an ob-gyn."

"That just means he knows his anatomy, Mae," Rose said in the tone of one addressing a half-wit. "It doesn't mean he can light my fire."

Mae pursed her lips. Considering how frequently and easily Rose's fire could be lit, Tom the ob-gyn must have been crushed by his failure.

Rose propped herself up on an empty autopsy table and dropped her messenger bag next to her. "How about I keep you company while you finish up? That way you won't run out on me like last time."

Mae sighed and brought her focus back to the saw.

CHAPTER TWO

"You know, I didn't actually run out on you, right? I had a family emergency."

Rose wrinkled her nose. "Your family emergency was your grandmother setting you up on another marriage meeting."

Mae couldn't well argue with that statement.

Even though she was born and raised in Queens, her South Korean family insisted on her and her younger sister Ryu So-Young following the customs of the country they had left behind when they emigrated to the States. Two of those traditions were *So-gae* and *Seon*, which literally translated to 'introduction' and 'marriage meeting.' At the ripe old age of twenty-eight, Mae was fast losing her value as a prospective bride, a fact her mother and grandmother never failed to remind her of.

Mae's mouth tightened.

She wasn't sure how much longer she was willing to indulge their desperate matchmaking attempts. She shuddered when she recalled the last suitor they had arranged for her to meet, the night she'd bailed on Rose.

The accountant's pasty complexion and stout appearance had reminded her of a *songpyeon*, the doughy, mung-bean-filled, half-moon rice cake her mother liked to make for afternoon tea.

Since Rice Cake had chosen a pricey place for their date and was picking up the bill, Mae had decided to overlook his sweaty hands and feverish eyes in favor of the delicious food. The meeting would have ended the way all of Mae's *So-gaes* did, if not for Rice Cake's wandering fingers. Guilt shot through her as she put down the saw and lifted the dome of Antonovich's skull.

I probably shouldn't have hit him as hard as I did.

Though there'd been plenty of witnesses who'd seen the guy fondle her ass without her permission as they were preparing to leave the restaurant, Mae still hadn't heard the end of it from her mother and her grandmother.

Apparently, kicking Rice Cake in the balls before finishing him off with a vicious left hook had been a step too far and not the kind of behavior expected from a polite young lady seeking a wedding match.

"It's a miracle he hasn't sued us," Ye-Seul Hwang had grumbled upon hearing the news of her granddaughter's violent transgression from their neighbor Mrs. Son-Ha, AKA Koreatown's official busybody and first-class muckraker. "Never mind what this will do to your chances of landing another marriage meeting. Mr. Poh thinks you should lie low for a few weeks."

"For the hundredth time, I'm *not* interested in getting married right now," Mae had objected, doing her best not to make her words come out a wail. "Nor do I want you and Poh to set me up on any more crazy-ass dates."

"Language, young lady," her mother Yoo-Mi had warned coolly. "Mr. Poh is the best matchmaker in the city." Her mouth flattened to a thin line, a sure sign she was moments away from blowing a fuse. "You should be grateful your father and I even allowed you to leave home and get your own apartment. You don't know half the gossip we have to suffer through from Mrs. Son-Ha and her friends about having an unmarried daughter not living under the family roof." She sniffed. "They think you're fornicating with foreign men."

Bob the vibrator and the handful of guys she'd slept with since she lost her virginity in college had flashed before Mae's eyes at that.

"Why, they practically called you a jizz," Ye-Seul had added with a soured expression.

Mae had choked on her tea. Yoo-Mi had turned an alarming shade of red.

"Do you mean Jezebel?" Mae's sister Ryu had asked carefully. "Jizz means something, er, different."

"Yes, that Jeze word," Ye-Seul had concurred with some vigorous head bobbing. "What does jizz mean?" she'd asked curiously, much to Yoo-Mi's horror.

Ryu had waved a dismissive hand. "Never mind

that. Personally, I think Mae should have ripped that guy's dick off and fed it to Mrs. Son-Ha's dogs."

She'd made a slicing movement across her raised left middle finger and ignored the glare Yoo-Mi had shot at her.

"What am I to do with the two of you?" their mother had finally said in a heavy voice. "All I want is your happiness. After everything you've sacrificed for this family, you both deserve that."

Her chin had wobbled and her eyes had glistened with a shimmer of tears.

Remorse and frustration had swept through Mae at the quiet accusation behind Yoo-Mi's words. She'd seen the same emotions flash in Ryu's eyes and almost wished she hadn't come home for Sunday dinner.

Their mother still hadn't forgiven herself for the fact that Mae had had to give up her surgical residency at Grandview General to manage the family's funeral home three years ago, after their father's sudden death from a heart attack. Or that, instead of pursuing a promising MBA, Ryu had taken over the job of funeral home director from Mae a year and a half later, after graduating in the top ten percent of her class from one of New York's most prestigious business schools.

Mae had forgone returning to her surgical residency program and signed up to be a mortuary assistant at Grandview General, mostly so she could carry on helping out at the funeral home until they appointed someone they trusted to assist Ryu. Since theirs was the main funeral parlor catering to traditional death rites in Koreatown, the business was hectic even at the best of times.

Yoo-Mi had tried her best to learn the ropes and support Ryu. Having spent most of her adult life successfully running a home and bringing up a family, she had proven to be more of a hindrance than a help to Mae's younger sister.

It wasn't long after that that their mother had convinced herself marriage was the answer to her daughters' future happiness, something Mae and Ryu strongly suspected Mrs. Son-Ha had a hand in. Yoo-Mi and Ye-Seul had since pursued this avenue of action with a devotion that gave the two sisters regular indigestion.

"You heard anything from Rice Cake's lawyers yet?" Rose asked presently.

"Nah." Mae removed Antonovich's brain from the cranial vault and placed it on the examination table. "He was caught feeling me up on camera. He'll lose his state license if he tries to come after me. And technically, my reaction was self-defense, not assault."

Rose grinned. "You didn't tell him you were a kickboxing black belt, huh?"

"He found that out the hard way."

The bullet had crossed Antonovich's left frontal lobe and carved a destructive path straight through his midbrain before lodging in his right cerebellum. Which meant the shot had originated from high up. Considering the preciseness of the entry wound, Mae was willing to bet a hundred dollars this was a contract killing involving a sniper.

She carefully extracted the slug with some forceps and held it up to the light. Her eyes narrowed when she saw the striations on the surface. They were etched into the metal, as if the round had been ejected under super-heated conditions through the rifling. Mae placed the bullet in a petri dish, wondering what kind of gun could have produced such a devastating effect.

That's gonna be hard to match on the ballistics database.

An area in the midbrain caught her eye. She leaned in to take a closer look.

"Found something interesting?" Rose said.

"The pineal gland is enlarged." Mae paused, puzzled. "It doesn't look like a tumor though." She gently lifted the left thalamus aside. "It's almost as if—"

A beeping noise distracted her.

Rose reached for her messenger bag and took out her pager. Her face tightened when she read the message on the screen.

"Dammit. I gotta go. The guy I just operated on is hemorrhaging." She jumped down from the table and headed briskly for the door. "Looks like we're not gonna make that dinner date after all."

"Catch you on the rooftop when you're done?" Mae called out. "I'll get some sandwiches from the deli across the road."

Rose waved a hand on her way out of the room. "I want extra mustard on my pastrami!"

Mae smiled faintly as she listened to the door close.

However down she got about her life sometimes, Rose was always there to pick her up. They'd been best friends since their first day at college and roommates for most of their medical training. To Mae, Rose was the older sister she'd never had, even though their birthdays were barely a few months apart. Nothing would have made her happier than the two of them navigating their grueling surgical residencies together.

They'd even spoken of opening a clinic in Queens after they finished.

Alas, that dream had come to a crushing halt with the death of Mae's father. Still, she hoped they would eventually accomplish it. It might take a few more years than they'd anticipated, but Mae knew Rose would wait for her.

That's what best friends did.

Magic poured out of Nikolai Stanisic's soul, raw and powerful. Moonlight bathed him in pale radiance as he clenched his jaw and directed it into the complex runes he'd drawn out on the roof of the skyscraper overlooking 42nd Avenue. The air trembled around his fingers, subtle waves of heat and power distorting the atmosphere. The lines and symbols linking the six concentric circles started to shimmer as the spell took hold.

The crow on his shoulder shifted, claws gripping his jacket firmly. Alastair's wings trembled and his eyes glowed with an orange light as his own soul focused Nikolai's magic.

Nikolai blinked sweat out of his eyes and looked around the empty rooftop. He would have but minutes before his location was uncovered once the spell came to life. As a fugitive on the run from the Dark Council in a city teeming with magic users, he doubted there would be many who could resist the million-dollar bounty on his head.

His limbs grew heavy as the runes sucked out the power buried deep inside his body. Nikolai felt his familiar sway and steadied the bird with a gentle hand.

"Hold on, Al. We're almost there!"

The crow shook out his wings and rubbed his head gratefully against Nikolai's palm. Relief shot through him when he felt the bird's soul bind even more strongly with his own. They both needed to have their wits about them if this was to work.

A pillar of light some twenty feet tall flashed into existence around them seconds later, the ancient scripture making up its substance raising chills on Nikolai's flesh as it imprinted onto his and Alastair's bodies. Magic swamped the air. Nikolai gritted his teeth, the artifact he'd stolen from the Dark Council a cool presence against his chest.

It was the second time in as many days that he and Alastair were utilizing their powers at full strength. Still, compared to the spell they were about to unleash, the ritual they'd undergone the day before had been ten times worse.

Having succeeded in shielding his presence from the Dark Council sorcerers and witches his father and brother had sent after him as he raced across Europe, Nikolai had finally reached Paris at nightfall yesterday. He'd spent several hours searching for the closest compatible ley line upon which to carry out the dangerous rite he intended to perform, aware that time and his luck were running out. Just when he'd thought he wouldn't find such a place, he'd stumbled upon a deserted clearing in a forest to the north of the city, where the full moon had shone the brightest.

The silence of the glade he and Alastair had uncovered had been so eerie, Nikolai had been half-convinced it was a trap laid by his brother. It had taken nearly twenty minutes for him and his familiar to probe the area and ascertain there were no enemies around. Still, the absence of even nocturnal animal sounds had made the place seem unnatural and rendered Alastair restless.

It was as if the world itself had been holding its breath, waiting to see which devil would dance under the light of the moon that night.

The scrying ritual Nikolai had performed would normally have required at least six sorcerers or witches. To do it on his own risked him not only losing his mind and his soul to Hell itself, but his flesh to demonic possession. He'd had little choice in the matter though.

He'd needed to find the body of the woman whose soul was about to awaken if he wanted not just to avenge his mother's death and preserve the world of magic, but also to save the world itself.

The dark energy of the fallen angel who had gifted his race with Heavens' powers had almost overwhelmed Nikolai and his familiar halfway through the ceremony. They'd clung to each other grimly and to the white light that was ever present within them, the brightness of the first witch's energy a warm balm that had tempered the coldness of her demon lover's magic.

Nikolai had woken up on the cool, damp forest

floor at dawn, alone but for the crow who'd kept watch over him after he'd lost consciousness. The dullness of Alastair's feathers and eyes had spoken of the toll the ritual had taken upon the creature. Though Nikolai had wanted them both to rest and recover their energies, there had been no time to waste, for the scrying ceremony had worked.

Nikolai had seen the Witch Queen's soul awakening in the City of the Empire, AKA New York.

He'd used his contacts to find him a private plane to take him across the Atlantic and had landed at JFK Airport an hour ago. It hadn't taken him long to sense the all-too-familiar magic of the Dark Council as he'd made his way into the city.

His father and brother already had their forces in place.

Nikolai wasn't too worried about this yet. He suspected this was the case in every major city in the world right now. The seer whose vision had propelled his father to take action a couple of weeks ago had spoken of the Witch Queen's revival in a crowded metropolis, under a waning gibbous moon.

Nikolai had chosen a high-rise in Midtown Manhattan to create his and Alastair's next spell, this one also of a grade and complexity that should have necessitated several powerful magic users to put it in play. But it was yet another conjuration he and his familiar would have to do on their own.

What they were about to unleash on New York had one purpose and one purpose only. To hasten the awakening of the soul whose return his father and every Sorcerer King before him had long awaited. Once the spell took effect, it would give away his position to his father and brother's army. Nikolai just hoped he had enough strength to fight them off and find the Witch Queen before they did.

Static charged the atmosphere. The light making up the runes grew dazzling. Nikolai took a ragged breath.

Here we go.

He sensed the presence of the Dark Council even as the magic storm exploded across New York, its brilliance causing him to squint. The clouds parted on a violent wave of energy, roiling masses twisting angrily as they were unceremoniously pushed aside in an expanding circle several miles wide. The waning moon pierced the inky firmament in the fading brightness, a brilliant globe surrounded by glittering stars.

Darkness fell over the city, lights blinking out in large swathes across the boroughs, starting with Manhattan.

Nikolai's heart thundered against his ribs as he rose and turned to face the group of black-caped sorcerers and witches who'd appeared on the rooftop behind him, magic blazing from their hands and weapons, the eyes of their familiars full of loathing.

The watch on his right wrist transformed into a dark, double-ended spear as he directed what remained of his power into it. Alastair let loose a threatening squawk where he perched on his shoulder, wings fluttering agitatedly and body braced for battle.

Once again, Nikolai was thankful for the familiar his mother had gifted him when he was a child.

He clamped down on the dread swirling in the pit of his stomach and glared at the Dark Council members as they closed in on him.

"You're too late. The Witch Queen will awaken before you can get to her!"

"We'll see about that," someone said coldly to his left.

Ice filled Nikolai's veins.

Oscar Beneventi alighted soundlessly on the roof, his magic a black haze that cloaked his body and the wicked sword he wielded. His lynx, Drabek, coiled sinuously around his legs, the wild cat's hateful eyes aglow with a dark light.

Shit! What the hell is he doing here?

Nikolai ignored the cold fingers dancing down his spine.

"This is a surprise," he told his brother in a hard voice. "I thought you were in Budapest, licking our father's boots."

One of the sorcerers cursed and took a step forward, his weasel hissing at his feet. "How dare you insult our future king?!"

Oscar raised a hand. The sorcerer halted in his tracks and reluctantly returned to the offensive line at the silent command. Nikolai's brother pushed back his hood, exposing his red hair and gray eyes.

"Father wants to have a word with you, *Niko*."

Nikolai masked a shudder at the diminutive. He knew exactly what the current Sorcerer King intended to do to him if he got his hands on him. It didn't matter that he was one of two surviving heirs to his father's throne. He wouldn't walk away with just broken bones and bruises this time. Not after stealing the most closely guarded and valuable artifact in his father's personal vault.

A contemptuous expression distorted Oscar's face. "I'm going to enjoy watching you die, little brother. Just like your whore of a mother."

The scar on Nikolai's back flared hotly. Rage flooded his veins, ridding him of his fatigue. He straightened, his knuckles whitening on his spear.

Alastair's fury swirled inside him in a dark wave. The bird had been there the day Oscar had killed Nikolai's mother.

"Our father didn't marry any of the women he bedded and had children with, Oscar." Nikolai arched an eyebrow and smiled thinly. "Technically, that makes Ivanya the biggest whore of them all, don't you think?"

Oscar's pupils flared at the mention of his mother's name. His lips pulled back, baring his teeth. "Let's dance, little brother!"

He charged across the rooftop. Nikolai widened his stance and reached for his magic, his jaw set in a hard line.

A golden sphere streamed down from the sky and exploded on the ground next to Oscar's left foot. He cursed and staggered to a stop.

Nikolai looked up in time to see a powerful purple spell drop on his brother. He shielded his eyes, the light of the explosion dazzling him for an instant. The heat from the blast washed over him and ruffled his hair.

Who—?!

"Incoming!" someone shouted jovially above them.

"We were supposed to blast him together, you ass!" someone else snapped.

Before Nikolai could seek out his unknown allies, a beam of crimson light detonated silently half a mile southeast of the high-rise, close to the river. It shot up into the sky and lit the gibbous moon, turning it a glorious vermilion.

Magic rolled across New York in a blood-red wave that made the very air tremble. It was wild and free and so formidable Nikolai had to grind his teeth and lean his body into it to stop from falling over. He shuddered when he sensed its echo deep inside his body and within his soul, the magic seeping into his flesh to seek out the core of power that dwelled in his very bones. He didn't doubt that everyone on that rooftop was experiencing the same overwhelming feeling of dread at what they could sense.

They all stared at the column of red light as it slowly fizzled out. Even Oscar looked pale where he stood wiping a trickle of blood from his temple, fear a heavy weight in the depths of his dark eyes.

The moon slowly shifted back to its pale radiance. The clouds surged back in. Lights winked back on across the dark metropolis. A breathless stillness fell across the city, the silence broken by a cacophony of alarms and the muted roar of traffic from the avenue below.

Their queen had just awoken.

CHAPTER FOUR

MAE GRABBED THE STEEL TABLE AND BLINKED SWEAT OUT of her eyes. Her stomach clenched on a violent spasm of nausea. She yanked off her splash shield and vomited in the sink next to where she'd been examining Antonovich's brain.

It took nearly a minute for the heaving to die down.

Mae rinsed her mouth, splashed water on her face, and clung weakly to the edge of the basin. The room spun sickeningly around her as she gazed blindly at the water swirling down the drain, her heart thumping in her chest.

What the hell is happening?!

She'd been studying the dead man's pineal gland when a tremor had shaken the lab and sent the lights flickering above her head. Earthquakes were not unheard of in New York, but she'd never felt one that strong before. She'd stripped off her gloves and had been about to take cover under the table when she'd been overwhelmed by dizziness.

Was it something I ate?!

She'd had a bacon and egg sandwich for lunch. Though she would have loved to blame it for her current state, her instincts told her this was more than just a simple case of food poisoning. She could feel something. A heaviness deep inside her body that was sucking all her energy. The room shook again before she could make sense of what it was. The lights went out. Mae startled.

Fear wrapped her heart in an icy grip. It wasn't a tremor that was making everything shudder around her.

The air around her body was shimmering violently, as if in the grip of a heat wave. A red glow accompanied it, the unholy radiance growing stronger by the second.

Wait! Am I the one doing this?! But—how?!

The lab door clattered open. Hodge dashed in, face pale and eyes bright with panic in the half-gloom.

"Mae! Are you okay?!" The lab director staggered to a comical stop at the sight of her. He froze before backing away a step, terror and incomprehension widening his pupils. "What—?!"

"Help me!" Mae mumbled.

She reached a trembling hand out to him. Hodge faltered for a second before swallowing and taking a step toward her.

Heat detonated inside Mae, so fierce and scorching it felt as if her very body had gone supernova. She gasped and bent over. Tears sprung to her eyes. She clawed at her belly, desperate to dig out the source of the agonizing inferno raging through her bones. Her spine arched the next instant, drawing a shocked cry from her lips. Her head snapped back and her limbs grew rigid, every joint locking in place.

Mae heard Hodge shout something above the buzzing in her ears. She gazed blankly at the ceiling, unable to move a single muscle, the coppery tang of blood filling her mouth.

Dammit! I must have bitten my tongue! Am I—am I having a seizure? Is this some kind of stroke?!

A crimson explosion filled her world. Sound and sight faded.

Fire surged through Mae's veins and flooded her flesh, a vengeful storm she feared she would not survive. Her heart thudded louder and louder with every painful, wretched beat, as if it were trying to leap out of her very chest and escape her treacherous body. She blinked.

The echo of another heartbeat was rising beneath it. One that felt strange yet achingly familiar at the same time. It was as if it had always been there, waiting quietly for the right time to make its presence felt.

Mae shuddered.

Why did I just think that?!

The other heartbeat grew exponentially until it merged seamlessly with her own, a savage pounding that sent pulses of red throbbing across her darkened vision.

At last...

The voice danced through her mind, soft and

feminine, yet filled with such strength and menace Mae could only tremble in fear.

"Who—who are you?!" she choked out.

She wasn't sure whether she'd spoken the words out loud or just said them in her head. She wasn't even sure if she was alive right now.

The presence focused on her.

A wave of kindness washed gently through Mae's consciousness. Tears came to her eyes once more. But this time, they were of grief and loss.

I am you and you are me, Mae.

Images flashed before her sightless eyes. Mae's breath locked in her throat. She knew instinctively that these were memories.

The battlefield she saw was like nothing she'd ever experienced. An army of monsters crowded an immense landscape all the way to the horizon, their numbers legion. On the blood-soaked grounds they left in their passage were hundreds upon thousands of mutilated corpses, many piled in mounds dozens of feet high. Ash darkened the sky from the fires raging through a burning palace and the city around it, the clouds tinged orange by the fierce flames and the screams of the dying reaching up to the very Heavens.

It was a scene of devastation on a scale Mae had never witnessed and could not even have begun to imagine. And she knew, deep in the marrow of her bones, that it was all because of her and the voice inside her.

Because of who they were.

Another vision flitted before her eyes.

A man, no, a demon with curved horns and crimson eyes stood looking down at her. And beside him, as bloodied and broken as he was, a woman whose beauty was dazzling despite the injuries marking her fair skin. They were holding her in their arms, their tears falling upon her cooling face. Their love for her shone brightly in their grief-stricken gazes, their words a faint whisper she could not make out.

The memory faded. The voice inside her spoke again, its tone steely.

Get ready. They are coming.

Mae woke up with a gasp. She blinked, her vision swimming for a moment. A dark floor came into focus.

She was lying on her front, cheek pressed against the cold linoleum. Her nails bit into her palms where she'd clenched her hands so hard, her knuckles blanched.

The emergency lights had come on in the corridor outside. Alarms blared from the upper stories of the hospital.

Mae unfisted her fingers and crawled onto her hands and knees. She shook her head dazedly, the taste of ash in her mouth and the beginning of a headache throbbing between her temples. Sweat cooled on her skin under her clothes and the protective gown she wore.

The red glow had faded from her body.

Mae inhaled shakily.

Wait. Was any of that even real or did I imagine it?!

The voice inside her head stayed silent. She looked

around. Hodge lay unconscious some twelve feet from her.

Mae rose unsteadily to her feet. "Steve!"

Glass crunched beneath her shoe when she took a step toward the director. She looked at the glittering fragments on the ground before glancing at the ceiling and around the rest of the lab. The lights had all exploded, as had the glass in the cabinets where they stored equipment and autopsy samples.

A thousand questions stormed Mae's mind as she carefully navigated the shard-strewn floor to her boss. She didn't know what had just happened, but whatever it was hadn't been natural. And she suspected even stranger things were about to unfold.

Though she couldn't hear the voice whose heartbeat she had sensed, she knew the presence was still there. There was a warm spot in her heart and one in her belly that hadn't been there before.

The words the voice had spoken flashed through Mae's consciousness.

I am you and you are me.

Mae grimaced. She hated cryptic stuff like that; she had enough of that hoodoo from her grandmother. It dawned on her that she was surprisingly calm considering the circumstances.

Maybe I'm in shock.

She checked Hodge over and carefully rolled him onto his side. He started to come around.

"Can you hear me?" Mae asked anxiously.

The director groaned and opened his eyes. "Mae?"

"Yeah, it's me."

Hodge swallowed heavily and sat up, Mae supporting his back with one hand. A lump was forming above his left eye from where he'd banged his head when he'd fainted. He rubbed it gingerly before staring at her dully.

"What happened?"

Mae bit her lip.

I can't exactly tell him I just got possessed by some kind of entity.

"I'm not sure. I think it was an earthquake."

"Damn strange earthquake," Hodge muttered as Mae helped him to his feet. "Did you see that red light?"

Mae shook her head and swore she heard her ancestors roll over in their graves at her next words. "I don't remember much. I woke up on the floor a minute ago."

The words *"Liar, liar, pants on fire"* flitted through her mind in Rose's wry voice. Mae's stomach lurched.

Rose! I hope she's okay!

"We should get out of here," she told Hodge briskly. "Let me grab my phone."

She'd taken two steps toward the worktop where she'd left her cell when Hodge made a gargled noise.

Mae stopped and looked over her shoulder. "Steve?"

The color had drained from the director's face. He was staring at something to her left. Mae followed his terrified gaze. She froze, shoulders growing tight.

Antonovich was sitting up on the autopsy table.

CHAPTER FIVE

That's not Antonovich!

A dark miasma crowned the dead man's head and coiled around his body, wisps of blackness that screamed of corruption. The whites of his eyes had turned an unearthly obsidian; in their center, shining with the light of Hell itself, were ochre pupils full of menace.

Mae's gaze strayed to the organs lined up neatly in their respective system blocks on the examination table next to Antonovich. The dead man looked over at his innards before staring down blankly at the gaping hole in his chest and abdomen, the scalp flap on his head dangling over his face.

Antonovich reached a hand inside his own body and ripped out a section of his spine. Hodge gagged and threw up.

The dead man studied the bloodied bones and ragged cord for a moment before shoving the whole thing inside his mouth, his jaws splitting into a monstrous maw so he could fit it all in.

Bile surged at the back of Mae's throat as the sound of crunching and chewing filled the lab. She swallowed convulsively and stole a glance at the equipment tray next to Antonovich.

The rib shears and bone saw were underneath the retractors and smaller postmortem instruments.

Antonovich, or whatever creature had possessed the man, for he was most definitely no longer human, followed her gaze. He smiled, his mouth widening until it stretched from ear to ear in a horrifying grimace that knotted Mae's stomach. His body started to swell, muscles bulging and frame growing.

His figure blurred before he'd fully transformed.

Shit!

Mae blocked his strike by sheer instinct. His fist landed on her forearms with a powerful crunch where she'd tucked them up in front of her chest, jarring her bones. She gritted her teeth, stomped down on his left foot with her heel, and felt something crack beneath her axe kick. Antonovich's head snapped sharply to the side as she jabbed him viciously in the jaw.

She never saw his left fist move.

Fire erupted in Mae's belly as he punched her in the gut, his movement lightning fast, just like when he'd jumped down from the table and charged her. She sailed across the room and struck the worktop with her back. Her cell phone clattered to the ground and pinwheeled under the counter.

Mae choked and wheezed, the pain in her stomach

and spine an agonizing fire that seared her very nerves. Her knees folded beneath her. She sagged to the floor, legs going numb.

Focus, Mae. Breathe.

Dark spots swam across Mae's vision. She finally managed to suck in air.

"Focus?!" she snarled with her next breath. "Focus on what, dammit?!"

Hodge and Antonovich stared at her.

"Great," she mumbled. "Now they both think I'm losing my mind!"

Use your powers.

Mae blinked. The warm spots in her heart and belly were growing hotter. Her hands rose to her chest and stomach, unbidden.

The heat spread through her veins and filled her body. Unlike what she'd experienced before she'd lost consciousness, there was no pain this time. Only a growing sense of…potency.

A ringing sounded in Mae's ears. "What—what is this?!"

Magic.

Hodge finally unfroze.

Antonovich's head twisted around at the flicker of movement. He leapt toward the director, nails lengthening to vicious, black claws, an inhuman shriek rising from his throat.

"*No!*" Mae yelled.

She raised a hand instinctively toward the dead man.

Red light exploded around her fingers. It flared and

twisted into a ball that pulsed with her heartbeat. She stared at it blankly before drawing her arm back and hurling it at Antonovich.

The crimson sphere struck the dead man's flank with a detonation that rocked the lab. Antonovich screeched and flew across the room. His scream ended abruptly when he crashed into a cabinet, metal denting under the impact. He froze for an instant before slumping to the ground.

Mae blinked rapidly, her heart in her mouth.

Smoke sizzled around the jagged, gaping hole where Antonovich's right abdomen and chest had once been. She looked dazedly at her hand.

"That's new," she mumbled, an edge of hysteria underscoring her words.

The cabinet wobbled and crashed down on the dead man, startling her and waking Hodge from his stupor. The director jumped, an incoherent yelp leaving him. His head swung jerkily from the creature under the cabinet to Mae.

"What—what just happened?!" he squeaked.

Mae rose to her feet. The pain in her belly and back was already easing.

Is that the effect of magic too?

Hysterical laughter bubbled up her throat at that thought. She clenched her jaw and cut it off.

Yeah, right. It's probably just adrenaline.

Her subconscious told her adrenaline did not produce powerful red balls of light that could take chunks out of human bodies. She thought she heard the other her sigh.

"Mae?" Hodge quavered.

Mae frowned. "I don't know, Steve. But I suggest we get the hell out of here."

She retrieved her cell from under the worktop. The screen was cracked. Mae stiffened.

A text had come through from Rose five minutes ago. She'd gone to the roof to wait for her. Mae frantically messaged back. Her heart sank as she tried to send the missive.

There was no signal.

Cold fingers skittered across her skin. She discarded her protective gown and shoe covers, slipped her phone inside the back pocket of her jeans, and headed briskly for the door. Hodge hesitated before following, his face ashen.

A sound made them stop.

Antonovich was trying to crawl out from under the cabinet.

Hodge recoiled, a whimper falling from his lips. "Oh God!"

Mae scowled, walked over to the equipment tray, and picked up the bone saw.

"Er, Mae? What are you—?" Hodge's eyes bulged. "Wait. You're not really gonna—? Oh, shit. You are."

He heaved and pressed a shaking hand to his mouth.

Mae squatted next to Antonovich, clutched him by his bloodless scalp flap, and proceeded to cut his head off. The dead man struggled feebly until she severed his spinal cord. He finally went limp, the sulfurous light fading from his eyes.

His lips parted on a low hiss before he stilled. *"Na... Ri..."*

Goosebumps broke out on Mae's skin. She knew the voice didn't belong to Antonovich. Fury misted her vision with a red haze. She inhaled shakily, stunned by her sudden anger. This wasn't just a projected emotion.

The rage she was feeling was her own.

I am you and you are me, huh? In that case, I hope you tell me what the hell is going on—and soon!

The voice inside her stayed silent as she dropped the saw and rose to her feet. She took a lab coat from the rack next to the sluice room, opened the instrument drawers, and filled the pockets with as many scissors as she could find. Her gaze landed on a mop. She lifted it out of its bucket, kicked off the sponge at the end, and snapped the handle in half on her knee. She gripped the two ends firmly and crossed the floor to Hodge.

"What—" Hodge paused and licked his lips, "what are you intending to do with those?"

Mae stormed past him and exited the lab. Hodge joined her in the basement corridor, feet dragging.

"Can you hear that?" she said.

The director's eyes rounded when he finally registered what Mae had perceived a moment ago. Screams punctuated the alarms blaring through the hospital.

"What the devil is going on?!" Hodge mumbled, teeth chattering.

Mae recalled the sulfurous pupils of the creature

who had possessed Antonovich. Her eyebrows drew together.

The devil may very well be among us right now.

Rose's face swam before Mae. Her mouth went dry.

Please be okay!

They were halfway to the emergency stairs when a figure appeared at the end of the gloomy passage. It was a man with a colostomy bag. A woman followed, the drip stand she was attached to clattering across the concrete floor as she dragged it behind her.

Mae didn't have to be a genius to figure out they were no longer human. A cloud of darkness swirled above their heads and enveloped their bodies. Their pupils were yellow disks in a sea of black.

Their eyes flared at the sight of her.

Hodge flinched. Mae's fingers tightened on her makeshift weapons.

"Stay behind me," she said grimly.

CHAPTER SIX

Alastair squawked where he whirled in the night sky above Nikolai. The familiar dropped down onto his shoulder when he reached the intersection of First Avenue and East 33rd Street, his dark wings fluttering agitatedly against his neck.

Nikolai staggered to a stop, heart racing and breaths coming in short, sharp pants. His chest grew tight.

Panicked screams rent the air as staff and patients streamed out of Grandview General Hospital. Many wheeled, carried, or dragged the injured with them. Their fear had spilled onto the streets, bringing traffic to a screeching halt.

"Fuck!"

Nikolai could sense the corruption of demons and the magic of the Dark Council coming from the glass-covered buildings that took up the block overlooking FDR Drive and the river estuary separating Manhattan from Brooklyn and Queens. He clenched his jaw and bolted across the avenue toward the nearest entrance. Horns blared around him, the few cars and trucks trying to navigate the jam slamming on their brakes to avoid hitting him.

I can't believe these assholes actually attacked a human facility with this many witnesses around!

Then again, nothing should surprise Nikolai anymore when it came to his father and the Dark Council. He had witnessed their cruelty enough times in his wretched life to know they were arrogant enough to carry out such a barbaric attack.

Considering what was at stake, their desperation seemed to have made them even more reckless.

People ran past him as he entered the main bay of the Emergency Department, faces blank and eyes blind with terror. They stumbled and fell over the bodies of the dead before picking themselves up and racing toward the exits, unheeding of the blood staining their skin and clothes.

Rage churned Nikolai's stomach upon seeing the injuries on the fallen. They were the work of demons.

He located the emergency stairs and headed to the second floor, where the artifact seemed to be drawing him. A dark sphere sailed toward him when he entered the main corridor. Nikolai cursed and ducked. The spell crashed into the wall behind him, scorching plaster and concrete.

He reached for his magic and unleashed his spear. Alastair's claws sank into his flesh, the familiar amplifying his power. Their gazes found the black-caped witch who had attacked them where she skulked in the doorway of a medical bay.

Nikolai's stomach twisted as the witch brought forth another sphere of magic, a sibilant noise leaving the python coiled around her waist. The adrenaline rushing through his veins would only keep him going for so long before his exhaustion caught up with him and made him slip up.

Still, it could be worse. I really need to thank those two for saving my ass back there.

Had it not been for the unknown witch and sorcerer who'd appeared on the rooftop where he'd been surrounded by Oscar and the Dark Council, Nikolai doubted he would have made it this far.

The artifact around his neck grew hot under his shirt, its crimson light radiating through the cotton. He tensed.

And there's this thing too.

The Witch Queen's weapon had protected him from the brunt of his brother's attacks before he'd escaped the high-rise. How, Nikolai still wasn't sure. It was as if it'd known that it needed to keep him alive so it could reach its mistress. Nikolai shivered.

In all his time in the world of magic, he had never heard of a sentient magic tool.

The witch's eyes shrank to slits at the sight of the radiance over his chest. She knew what it was that he'd stolen from his father's vault.

"Give it back, traitor!"

She hurled her magic at him. Nikolai spun out of the way of the destructive spell and threw his spear.

The witch grunted and froze. Her eyes rounded. She grappled frantically with the weapon that had pierced her throat, gurgling sounds choking her breath. Her python hissed in alarm.

The pale glow of Nikolai's magic fluttered across his skin as he flexed his fingers.

The spear left the witch's flesh with a sickening sound and returned to his grasp, wood striking his palm with a clap. Horror leached the color from the woman's face as she clamped her hands to the gaping hole in her neck. Blood streamed thickly through the gaps between her fingers and fell on the swaying snake wrapped around her body.

The bond between a familiar and a witch or sorcerer was such that if the human died, so did the creature bound to them.

The witch's legs gave way. She thudded to the ground in an expanding, crimson pool.

Nikolai didn't even spare her a glance as he walked past her body and that of her dying familiar. He had no pity for the Dark Council. Even if most weren't born evil, they were soon corrupted by their master, the Sorcerer King, and they reveled in the brutal acts he ordered them to carry out on his behalf.

Nikolai reached the end of the passage without encountering more magic users, turned the corner, and halted in his tracks.

A demon squatted on the ground some twenty feet ahead of him, claws and jaws dripping with gore as he ripped out the intestines of the male nurse he had killed.

Two women in scrubs and an old man in a dressing gown cowered under the nurses' station just beyond the creature, knuckles white as they clung to one another in abject terror.

The demon straightened when he sensed Nikolai's presence. He turned his head and fixed him with ochre-lit eyes. There was a nametag on his bloodied scrub top. It read 'Dr. Chavez.'

Tension knotted Nikolai's limbs. His hand strayed to the weapon that lay against his heart.

Please. Lend me your strength a little while more, so I may help these people!

The artifact thrummed under his fingers. Magic filled Nikolai, a red river of fire that replenished his reserves. Alastair flapped his wings, his eyes flashing orange as his powers recharged.

They headed toward the demon.

MAE SLIPPED UNDER A SET OF TALONS, KICKED THE demon's left leg out from under her, and drove a pair of scissors into her left temple as she fell to the ground.

The creature went rigid before slumping to the floor. Her eyes dulled and her claws shrank as her body slowly took on a human form once more. Mae bit her lip when she saw the woman's face.

It was a surgical nurse who worked with Rose.

"Go!" she shouted at the patients and staff who'd taken refuge inside a janitor's closet.

They darted out of the cupboard and headed for the

nearest emergency exit, stumbling and whimpering in horror. Mae wrenched the scissors out of the dead woman's head and climbed to her feet. Unlike the creature who'd possessed Antonovich, these ones died as long as she pierced their brain or the base of their neck. She dropped the blades in her pocket and headed in the direction of the stairs that would get her to the roof.

Her hands curled into fists as she observed the bodies littering the bays and side rooms she passed, rage a heavy weight in the pit of her stomach. She'd counted over fifty dead as she'd made her way through the hospital and up the floors of the surgical block. Many more had been wounded and were being moved to safety by those who'd managed to escape the savage attack by the sinister creatures who'd appeared in their midst.

Hodge had stayed behind to help with the evacuation. He'd begged Mae not to go farther inside the hospital. His pleas had fallen on deaf ears. There was no way she was walking out of Grandview without Rose.

The fire door that would take her to the rooftop finally came into view. Mae was twelve feet from it when the hairs lifted on the back of her neck. She spun around, saw a dark sphere whooshing toward her, and dove to the side.

CHAPTER SEVEN

THE GLOBE SMASHED THE WINDOW AT THE END OF THE passage and sent a spiderweb of cracks blooming on the wall around it. Plaster dust and glass rained down on Mae on a wave of heat as she hit the ground and rolled. She landed on her front, her pulse racing.

That was magic!

She lifted her head. Her gaze found the dark-cloaked men and women who'd emerged from the elevators next to the nurses' station. There were five of them in all. Surprise jolted her.

They had animals with them in the form of two cats, a parakeet, a chihuahua, and a hawk.

Mae rose shakily to her feet.

Who the hell are they? And why do they have—pets?!

"Hey!" the man with the chihuahua snapped at the woman with the hawk. "Remember, we need her alive!"

"Relax, Silvius," the woman drawled. "This is the Witch Queen we're dealing with. She won't die from a spell like that." A sneer twisted the brunette's mouth as she raked

Mae from her head to her feet, her gaze mocking. "Although, why anyone would take this woman for our queen is beyond me. She looks like a drowned lab rat."

The robed figures next to her looked at one another uneasily.

Mae stared.

Witch Queen? Wait. Are they talking about me?!

Her mind raced as she studied the strangers and the creatures with them. Though they weren't mired in the black mist she'd seen around the monsters with the ochre pupils, she could sense something from them. Something…sinister. She narrowed her eyes.

They must be the ones behind the attack on Grandview!

"Who are you people?" Mae asked coldly.

The woman smirked. "That's for us to know and for you to find out in the comfort of our king's dungeons, my *queen.*"

Her hawk screeched and flapped his wings.

"Agatha, wait," one of her companions muttered in a strained voice.

The woman raised her hands. The air wavered around her fingers. Her hawk's eyes flashed black.

A barrage of spinning, inky spheres erupted in front of them.

Mae's mouth went dry.

That's not good!

"*No!*" the first man yelled.

He lunged toward the woman. She laughed and released her magic.

The emergency lights exploded as the corrupt orbs

arrowed toward Mae, the force of their passage ripping tiles from the ceiling and the linoleum floor.

Fear rooted her feet to the ground. It was replaced by outrage.

Heat erupted inside Mae in response to her fury, a wave of wrath that filled her with glorious power. She recalled what she'd done in the autopsy lab, bared her teeth, and raised her left hand.

A globe of crimson light detonated into existence in front of her palm, the explosion sending her clothes and hair fluttering wildly around her body. Mae planted her feet wide and scowled as the black orbs drew close. A word danced through her mind, unbidden.

"Devour!"

The red sphere she'd manifested crackled and sparked as it swelled. It swallowed the dark balls of magic in a spiraling storm, expanding with each one it guzzled. It took but seconds for it to consume the dark orbs. A breathless silence descended inside the corridor once the last one vanished inside it with a gluttonous gulp.

Mae's heart slammed erratically against her ribs. She looked past the giant, writhing, scarlet globe floating in front of her to the pale faces of the group beyond it. She wasn't sure who was the most shocked, her or them.

"Here, you can have this back."

She lobbed the sphere at them. Magic roared as it left her grasp.

The black-robed figures turned to flee. They didn't get far.

The globe blasted into them and lifted them off the ground. Their screams echoed against the walls as they were carried clear to the end of the passage. Mae sucked in air as they smashed straight through the concrete and vanished into the empty ICU bay beyond.

Her pulse thrummed as she ran up the corridor. She maneuvered her way into the gaping hole in the bloodstained masonry and through the mass of twisted, exposed steelwork framing it. Her steps slowed as she crossed the dark room to the jagged opening that was all that remained of the exterior wall of the building. She swallowed, gripped the edge of the concrete gingerly, and peered out into the void.

Alarms whistled and blared where the black-robed figures had dented the roofs of the vehicles they'd landed upon, twenty stories below. Mae didn't need to see their faces to know they were dead.

No one could be twisted at that many angles and still be breathing.

Tightness filled her chest. She stepped back from the drop and studied her trembling hands.

I need to learn how to dial this shit down!

A scream came from the direction of the roof.

Mae's breath caught.

Rose!

She turned, sprinted out of the ICU, and bolted for the fire escape at the other end of the floor. Lights flickered in the gloomy stairwell beyond it. Shouts reached her as she started up the emergency stairs.

Mae stopped, leaned over the banister, and scanned the shadows below, her heart thumping.

Magic of all colors flared on the lower levels of the building. A group of strangers in street clothes and their animal companions had engaged the ochre-eyed monsters and the black-robed individuals who'd attacked the hospital.

Mae hesitated before turning and taking the stairs to the roof two steps at a time, teeth clenched so tight her jaw ached.

I don't have time to help them!

She smashed through the metal door at the top with her shoulder, staggered to a halt, and whirled around. Horror froze her limbs to the ground.

Rose stood flanked by three monsters near the south end of the building. Blood dripped from the steel pipe in her hands and the lacerations on her arms and thighs. Her gray eyes were full of resolve despite the fear that shook her body.

Four patients in hospital gowns and two nurses cowered on the asphalt behind Rose. Their getaway route to the fire escape down the side of the building had been cut off by the creatures who had surrounded them.

Mae's gaze moved jerkily to the mutilated bodies of a man in scrubs and the two patients who hadn't survived the assault. She flinched. It was Tom, the ob-gyn. He'd died protecting the man and woman next to him, the surgical blade he had used still lying in his slack grip.

Rage swept over Mae like a storm. She headed

across the roof.

CHAPTER EIGHT

ROSE'S GAZE FOUND HER. HER EYES WIDENED. "No! *Run!*"

This time, magic poured through Mae of her own free will, the fire licking her veins in a controlled flow. It was getting easier to access the power churning deep inside her.

She blasted the first two monsters with crimson orbs.

Rose recoiled as the creatures flew past her and fell off the building. The third fiend jumped out of the way of Mae's attack, dashed behind the blonde, and clasped her by the back of her neck, his wicked talons wrapping all the way around her throat.

"*No!*" Mae yelled.

Rose choked and kicked out as the monster dragged her to the edge of the roof and lifted her in the air. Her legs dangled feebly beneath her. The steel pipe dropped from her hands. She clawed at the creature's talons, fury and horror lending her desperate strength.

"Let her go!"

Mae's roar scorched the rooftop in a red wave of magic.

The people Rose had been protecting collapsed, unconscious.

Her best friend blinked sluggishly. "M—Mae?!"

An oppressive pressure blanketed the rooftop. Mae gasped, her legs buckling beneath the heavy mantle until her knees struck the ground. The air grew thick, so much so she found herself struggling to breathe.

What the hell is this?!

A sound reached her through the buzzing in her ears.

Mae looked up. She froze.

The world faded around her, the alarms blaring through the city and the streets below dimming to nothingness.

Blood burst from Rose's lips and dripped down her chin. She looked blindly at Mae, her body rigid with shock.

Evil talons had pierced her chest from the back.

The creature who held her in his grip had morphed into an eight-foot-tall devil with dark skin, curved horns, and black wings. Smoke curled from the fiend's nostrils and mouth as he studied Mae, crimson pupils bright in the night. His lips curled in a cruel smile.

"Do as I say and the girl lives," he growled.

Tears blurred Mae's vision. She wiped at them angrily with one hand.

"What—what do you want?!"

"Don't!" Rose gasped. "Don't give them what they want, Mae!"

The devil observed Rose with a calculating look. "I'm surprised you can still talk, little girl."

Rose looked over her shoulder. She swallowed when she saw the fiend's horns and eyes. A scowl darkened her face despite her fear.

"Screw you, asshole!"

The devil's smile widened. "How amusing." His gaze switched to Mae. "Give us your power, witch, and I will let her go."

Never.

Mae's eyes rounded as the denial left her lips without her volition. It had come from the voice inside her.

The devil's pupils flared. "So be it."

Rose grunted.

Mae's pulse stuttered. A cry of denial left her throat.

The fiend had ripped her best friend's heart out of her body.

Rose looked blankly at Mae. A gentle smile curved her mouth.

Her lips parted on a whisper. "I love you…Mae."

Rose's eyelids fluttered closed. She sagged in the devil's grip.

Fury filled Mae's world, so potent she felt it would swallow her whole. She raised her face to the sky and screamed.

A crimson storm erupted around her. It blasted across the rooftop and rolled across the city, ripping the clouds to shreds and startling the devil who stood facing her, her best friend's corpse in his hand.

The building trembled as Mae straightened, her body vibrating with a power that threatened to break her bones. She levitated some ten feet in the air, no longer surprised at what she could do.

A single conviction occupied her mind. The devil had to die.

Calm your anger. His death leads to nothing!

"*Shut up!*" Mae roared at the voice inside her. "*This is all your fault!*"

A spell came to her mind. She reached for the blaze scorching her insides.

No, Mae! You know not what you—

Mae scowled and raised her hands to the sky. "*Eclipse!*"

A black orb exploded into existence above her. It expanded rapidly, the currents inside it twisting at a dizzying speed. The air quivered and the clouds drew in.

The rooftop started to crack.

Chunks of asphalt broke free and shot up into the growing void. The devil cursed, clawed talons raising sparks on the blacktop as he was dragged inexorably toward the dark vortex.

One of the nurses came to just as the whirlwind started to lift her off the ground. Her scream jolted Mae out of her daze.

"*Stop!*" someone yelled behind her.

She looked over her shoulder.

A man with dark hair and eyes had appeared from

the direction of the stairs. There was a crow on his shoulder and a bloodstained spear in his hand.

Something underneath his shirt captured her gaze. An object that glowed with the same power surging through her. Mae shivered and turned in mid air. She drifted toward him, unable to resist the call of whatever the item was.

"Undo the spell!" the stranger shouted above the raging wind. His gaze shot past her. "Quick, before it's too late!"

She twisted around.

The far end of the building was shuddering with violent tremors, the people Rose had been trying to protect clinging grimly to the crumbling asphalt.

Mae's blood turned to ice.

No!

She took a ragged breath, clenched her jaw, and focused on the power that had overwhelmed her consciousness.

The voice inside her reached her faintly.

Breathe, Mae. Control it!

Her throat hurt as she did just that, her neck so tight she thought her tendons would rupture. She drew air in and out of her lungs with painful gasps. The crimson core inside her resisted for a moment. It fluttered before gradually shrinking.

The fire in her blood abated.

The devil snarled and broke free of the vortex. His crimson pupils flared in the next instant.

The section of the roof he was standing caved under him.

He started to fall, his victim in hand.

"*Rose!*" Mae bellowed.

Her magic faded as she landed on the ground. She stumbled and fell, scraping her palms raw. She was up in a heartbeat, desperation giving her a final burst of speed.

Mae reached the edge of the collapsing building and lunged over the abyss. Her fingers closed on something warm as she hit the asphalt. She blinked through the debris and dust clouding the air, her heart in her mouth.

It was Rose's right wrist.

The sapphire bracelet she had given her best friend scratched the wounds on her palm. Movement below caught her eye. The devil dangled from Rose's left arm, a mocking grin on his monstrous face.

Their combined weight dragged Mae forward. She cursed and tightened her grasp on Rose as she slid farther over the chasm. Another segment of the roof disintegrated next to her.

Someone grabbed her legs and yanked her back from the void.

It was the guy with the crow.

She kicked at him, despair making her clumsy. "No! Let me go!"

"Your friend is dead!" he yelled. "Release her or he'll take you both down!"

The devil cackled at the stranger's words. "The traitor is right, witch! In fact, why don't you just give up and come with me? Do not fear. The king and I will treat you well."

Mae's throat grew tight. The blood on her skin was making her hold slippery. Rose's arm slid through her grip.

Let go, Mae.

"No," she mumbled. "I can't. I won't!"

She dug her fingers into Rose's flesh. A sob left her as her best friend continued to slip through her hands.

"Don't leave me." Mae's vision swam with tears. "I need you, Rose. I—"

Her breath locked in her throat as she finally lost her grip. The devil pulled Rose down into the night, his crimson gaze taunting.

The sapphire bracelet Mae had ripped from Rose's wrist dug into her clenched fist, a cold blessing against her palm. Heaviness filled her heart and mind. Her consciousness flickered. The last thing she saw before darkness claimed her was the devil unfurling his wings and wrapping Rose in his arms.

CHAPTER NINE

Nikolai's heart drummed violently in his chest where he sat on the edge of the building's decimated rooftop, the motionless woman in his hold a burden that weighed heavily on his conscience.

What have I done?!

The people the Witch Queen had saved lay unmoving some twenty feet away, minds and bodies rendered senseless by all they had just experienced. Remorse brought a sour taste to Nikolai's mouth as he looked out over the dark city.

The devastation the magic storm and the Witch Queen's awakened soul had wreaked would be felt for days, not just by the magic users who inhabited New York, but also by the humans who had unwittingly found themselves in the middle of a battle they hadn't even known existed.

He clenched his jaw. Still, the outcome would have been worse had the Sorcerer King and the Dark Council gotten their hands on the Witch Queen before she awakened. His stomach twisted as the image of the devil danced before his eyes.

I can't believe he *came!*

It was only recently that he'd uncovered the shocking truth of how his father and every Sorcerer King before him could control and call forth fiends from Hell. It was a secret his father had kept close to his chest, one likely only known to Oscar and his most trusted circle.

That horrifying information and the imminent awakening of the Witch Queen had finally propelled Nikolai to take action. What he had achieved tonight was the culmination of a path he had chosen a long time ago, under a moonlit night in an amphitheater thousands of miles from here. There would be no walking away from the bloody fate he had espoused, nor the woman at the center of it all.

Nikolai studied the Witch Queen. He hadn't been able to make out her features through the debris flying across the rooftop and the power engulfing her earlier.

She was tall and lean, the tone and definition of her muscles speaking of someone used to regular physical training. Her long, black hair fell midway down her back, framing a slender neck and a heart-shaped face. Her skin was so fair it almost glowed under the moonlight, the faint blush of color on her sharply defined cheekbones and full lips a sharp contrast to her snowy complexion.

Something tugged at his heart. He blamed it on the artifact hanging around his neck, took it off, and carefully slipped it over her head. The pendant glowed crimson as it nestled against its mistress's flesh. She shuddered, red lines flashing across her skin briefly as the weapon bonded with her soul.

The heat of the connection seared Nikolai's skin, her magic so potent it caused his own to stir in response. He laid her on the ground and climbed to his feet, eager to get away from her all of a sudden.

Alastair's claws sank into his shoulder, the familiar's curiosity flitting through his mind. Nikolai took a shaky breath and shielded his thoughts from the crow.

Their job here was done for now. He doubted the Dark Council would attack the Witch Queen again tonight. Not with the eyes of every coven in the world and the U.S. government Special Affairs Bureau locked on New York.

He turned to walk away, felt a presence at his back, and spun around, his watch transforming into the spear once more.

"Steady there." A young woman with purple hair and blue eyes landed on the rooftop. "If we'd wanted to attack you, we would have done so back on that high-rise."

She observed him with a probing stare as the arming sword in her hand retracted to a silver ring on her right middle finger. The white rabbit on her shoulder twitched her nose, pink eyes gleaming with intelligence.

A guy with brown hair and eyes who looked a few years older alighted next to the woman, a frown on his face and his saber shrinking to a bracelet on his left wrist.

"Man, you dropped us like we were horse shit back there," he muttered.

The boa constrictor around his chest tasted the air curiously with her tongue.

Nikolai watched them stiffly. It was the witch and the sorcerer who had helped him fight off Oscar and the Dark Council. They looked remarkably unscathed considering whom they'd been facing, the only signs of the battle they had engaged in the singe marks on their clothes.

They're strong.

Alastair's head darted forward as he focused on the rabbit and the snake. Nikolai sensed only interest from the crow. The bird evidently didn't consider the other familiars his foe.

"I'm sorry about that," he said gruffly, relaxing slightly. "I needed to get away from there."

The witch's gaze shifted past him. She arched an eyebrow.

"Is that her?"

Nikolai found himself standing protectively in front of the still figure on the ground. He blinked rapidly.

His body had moved of its own volition.

He turned and narrowed his eyes at the pentagram pendant around the Witch Queen's neck.

Wait. Did that thing just manipulate me into protecting its mistress?!

The weapon projected an air of blissful innocence where it lay against the woman's chest.

Alastair cocked his head at Nikolai, puzzled.

"Hey, Vi," boa constrictor guy hissed out the corner

of his mouth. "You sure that's the Witch Queen? She kinda looks, I don't know—weak."

Nikolai's hand clenched on his spear. "How did you know?"

The purple-haired witch heaved a heavy sigh. "You'd have to be a moron not to sense her magic."

"Yeah." Boa constrictor guy nodded briskly. He stopped and glared at the witch. "Wait. Did you just call me a moron?!"

She ignored him. "Why is the second son of the Sorcerer King helping the Witch Queen, his sworn enemy?"

Nikolai kept his expression neutral as he met her piercing gaze.

These guys know a lot.

"Hey, should we really be having a chat with him?" Boa constrictor guy pursed his lips. "Aunt Barb and Bryony will read us the Riot Act if they learn we've been fraternizing with the enemy."

Nikolai stiffened. "Bryony? As in Bryony Cross, the High Priestess of the New York coven?"

"Way to go, dumbass," the witch told her companion scathingly.

Relief shot through Nikolai.

Good. I can leave her in their hands.

Bryony Cross wasn't just the head of all the registered witches and sorcerers in New York, she was also a member of the High Council, one of the principal bodies governing magic users in the world. Though the three magic councils had been forced to overlook the worst of the Dark Council's deeds following the Treaty of Argentheim, they had all secretly been praying for the Witch Queen's rebirth and would stand firmly by her side.

"I have no grievance with the Witch Queen," Nikolai said firmly. "If anything, it's the opposite. I need her help to stop my father."

"Is that why you unleashed such a dangerous spell on the city?" Anger darkened the witch's eyes. "Do you know how many deaths you've caused, not just among magic users, but humans too?"

"I didn't choose to attack this place!" Nikolai grated out. "That was my brother and the Dark Council's doing. And I couldn't very well let her fall into their hands. If they'd gotten to her before she awakened—"

A low mumble sounded behind him. He whirled around.

Color was returning to the Witch Queen's face. Her lips parted on a name.

"Rose…"

Her sorrow drenched the air with a pressure that almost brought Nikolai to his knees. The witch and the sorcerer startled, legs similarly buckling. They had not yet experienced the influence of their queen's emotions up close.

The heaviness in the air abated as the unconscious woman settled back down.

Nikolai shuddered before heading for the rooftop door hanging off its hinges. His body grew heavy, his adrenaline finally wearing off and his depleted magic making itself felt.

"Take care of her."

"Hey, wait up!" the witch protested. "You can't just leave!"

"He already did, Vi."

Their voices faded behind Nikolai as he headed down the dark stairwell on shaky legs, Alastair trembling with exhaustion on his shoulder.

They needed to recover their strength for the next step of their plan.

CHAPTER TEN

"Bar a few cuts, your body is okay. And your scans are all normal." Dr. Mehta hesitated, lines wrinkling his brow. "We think the reason you were out for so long is shock from the trauma you suffered."

Mae looked blindly at her hands where they lay on her lap.

"Mae, can you hear me?"

She swallowed and looked up. "Yes."

Concern darkened the physician's kind eyes. He was a familiar face, having been her mentor during her ICU residency. Yet, he felt like a complete stranger. Everything seemed strange to her right now. It was as if she were looking at the world through a dream. One she wished she would wake from.

Movement beyond the window to her right drew her deadened gaze.

She looked past vases brimming with flowers to the surgical block rooftop. It was being taken apart by a crane, the contractors who'd been assigned the demolition project bright figures in yellow jackets on the elevator platforms around the building.

It had been three days since the attack on Grandview General.

Three days since her world changed forever.

Three days since she lost Rose.

Even now, it all seemed surreal. The risen Antonovich, back from the dead. The attack by the monsters who had swarmed the hospital. The black-caped figures who had been after her. The devil and the man with the crow. And the being at the center of it all. The one who had taken possession of her body as if she were a tool to be used.

It all felt like a nightmare she would never be roused from. One that would see her bound forever in darkness, her heart broken and her soul swallowed by grief.

Mehta went over to the window and drew the curtains, his expression sympathetic. There was a knock on the door.

It was her mother and grandmother. Hodge hovered behind them.

The pathology director greeted Mehta with a somber nod.

"Hi, Ramesh."

"It's good to see you again, Steve." Mehta looked at Mae. "I'll leave you with your visitors."

He left the room.

Although access was usually restricted to one family member in ICU, the hospital had made an exception for the people caught in the unprecedented tragedy three days back. No one wished to deepen the victims' distress by separating them from their loved ones.

Mae wondered whether everyone else was enduring the same emotional detachment she'd experienced since she'd woken up yesterday.

Yoo-Mi and Ye-Seul approached the bed and took the chairs they'd occupied for most of the last three days.

"Ryu is parking the car," her mother murmured.

Her eyes were red-rimmed, as if she'd been crying all night.

"What about the funeral home?"

Yoo-Mi stared, her eyes widening slightly. "We closed up for the week. We couldn't very well operate as normal with everything that—"

She stopped and bit her lip.

"With everything that happened to me?" Mae finished.

Yoo-Mi nodded miserably. "You almost died, Hana Mae."

Tears sprung to her eyes. She sobbed and pressed a hand to her mouth. Hodge grabbed some tissues from a box and gave them to her.

"Thank you." Yoo-Mi sniffed. "Who are you again?"

"He's my boss, Mom," Mae said.

"Oh?" Ye-Seul brightened. "Steve who likes to wank."

Shocked silence descended on the room. Yoo-Mi paled. Hodge's jaw sagged open.

Mae cast an apologetic look at her boss. "If you mean Steve who likes the New York *Yankees*, then yes."

Hodge closed his mouth.

"We really need to get Grandma new hearing aids," Mae told Yoo-Mi.

"I know. But she likes the ones she has right now. She says they make her look cool."

Mae swallowed a sigh and studied her mother's pale face. She couldn't very well tell Yoo-Mi off in the state she was in right now. But closing the funeral home was going to cost them money.

Ye-Seul gripped Mae's hand where it rested on the covers, her liver-spotted, parchment skin warm against Mae's flesh. "We brought another one of your favorites today. *Samgyetang*."

Yoo-Mi took a large plastic container out of the food bag she'd brought and removed the lid. The smell of ginseng chicken soup filled the room. Nausea twisted Mae's stomach. She clenched her teeth and swallowed.

Everything tasted like sour ash since she'd woken up.

"Thanks, Grandma."

Hodge fidgeted where he stood at the end of the bed. His gaze flitted to the thank you cards crowding the surfaces of the hospital room.

"How are you feeling?"

Mae met his troubled gaze. She knew the gruesome events they'd witnessed together were still at the forefront of Hodge's mind. Despite his ardent protests, he'd been put on mandatory sick leave for the week. With the autopsy labs at Grandview closed until NYPD finished their investigations into the attack on the hospital, he was probably at his wits' end trying to keep himself occupied.

"I'm…okay. Or I will be."

She glanced at the flowers and cards filling the room and swallowed the tight ball in her throat. The staff and patients whose lives she had saved had sent them to the ICU. As far as they were concerned, she was their hero.

Remorse stabbed through Mae. She didn't deserve their thanks. Not when she was likely the reason Grandview had been attacked in the first place.

She maintained a neutral expression and studied Hodge steadily. "How are you holding up?"

A haunted look came over Hodge. He swallowed. "I still see it when I close my eyes. That…thing that attacked us."

Yoo-Mi and Ye-Seul exchanged an uneasy look.

Stories of the deadly creatures that had invaded Grandview General had made headline news since the night of the incident, the first reporters who'd turned up on site catching the terrified, first-hand accounts of those who had survived the ordeal before they were whisked away by police and paramedics. Yet, no traces of the monsters had been found. A few experts were now starting to talk about some kind of mass hysteria event and a collective murder spree caused by a nerve agent or other toxin.

When some survivors mentioned seeing black-robed figures among the creatures, their statements were also regarded with heavy skepticism. The security cameras had not captured any images of people who fit that description before they'd gone offline during the city-wide power cut, just as they hadn't recorded anything that looked like the monsters the survivors had described in graphic detail.

The missing innards and body parts from many of the victims was something that had evidently not been made public yet. And no one had mentioned the animals who had been present during the attack.

"Did they find Antonovich?" Mae asked Hodge.

The director shook his head. "No. The cops who interviewed me said there was no trace of his body in the basement. The only things they found were the organs you'd dissected out." He hesitated. "They're wondering if this whole mess is because someone wanted to steal the corpse and interfere with the murder investigation."

"That's far-fetched, even for NYPD," Mae muttered.

Talking to Hodge was making her feel better. She realized just speaking with someone who'd gone through the same experience as her was going to be the key to getting her out of her funk.

Ryu appeared. She slowed when she saw Hodge. "Hi, Steve."

"Hi, Ryu." Hodge cast a guilty look at Mae. "I best leave you. I'll drop by tomorrow."

"You don't have to go," Yoo-Mi protested. "You're more than welcome to stay and eat with us."

Hodge shook his head. "Thank you, Mrs. Jin. But what Mae really needs right now is her family."

An awkward silence fell inside the room when he left. Ryu pulled a chair over to the bed.

"I can't believe you let her talk you into closing shop," Mae whispered to her sister while Yoo-Mi and Ye-Seul unpacked the rest of the food they'd brought on the tray table.

"I was the one who suggested it," Ryu said.

"Why? You know how much money we stand to lose even shutting for one day!"

A muscle jumped in Ryu's cheek. "You almost died, Mae. Do you really think any of us were in the right frame of mind to carry on, as if nothing had happened?"

Remorse stabbed Mae at her sister's angry expression. Their conversation was interrupted by a nurse. She took Mae's vitals and charted them on the computer station at the side of the bed.

"Mmm, that smells good." The woman smiled at the spread Yoo-Mi and Ye-Seul had laid out before looking over at Mae. "I hope you'll eat something this time. You haven't had anything since yesterday."

Yoo-Mi bit her lip. "You didn't eat?"

"I wasn't hungry," Mae murmured.

Considering how much she loved food, her words made her family even more anxious. She could see the silent questions on their faces. They still hadn't talked about what had happened that night, or about Rose. One thing they had told her, though. Or Ryu had, at least.

Rose's remains hadn't been found among the rubble of the collapsed surgical block. For some reason, Mae had felt an incredible sense of relief at the news. As long as Rose's body was missing, then she could still be out there, injured but alive.

A memory flashed before her eyes. Of the bloodied hole in Rose's chest and the beating heart quivering in the devil's hand. Her head throbbed. She clenched the bed sheets with her fists, her own heart screaming in denial as her mind tried to force her to accept the reality of Rose's fate.

CHAPTER ELEVEN

"Are you okay?" Ryu asked, alarmed. "Should I get someone?"

She jumped from her chair.

"*No!*" Mae barked.

The window trembled. The table at the end of the bed shook slightly. Ripples broke out across the surface of the soup Yoo-Mi had served out in bowls.

Everyone stared at the quivering dishes until they stilled.

"Damn," Ryu mumbled, pale-faced. "Was that an aftershock?"

Mae swallowed. She was pretty certain she now knew the cause of the violent tremors that had shaken the city three days ago. It hadn't been an earthquake, like most people had originally presumed.

It had been the power that had awakened inside her. The power she could still sense in her heart and belly, points of heat she couldn't explain but which felt familiar, like they had always been there, deadly and dormant.

She hadn't heard the voice again since that night.

One of the ICU nurses popped her head through the door. "Is everyone okay? I thought I felt the floor shake a little."

"We're fine," Mae lied.

Ryu frowned.

"Alright. Call me if you need anything." The nurse left.

"Let's eat," Ye-Seul said in the strained hush.

Mae forced herself to chew and swallow, conscious of her family's stares. Her queasiness had thankfully abated. She wondered whether it had anything to do with the echo of magic that had just erupted from her core.

Ryu and Yoo-Mi made light conversation while they ate. Ye-Seul remained mostly silent, her expression thoughtful as she studied Mae. For some reason, Mae felt her grandmother could see right through her.

They left soon after, their unspoken words a heavy strain that filled the space between them. They were a close-knit household, which made the tension between them doubly worse. Mae knew she would have to talk things over with them soon. She just wasn't ready to have that conversation yet.

Her hand rose to the pentagram pendant under her hospital gown. It lay flush against her chest, the metal unusually warm where it kissed her skin. She lifted it out and scrutinized it, her thumb running absent-mindedly over the design.

She'd found it in the drawer next to her bed when she'd woken up yesterday, along with Rose's bracelet and the belongings Hodge had retrieved from the autopsy lab. The nurse looking after her had told her it had been around her neck when the rescue services had discovered her on the rooftop of the surgical block.

Mae had no recollection of ever owning a pentagram pendant. Still, she would not be parted from it. The pendant belonged to her.

She knew it in her bones.

The restless feeling that had been brewing inside her all day escalated as the afternoon wore on. Dusk soon leached the light out of the sky. Thunderstorms lit a bank of dark clouds to the north. Mae finally grew tired of flipping through TV channels, slipped into a dressing gown, and headed out of the room.

"I'm going for a walk," she told the nurses manning the station in the middle of the floor.

The ICU staff glanced uneasily at one another.

"We shouldn't really let you leave," one of them said.

"I need the fresh air," Mae insisted. "I won't go far, I promise."

The male nurse in charge of the shift sighed. "Well, seeing as you're back on your feet, we can let you go out for a short time. Be back within the hour, though. We need to check your vitals."

"Thanks."

The corridors of the hospital were unusually quiet, the subdued atmosphere a reflection of the mood inside the place. Though many of the injured had been transferred to other facilities across the city, Grandview General was still operating most of its services.

Mae soon found herself on the rooftop of the medical block.

Inky clouds billowed above her, the ozone in the air carrying the promise of rain. She walked over to the railing spanning the east edge of the building and looked out over the river. Lights twinkled brightly across the water, the boroughs of Brooklyn and Queens teeming with life and noise.

She hesitated before heading left, her legs growing heavy with every step she took.

Bar the spotlights erected by the contractors, the surgical block was dark. The beams highlighted the cracks that had torn down the south and west sides of the building, the areas worst affected by the destruction Mae's powers had wrought upon it. Almost all the windows had been smashed, the empty frames gaping holes in the night.

A chill danced down Mae's spine.

Did I really do all of that?!

Movement far below caught her eye. She glimpsed bright yellow letters spelling out NYPD on the jackets and protective suits of the figures milling around the base of the building. This was still an active crime scene, even though no one really knew what crimes had been committed or by whom. She'd been told to expect a visit from a couple of detectives tomorrow. Mae grimaced.

"That's gonna be interesting," she muttered. "Hi, officer, sorry about what I did to New York. I got possessed by something and couldn't help it."

The words rang hollow in her ears. She had no doubt where she'd end up if she actually said that to them. Mae turned, leaned her elbows atop the railing, and closed her eyes. A cool wind ruffled her hair as she raised her face to the sky.

Are you there?

The voice who had been with her that fateful night remained silent. Mae's jaw tightened. She wasn't sure what she'd expected but, still, some kind of reaction would have been nice.

Look, I know you weren't just a figment of my imagination. So, do something. Anything, so I know I'm not going crazy!

Warmth bloomed inside her chest, a wave of recognition that made her soul tremble. She blinked, startled, her heartbeat a loud thump in her ears. She felt...different. And she'd only become aware of that fact in that very instant.

It was as if the one who had awakened inside her was now an integral part of who she was. Mae shuddered.

She did say that I was her and she was me. Does that mean we're—we're one and the same being now?!

There was a noise somewhere on the rooftop. Mae

tensed, stomach lurching. She scanned the shadows around her wildly. There was no one there.

A low mumble reached her ears.

She clenched her fists and made her way carefully around the bank of elevator shafts and air vents crowding the north end of the building.

CHAPTER TWELVE

VIOLET NOLAN CHALKED OUT A CIRCLE IN THE MIDDLE
of the hospital rooftop. Her rabbit Trixie sniffed
curiously at her hand, pink nose trembling. Violet
stroked the familiar absent-mindedly as she carried on
tracing the outline of the ring.

Miles Nolan fidgeted where he squatted next to her.
"How long is this going to take?"

"Five minutes. Ten, tops."

Violet finished the first circle, drew a second one
inside it, and started linking them with complex
symbols. Though it was her first time mapping out the
greeting ritual, it hadn't taken long for her to learn the
spell. She had an eidetic memory and could retain
anything she'd read or seen once. Her brow furrowed.

It helps that Bryony is a good teacher.

Miles pursed his lips. "Should we really be doing
this?"

Violet sighed and met her older cousin's anxious
gaze. "Seeing as the woman who should be carrying

out this ritual is A, incapacitated, and B, wouldn't have a clue how to do it, yes. Besides, who knows what that thing will do if he lands on Earth and doesn't find his mistress? This city doesn't need another disaster."

"I still think Bryony should have asked someone from her own coven to take the risk," Miles grumbled. "I mean, what the heck are we supposed to do with this thing when it gets here?"

"Ideally, convince it not to rip our hearts out and listen to our explanation," Violet muttered.

Miles paled. "That sounds like a bad idea."

Millie, his boa constrictor, coiled around his arm with a concurring hiss.

Violet couldn't very well argue with them. They had been at the forefront of the showdown between the New York coven and the Dark Council a few nights ago, something unheard of since they didn't belong to the city's extensive family of magic users in the first place.

Then again, we're the ones who came to New York and told them what was about to go down.

Violet thought of the woman whose words had led them from Chicago to the East Coast a week ago. She knew she wouldn't have deliberately put them in harm's way if she hadn't thought they could cope with the situation.

Miles stiffened beside her.

"*Vi!*" he hissed under his breath.

"What?"

"The Witch Queen. She's here!"

He elbowed her sharply in the ribs. Violet tumbled to the ground, cursed, and looked around.

Mae Jin was staring at them suspiciously from across the way. Her black hair fluttered around her face, her fair skin almost luminous in the shadows. Now that Violet saw her awake, she realized again how beautiful the Witch Queen was. She wasn't glamorous by any means, but pretty in a no-nonsense kind of way, her athletic build toned by hours spent in the club where she practiced kickboxing and mixed martial arts.

There was a lot Violet and Miles had learned about Mae since the night Nikolai Stanisic had left her in their care.

Even though the woman who was now technically their queen looked ethereal and fragile as she stood there in only a hospital gown and a house coat, Violet was not fooled. The power that had rocked the city and destroyed an entire hospital block might not be evident right at this moment, but she could still sense the indomitable magic inside Mae.

Violet climbed to her feet and dusted off her hands, Miles rising beside her.

"Hi, there," she said in a light tone.

"Who are you?" Mae blurted out. "And what's that?"

She pointed at the circle.

"Oh, this?" Violet started scrubbing out the spell work with her boot, Trixie helping with her paws. "It's nothing."

"Wait!" Miles gaped. "We're not doing the greeting ritual? But—*that's* why we're here!" he spluttered.

Violet indicated Mae with an irritated wave of her hand. "With everything that just went down, I didn't think anybody would be on the rooftop, let alone her. She's gonna freak out if she sees this."

Miles's mouth pressed to a thin line. "Shit. You're right." He looked accusingly at Mae. "Why *is* she here?"

"You guys haven't answered my question. Also, are those your pets?" Mae studied Trixie and Millie with a disapproving moue. "You should know animals aren't allowed in the hospital unless they are therapy or service pets."

Violet grimaced.

Boy, is she in for a surprise.

"Millie isn't an animal!" Miles protested. "She's my familiar!"

Millie bobbed her head vigorously.

Mae squinted, her eyes full of distrust. "What's a familiar?"

Miles opened and closed his mouth soundlessly. He turned beseechingly to Violet.

"You just couldn't keep your trap shut, could you?" Violet muttered. "You know Bryony wanted to officially tell her about our world."

A tapping drew their gazes. Mae was drumming a slippered foot against the ground, her expression impatient.

Violet rubbed the back of her neck and looked at the ground.

"How is it I always end up in these shitty situations?" she mumbled to herself.

A sympathetic sound left Trixie.

Violet thought she heard faint laughter inside her skull. She grimaced.

I wonder if she saw this coming too.

She came to a decision, raised her head, and fixed Mae with a determined stare. "I'm Violet Nolan. This is Trixie, my familiar." She indicated the pink-eyed rabbit. "I'm a witch. Trixie helps me focus my power."

Mae startled as a bright purple disk exploded into life around her right wrist.

Miles shuffled his feet. "I'm Miles Nolan. Violet and I are cousins. This here is Millie." His boa constrictor hissed happily as he stroked her under the chin. "I'm a sorcerer."

A golden globe of magic flashed into life above his left palm.

Mae blinked. Awareness dawned on her face as her gaze swung between them. "You're the people who fought those monsters that night!"

"It wasn't just us." Violet shrugged. "Half the New York coven was there too."

"Coven?" Mae said. "As in a gathering of witches?" She wet her lips nervously. "Like, naked women on a hill, under a full moon at midnight and stuff?"

Violet tried not to roll her eyes hard.

"That's just a load of bull crap," Miles protested. "Covensteads are pretty normal meetings. Except for the yelling and occasional hexing." He paused. "The only time someone disrobed was when Regina Nox got drunk at the annual Grand Meeting in Vegas two years ago and stripped down to her underwear."

"Jeez, thanks." Violet made a face. "I'm gonna keep seeing that image for the rest of the night."

Trixie covered her face with her paws.

"You're lucky," Miles said with a pinched expression. "I was sitting next to her. I swear Erik's hair turned gray when she threatened to pole dance naked."

Violet's brow knitted at the mention of her ex-boyfriend. Guilt flashed in Miles's eyes. A restless sound reached them. They met Mae's irate stare.

"Each city has its own coven and High Priestess," Violet explained with a sigh. "Miles and I are part of the Chicago coven. We've been…temporarily assigned to the New York coven for now."

Thunder boomed in the sky, interrupting them. Mae jumped. Miles studied the angry clouds uneasily.

"Looks like he's gonna be here sooner than we expected," Violet murmured.

"Do you think he'll be upset there's no greeting ritual?" Miles asked worriedly.

Violet indicated Mae with a jerk of her head. "He can take it up with his mistress if he is."

"What are you two talking about?" Mae said, her face tight. "Who's coming? And what's a greeting ritual?"

Violet chewed her lip. "We got a tip-off that your familiar would be making an appearance tonight. A greeting ritual will ease his passage into this world. Otherwise, his entrance might be…somewhat bumpy."

Mae's jaw dropped open. "My—my familiar?!"

"Yes." Violet dipped her chin. "The Witch Queen's

familiar is said to be the most powerful of all the creatures ever bonded to a magic user."

Mae sucked in air. "*Witch Queen!* Those people who attacked me that night called me that too. What does it mean?!" Her hands fisted at her sides, an echo of power pulsing from her. "Do you know what that red light was? And whose voice I heard inside my head?!"

Violet exchanged a startled glance with Miles. "You heard a voice?"

The wind picked up. The clouds started to spiral above them.

"He's coming," Violet warned.

Lightning flashed in the Heavens. Mae's eyes widened.

A dark void had appeared where none should be, some two hundred feet above the rooftop. A sickening, crimson light oozed out of it as it grew.

"What is that?!" Mae shouted above the rising gale.

"Hell!" Violet yelled back.

Mae looked at her blankly. "Huh?!"

Violet indicated the black hole. "That's a portal to Hell. Let's just hope nothing else comes out of this one." She narrowed her eyes. "Maybe we should have done the greeting ritual after all."

A crimson light throbbed on Mae's chest. The pentagram pendant Nikolai had stolen from the Sorcerer King and bestowed upon her levitated out the top of her hospital gown, metal aglow with a scarlet light. Mae flinched.

Miles blanched. "That thing was on her all along?!"

Violet's pulse quickened as she observed the medallion. She could feel its deadly magic.

It flashed, blinding them for a moment.

Something on the ground caught Violet's eye once her vision cleared.

"Oh."

Mae and Miles followed her dull gaze.

A circle overlaid by a pentagram and interlinked with radiating runes had formed around the Witch Queen, the lines blazing with the same red glow emanating from the pendant. It looked different from the spell Violet had intended to create but she could tell its purpose from the strong magic emanating from it.

"There's our greeting ritual."

The medallion hummed, the sound it made pleased.

"That's creepy," Miles mumbled.

Mae hesitated before raising a trembling hand to the pendant. The humming intensified, the weapon pulsing vermilion as it kissed its mistress's skin. She shuddered and blinked slowly, as if recalling something.

"There was a man with a crow. He was here that night, on the rooftop." She met Violet's eyes, her own wild. "He gave me this thing, didn't he?!"

Violet maintained a neutral expression. They hadn't seen nor heard of Nikolai since that night. It was as if he'd vanished into thin air.

Then again, I would be keeping a low profile too if I had the Sorcerer King and the Dark Council after me.

Still, Violet was certain he wouldn't be far. There was too much at stake for him to leave New York.

"We have incoming!" Miles warned, his eyes on the sky.

Violet and Mae looked up.

Something was falling out of the crimson portal.

"Wait." Miles squinted. "Is that a—?"

Violet drew a sharp breath as the shape spun and grew in size.

"Maybe you should step out of that circle," she told Mae.

Large, orange eyes appeared in a rich, red and black triangular face, the vertical irises wide with panic.

Violet shot an alarmed glance at Mae. "Like, seriously, move!"

"What the heck—?" Mae started.

A fox landed on her face with a wet plop.

CHAPTER THIRTEEN

"T HAT THING'S FERAL," M ILES SAID IN A DISGUSTED
tone.

Violet sighed. "He's not feral. He's just disorientated."

Miles indicated the livid red lines on his forearms with a scowl.

"Oh yeah? Tell that to my scars!"

Millie made a worried sound where she and Trixie loitered in the doorway of the bathroom, the two familiars too anxious to come inside.

The fox that had dropped on Mae's head hissed and spat at them from where he'd taken refuge at the far end of the shower cubicle, fur wet and dripping.

They were back in the hospital room. Violet and Miles had come in through the window after Mae had returned to the ICU. Violet had carried the fox in her leather jacket, which now lay in tatters on the floor.

He'd practically ripped the thing apart with his claws and teeth.

The fact that Violet and Miles had floated down from the rooftop using magic and had not been seen by the dozens of cops still swarming the grounds was something Mae had decided she would question later.

Violet had proposed they give the creature a wash to get rid of the sulfurous scent tainting his fur. When Mae had asked why he smelled like that, Violet had said one word.

Hell.

It had been enough to bring Mae to her senses. Though most of what had happened three days ago and tonight still felt like a dream, this moment didn't. She suspected the reason she'd been feeling restless all day had something to do with the creature currently studying them with menacing suspicion.

She'd been waiting for him.

It was a truth that resonated deep inside her, just like the fact that the pendant she'd been born to wield was a heck more powerful than she'd initially thought.

Mae blinked at that stray thought.

Wait. Why did I just think that?

The medallion trembled against her chest.

The fox stopped growling. His orange eyes locked on the pentagram pendant. He made a soft keening noise and strained forward slightly, as if he wanted to get closer.

"You need to talk to him," Violet advised. "He's probably still shocked by what he just went through."

"He's shocked? What about me? I just got a faceful of fox genitals." Mae hesitated. "What do I say to him?"

"Something. Anything."

Mae took a shaky breath. She lifted the towel in her arms and shuffled closer to the fox.

"Come here," she said gently. "I'm not gonna hurt you."

The fox's eyes flared with wariness. He bared his teeth, the sound that left his throat too loud for his tiny body. The air around him turned crimson as his hackles rose.

Miles and Violet traded a worried glance.

The force radiating from the fox made Mae's core and the pendant tremble with resonance. Her lips flattened to a thin line. "Look, I'm not enthused about this either, pal. So, how about you get your skinny runt ass over here and I dry you so you stop looking like a drowned rat?!"

"Oh wow," Violet muttered.

"If that doesn't piss him off, I don't know what will," Miles said, pale-faced.

Trixie and Millie uttered sympathetic noises.

To everyone's surprise, the fox approached slowly. He stopped and started several times, his body language screaming that he still didn't trust any of them. A yelp of surprise left him seconds later.

Mae had lunged forward and scooped him up in the towel when he'd come within arm's reach. She sat back on the floor, laid him in her lap, and started rubbing him down briskly.

"There, that wasn't so bad, was it?"

The shocked look he gave her was so comical Mae couldn't help chuckling. He stilled at the sound, his gaze roaming her face. He straightened as Mae carried on drying him, his head inching closer and closer to her face.

Mae blinked when he tentatively licked her chin.

"That tickles."

The fox seemed pleased by her words.

Mae faltered before stroking his soft, rich fur. "What's your name?"

The fox observed her solemnly.

"You have to give him one," Violet said.

Mae looked blankly at the witch. "What?"

Violet reached out and scratched Trixie's head. "All familiars are given a name by the witch or sorcerer they bond with. It's tradition."

The rabbit made a happy purring sound.

Mae cocked her head to the side and studied the fox. "Hmm. I don't know why, but I feel like he has one already."

She drew a sharp breath when the fox pressed his forehead against hers. His eyes glowed as he gazed into hers.

Sotsuna.

Mae froze. She knew the voice inside her head belonged to the creature gazing at her.

My name was...Sotsuna.

Mae's hands clenched on the fox. "Sotsuna."

"What?" Miles said, puzzled.

Mae looked over at him and Violet, her pulse quickening. "He just told me his name. It's Sotsuna."

Violet's brow wrinkled. Miles's eyes bulged.

"He—he told you?!" the sorcerer stammered, his gaze swinging jerkily between Mae and the fox.

"Yes. Like a voice in my head." Mae's stomach knotted. "Wait. You guys don't hear your familiars' voices?!"

"No," Violet replied grimly.

They all stared at the fox, Violet and Miles in dread and Mae in wonder.

The fox nuzzled Mae's cheek.

Sotsuna was the name your former self gave me. I think I should have another one for this era.

Mae shivered at his words. *Does he mean the voice I heard that night?*

"He says he wants another name," she murmured.

"He does?" Miles said in a strained voice.

"Ah-huh." Mae chewed her lip. A word came to her mind as she studied the creature's sumptuous red and black fur. "How about…Brimstone?"

The fox repeated the word in her head. *Brimstone.* His chest vibrated with a low rumble. *I like it.*

The pendant hummed against Mae's chest.

Brimstone lifted a paw and touched it.

Crimson magic detonated around Mae, wrapping the three of them in a bubble that distorted the air and made the lights flicker. She heard Violet and Miles gasp in the far distance.

Mae's heart slammed against her ribs. She could feel something happening inside her as the scarlet light swirled and pulsed around them. Something changing. No. Something…*forming* between her, the fox, and the pendant. Something she knew instinctively would link their fates forever more.

A red bond of power. A promise of souls. A contract forged in blood.

How long the moment lasted Mae wasn't sure. It ended just as abruptly as it'd started, making her ears pop and leaving her dizzy. The pendant hung heavily around her neck, as if showing its true weight for the first time. Brimstone swayed in her lap.

Mae steadied the fox with one hand and clutched the medallion. The connection between them raised the hairs on her arms and seared her senses.

The fox blinked sleepily. *Thank you.*

He licked her face, yawned, and curled up in a ball on her lap. He was asleep in seconds.

Mae met Violet and Miles's stunned stares. "What just happened?"

"I honestly have no idea," Violet murmured.

CHAPTER FOURTEEN

NYPD Lieutenant Jared Dickson stood a good six-foot-three-inches and towered over FBI Special Agent Alicia Calvarro. The African American detective's business-like smile contrasted sharply with the Hispanic woman's cool expression as they observed Mae from the end of the bed.

"Thank you for agreeing to see us, Miss Jin," Dickson said affably.

Mae wasn't fooled by the lieutenant's smile or tone. She'd seen enough good-cop-bad-cop movies to know he and the FBI agent were playing to a script.

"No problem."

Her head felt heavy, as if she hadn't slept in days. She suspected it was an after-effect of whatever had taken place between her, the fox, and the pendant last night.

Dickson pulled a chair over and sat down, a notepad in hand. "How about you tell us what happened the night of the incident in your own words?"

Calvarro stepped over to the window and looked at the contractors working in the grounds of the hospital before turning and focusing a laser-like stare at Mae, the afternoon sun streaming inside the room casting her face in shadows.

Mae's voice was calm as she narrated her account of the events from four nights ago, keeping to the details she knew Hodge would already have provided in his interview, as well as the witness statements from those who had seen her fight the possessed hospital staff and patients who had wreaked so much havoc on those around them. The only things she didn't speak about were being taken over by another being herself and the magic that had awakened inside her and helped her defeat the dark-cloaked figures who had been after her. As for what had happened with Rose and the devil, Mae omitted mentioning those details completely.

Violet had already told her the people who had survived the attack on the rooftop didn't recall much about what had transpired in those dreadful minutes. How the witch knew this Mae had chosen to ignore for now. What she did question was whether it was her awakened powers that had caused their memory loss.

"I don't know," Violet had told her before she and Miles had left last night, an unhappy Brimstone in tow. The witch had hesitated as she'd climbed out of the window. "But my gut tells me it probably did have something to do with it."

Silence descended when Mae finished talking.

"The body you were dissecting at the time of the incident was that of one Alexei 'Colin' Antonovich, correct?" Dickson asked.

Mae stiffened slightly.

Where are they going with this? They already know the answer to that question.

"Yes, it was."

"Did you find anything—odd when you were examining Mr. Antonovich's remains?" Calvarro said coolly.

Mae's pulse spiked. She recalled the strange bullet and the enlarged pineal gland she'd found inside the dead man. What with everything that had happened, she'd completely forgotten about them.

She remembered what Hodge had told her yesterday about one of the NYPD's lines of inquiry. Her brow furrowed.

"Wait. You guys don't seriously think all of this happened because of Antonovich?!"

Dickson's eyes gleamed with a shrewd light. "His body is still unaccounted for."

Mae's jaw jutted out. "Like I already told you, I decapitated him and left him in that autopsy lab."

Dickson raised an eyebrow. "Dr. Hodge said the same thing. Do you make a habit of decapitating corpses, Miss Jin?"

Mae clenched her hands. "I do when it's an undead one trying to kill me and my boss."

Violet and Miles had told her the identity of the ochre-eyed creatures who had taken control of the bodies of the people inside the hospital that night.

According to the witch and the sorcerer, they were demons.

The old Mae would never have believed them. The new Mae did.

The fact that she was so ready to accept the strange reality she was now living no longer surprised her. She wasn't the woman she had been before that fateful night. And, however much she resented the change, she knew it was her fate. Her connection with Brimstone and the pendant had shown her that.

Calvarro cocked her head to the side. "You believe in the undead, Miss Jin?"

Mae met the FBI agent's probing gaze. "I believe in the evidence of my own eyes, Agent Calvarro."

Calvarro's mouth shrank to a thin line. "You still haven't answered my question, Miss Jin. Did you or did you not find anything strange during Antonovich's autopsy?"

"No, I didn't," Mae lied. "Now, if you'll excuse me, I believe I've told you everything you wanted to know."

She reached over and pressed the call button.

Her nurse Jen appeared. "You okay, Mae?"

"I'm tired. Please see the lieutenant and the special agent out."

Dickson and Calvarro looked unhappy as Jen ushered them from the room.

"We still need to ask you more questions, Miss Jin," Dickson protested.

"You know where I live."

"Don't leave the state," Calvarro warned.

Mae managed not to roll her eyes. Jen wasn't as subtle.

The ICU nurse came back a moment later. "You okay?"

Mae smiled wearily. "Yeah. How's my paperwork coming along?"

"It'll be done within the hour." The nurse hesitated. "You sure you want to self-discharge? Dr. Mehta won't be happy when he hears the news. He wanted you under observation for another couple of days."

"There's nothing wrong with me." Mae grimaced. "Besides, I'm going stir crazy in here. It'll do me good to get out."

Ryu appeared behind Jen, Ye-Seul in tow. They'd insisted she come to the house for dinner before going to her apartment after they heard she was discharging herself.

"You ready?" Ryu said.

Mae was relieved to see her sister acting her normal self. "Almost."

They left a short while later, the overnight bag Mae's family had brought for her stuffed to the brim with chocolates and thank you cards. Ryu made two trips to get the flowers that had filled her hospital room.

They'd just passed St. Vartan Park and crossed the intersection of First Avenue and East 36th Street when Mae started seeing and feeling strange things. She thought it was her imagination at first. By the time they exited the tunnel under the East River and entered

Queens, she knew what she was experiencing was a direct result of her new abilities.

She could sense magic all around her. It came in waves, some subtle, some more powerful. She wondered if the variety in the pulses that washed across her skin had to do with the strength of the magic user and whether all witches and sorcerers could detect this too.

A thought came to her. She closed her eyes and was unsurprised to see brightly colored orbs appear in her mind, the wavering dots mapping out the locations of what seemed to be hundreds of magic users across the city.

But it wasn't just magic she discerned.

Mae opened her eyes and looked to her left. Wisps of darkness swirled above the bus driver in the next lane. The man glanced her way. Ochre flashed in his pupils. Her nails dug into her palms.

New York wasn't just full of magic users.

It was teeming with demons.

CHAPTER FIFTEEN

Mae burped politely behind her hand. "Excuse me."

Yoo-Mi beamed at her across the kitchen table. "I'm glad to see you've got your appetite back."

Mae patted her overfull belly and studied the remains of the feast. Her mother had excelled herself, as always. Meanwhile, she'd pigged out as if this were her last meal on Earth. She eyed the leftover rice cake in front of Ryu.

Her sister pushed the plate over. "Here, have it."

"Thank you."

It was past nine o'clock by the time Mae got up to leave. Ryu had brought her Vespa over from the hospital a couple of days ago. Betsy the Scooter had miraculously survived the destruction at Grandview despite being parked close to where the roof of the surgical block had collapsed onto the grounds.

"Won't you stay the night?" Yoo-Mi twisted her hands where they'd gathered in the hallway. "I don't like the idea of you being on your own."

"I'm okay, Mom." Mae secured her helmet strap under her chin. "Besides, I need to take out the garbage. My apartment must stink to high heaven by now."

Never mind the unexpected guests waiting for me there.

"Mr. Seong already aired out your place. And he put your mail on your kitchen table."

Mae froze. Mr. Seong was her landlord and the owner of the old cinema beneath her apartment.

"He did?" Mae pursed her lips. "When?"

"This morning."

Mae's stomach lurched. *Shit.*

"He, er, didn't say anything weird to you after, did he?"

Yoo-Mi's eyebrows drew together. "No. Why would he?" She squinted. "Are you hiding something from us?"

Ye-Seul straightened, an eager gleam lighting her rheumy eyes. "Is it one of those foreign men? You know, a guy with a big ding dong?"

She made a suggestive gesture with her hands.

"No!" Mae said, horrified.

"Jeez, Grandma," Ryu muttered.

Yoo-Mi's expression grew pinched. Mae swallowed a sigh.

Violet and Miles must have been out when he went there. That, or they were hiding in one of the bedrooms.

"I'm surprised Mr. Seong climbed the stairs to my place," she muttered. "He's frail and prone to falls."

Ryu brightened. "That's because you're the official hero of Koreatown."

Mae stared. "What?"

"It's the truth." Yoo-Mi bobbed her head. "Even Mrs. Son-Ha acknowledged it. By the way, she wants to introduce her son to you and Ryu."

"Over my dead body!" Mae and her sister snapped at the same time.

Kwon 'Michael' Son-Ha was a cheating little snake who liked to dip his stick in as many unchartered honey pots as he could find. They'd known him since high school, where he'd tried vainly to hook up with Mae or Ryu on many an occasion. The last time he'd asked Ryu out, he'd gotten overly friendly and earned himself a black eye.

Mae met her sister's gaze. They shared a faint smile.

The tension between them had dissipated.

"I think it would be best if I didn't date anyone for a while," Mae said firmly.

"Oh." Yoo-Mi's face fell. "Of course. It's too soon. Especially with everything that happened with Rose."

The funeral invitation in Mae's back pocket burned her skin through her jeans. Though Rose's body had not been recovered, she had been declared dead after having been seen falling from the rooftop of the surgical block at Grandview. Her parents had sent the funeral notice to Mae's home two days ago. The service was tomorrow, at Union Field Cemetery. It was going to be a closed casket burial, as per Rose's Jewish faith. Her family intended to fill the coffin with all her favorite things.

Her best friend's sapphire bracelet warmed Mae's skin where it kissed her wrist. She'd originally planned to place it in Rose's casket. But something had dissuaded her from doing so. It had taken her a while to figure out what it was.

Burying the bracelet would mean she had accepted Rose's death.

Mae became aware of the stilted silence in the hallway.

"I'll be off then."

She opened the door, saw an irate Violet trying to lift Brimstone from where he was sniffing the Vespa parked in the driveway, and slammed it shut.

"On the other hand, why don't I stay the night?" Mae said brightly.

Yoo-Mi's eyes sparkled. Ryu stared. Ye-Seul nodded wisely.

"I'll show myself to my room."

Mae took off her helmet and climbed the stairs to the second floor before anyone could stop her. She turned left at the top, stormed down the hallway, and entered the bedroom at the end.

Violet froze, one leg over the windowsill. Trixie startled on her shoulder.

Miles was cursing on the floor, Brimstone struggling in his hold. Millie bobbed in alarm where she'd coiled around the sorcerer's arm.

"What the hell?!" Mae whispered fiercely. She closed the door and dropped the helmet on a chest of drawers. "I told you guys to wait for me at the apartment!"

"We did." Violet came in, closed the window, and

drew the curtains. "Until your fox decided to run away."

Brimstone slipped out of Miles's hands, bounded over to Mae, and coiled around her legs. Mae sighed. She could feel the creature's distress at being parted from her.

She squatted and petted his head. "I was coming back."

Brimstone made a happy rumbling sound and rolled over onto his back. She scratched the fox's belly.

Truth be told, she'd felt an ache in her chest after he'd left with Violet and Miles last night. That ache faded as the bond between them tightened, warming their hearts. The pendant trembled against her chest in resonance.

"What am I going to do with—?"

The door opened and hit Mae on the ass. She tumbled face down on the floor, taking Brimstone with her.

"Here, I thought you might need a fresh—" Ryu froze, one hand on the doorknob and a pair of pajamas hanging limply in the other. Her eyes rounded. "Is that a *fox?!*" Her gaze shifted from Brimstone to Trixie and Millie. She paled. "Shit! Why the hell is there a snake in your room?!"

Mae sat up, her heart pounding in her chest.

Violet had told her familiars could only be seen by people who possessed magic in their souls or if the animals chose to make themselves seen. That was why their presence at the hospital had not been reported by any of the survivors. And since Mae's magic had been sealed inside her, she'd lived her whole life oblivious to the existence of the hundreds of familiars in the city until the night her powers awakened.

It seemed that wasn't the case for her sister.

Mae gawped at Ryu. "You can see them?!"

CHAPTER SIXTEEN

VIOLET STUDIED THE TWO SISTERS WHERE THEY SAT ON the bed.

Ryu was shorter than Mae by a few inches and sported a round face and wide-spaced, almond-shaped eyes. Despite the differences in their physical appearance, she carried herself with the same gritty determination as her older sister.

Ryu cut her eyes to the familiars in the room. "How long have I been able to see people with strange pets? Since middle school."

Violet chewed her lip.

So, the right age for someone's magic to start to awaken.

"Oh." Mae grimaced. "I remember you saying something about that. We all thought you were making it up."

Ryu shrugged. "Yeah, well, I decided to ignore it after that time. New York is full of weirdos anyway." She licked her lips nervously. "What's going on, Mae? Who are these people?"

She indicated Violet and Miles.

Mae clenched her jaw. She seemed to come to a decision.

"Don't," Violet warned.

Mae met her cool stare.

"The less your sister knows about our world, the better. It will only put her and your family in danger."

"I agree," Miles said in a strained voice.

Mae hesitated.

"What world?" Ryu's brow wrinkled. "Wait. Does this have anything to do with that crazy red light I saw that night?"

Mae paled. Violet clenched her jaw.

"Damn," Miles mumbled, his expression reflecting her disquiet as they exchanged a glance.

It seemed Ryu had seen too much already.

"You saw that?!" Mae blurted out.

"Yeah." Ryu clutched Mae's hand, her eyes darkening. "I don't know why, but I thought of you when it happened. I called your cell but I couldn't get through."

"The magic storm took out all the telecommunication masts in the city," Violet said grimly.

"Magic storm?" Ryu repeated.

Mae looked equally perplexed.

Violet fiddled with her ring.

She's not going to be happy when we tell her about Nikolai and what he did that night.

Mae hesitated before taking a deep breath.

The window trembled as she let loose a faint aura

of crimson magic. Her hair fluttered around her, the pendant at her neck glowing with power. Brimstone leapt onto her lap and closed his eyes, the same aura radiating from him.

Violet's scalp prickled. She glanced tensely at Miles.

They knew what they were seeing and sensing was but an infinitesimal fraction of the Witch Queen's true power. And something told Violet it would only grow with time. Mae Jin had barely begun to tap into her magic core.

Ryu stared unblinkingly at her sister. Mae retracted her magic and met her wondering gaze.

"That was you?" Ryu said weakly.

Mae dipped her chin. "Are you—" She stopped and swallowed. "Are you scared?"

"No." Ryu shook her head. "Why would I be? You're my sister."

Mae sagged. She gripped Ryu's hand tightly, her voice tremulous when she spoke.

"Thank you. I thought you would think me a monster."

Brimstone keened and pressed a paw against her chest. Mae stroked the fox's head. Then, she told Ryu everything about what happened that night, including Rose Blake's true fate. Ryu listened quietly without interrupting.

Violet could tell she never doubted her sister's words.

A stilted hush fell inside the bedroom once Mae finished talking.

Ryu met Violet and Miles's stares. "You're magic users too?"

"Yes," Violet replied reluctantly.

Ryu indicated Trixie and Millie. "And they are your…familiars?"

Miles dipped his chin warily.

Violet knew he shared her concerns about Mae revealing the truth to Ryu. But she could also see why Mae had chosen to do so. Ryu evidently possessed magic in her soul and would be at risk from Mae's enemies from now on. It was better to arm her with some knowledge so she could be on her guard.

"There's something I don't understand," Mae told Violet. "How come Ryu has magic?"

"Because it is in our bloodline."

Violet jumped, as did everyone else.

Mae and Ryu's grandmother was standing in the doorway of the bedroom, a small stone bowl clasped in her hands.

Shit. I didn't hear her come in!

MAE'S HEART THUMPED VIOLENTLY IN HER CHEST AS SHE looked at Ye-Seul's wizened face. The older woman's eerie words echoed in her ears.

"What are you saying, Grandma?" Ryu said shakily.

Ye-Seul came inside the room and closed the door. She walked over to the bed. Mae and Ryu shuffled aside to create space for her.

She sat between them and indicated the stone bowl she held.

"Do you know what this is?"

Mae's stomach clenched as she studied the pile of gray ash filling the vessel. "No."

"It's the remains of the stupa I brought over from our family shrine when we left South Korea."

Ryu bit her lip. "But—we already have a family stupa. It's on the altar in the hallway."

"That one's a fake," Ye-Seul said.

Mae sucked in air. Ryu's eyes bulged.

"What's a stupa?" Miles said blankly.

"It's an item found in temples of various faiths related to Buddhism," Ryu replied, her voice quavering. "It represents the remains of a religious relic. Many places of worship were built in its form, some dating as far back as over two millennia ago."

"All family shrines in South Korea have a version of the stupa," Mae added. "Many are several hundred years old." She chewed the inside of her cheek as she observed Ye-Seul. "Did you overhear what I said to Ryu? About what happened the night of the attack?"

"Yes."

Mae's pulse stuttered. She hadn't wanted Yoo-Mi and Ye-Seul to know the truth yet, if ever.

Ryu groaned. "You shouldn't eavesdrop, Grandma."

"I had no choice, since my granddaughter is intent on keeping secrets from me," Ye-Seul retorted, unrepentant.

Mae hunched her shoulders. "I'm sorry. I just—"
She lapsed into a guilty silence.

"You didn't think this old lady could handle the facts?" Ye-Seul said quietly.

Mae's mouth pressed to a thin line. She dipped her chin.

Ye-Seul watched her steadily. "You'd be surprised at what I've seen and experienced in my life, child. Now, I want you to pay close attention to what I'm about to tell you. Both of you, but especially you, Mae." She cast a shrewd stare at Violet and Miles. "I suspect the two of you know some of this story already."

The pair traded a puzzled look.

Mae's gaze strayed from Ye-Seul's resolute face to the stone bowl. She had a feeling she didn't really want to hear what her grandmother intended to reveal to them.

"What does this have to do with our bloodline and magic?" she asked reluctantly.

Ye-Seul was silent for a while.

"What I am about to tell you is a secret passed down the generations of the Hwangs, since time immemorial," she finally said, her tone grave.

Mae blinked slowly. "What?"

"The Hwangs are related to the Jee family. And the Jees possessed magic in their souls."

Ryu flinched. "Wait. You're not talking about—?"

"The Jee family?" Mae said hoarsely, her chest tight. "As in the nobles who united the Three Kingdoms and gave rise to the most powerful emperors of the Goryeo and Joseon Dynasties?!"

"Yes."

Mae shared a stunned glance with Ryu.

Since Korean history wasn't taught in the U.S. education system, their father had enrolled them in private Korean language and literature evening classes when they were kids. They knew all about the turbulent past of the Korean Peninsula, from the inception of its first kingdom in the 7th century B.C. to the 20th century war that tore it into two nations a mere hundred years ago. The geopolitical, cultural, and scientific achievements of the dominant dynasties meant that time had long been seen as the golden age of prosperity during which Buddhism thrived.

Mae swallowed, the ramifications of this revelation echoing through her.

"Does that mean the Jee family used magic to reign over their empires?" Ryu asked, pale-faced.

"That I do not know," Ye-Seul said. "If they did, it was never practiced openly, nor written down in any historical documents. But it is not the Jee family that I truly wish to tell you about."

CHAPTER SEVENTEEN

"It isn't?" Mae mumbled.

"No," Ye-Seul replied with a gentle smile. "I wish to tell you the story of Ran Soyun, the Jee family's ancestor."

And so, she spoke. Of a woman of incomparable strength and spirit, born in a time of strife and terror, in an Eastern kingdom ruled by war. Of the demon who sought her presence and made a pact with her, in which she promised him her soul in exchange for the arcane knowledge he would teach her to make her the very first witch on Earth. Of a love story that should never have been but was. Of the child born of their union, a being of unimaginable power destined to rule the magic world in her father's stead. Of the tragedy that befell the couple and their newborn daughter, and the Sorcerer King who gathered a monstrous army to destroy their kingdom and murder the infant before she could take her very first steps.

Ye-Seul studied the remains of the stupa, her

expression melancholic. "But though he succeeded in destroying the child's body, the Sorcerer King could not—"

"—*annihilate her soul*," Violet quoted in a dull voice. The witch sat down heavily at Mae's desk, her face pale. "*And so, the child's spirit lingered in limbo, neither alive, nor quite dead.*"

"*But the Fates had one last trick up their sleeves,*" Miles recited slowly, his complexion similarly ashen. "*As the first witch breathed her last breath and Azazel was forced back to the depths of Hell, the child's soul found a place to hide on Earth. And she vowed that she would be reborn again in the future—*"

"—once her body returned to this realm, in the never-ending cycle of death and reincarnation. And she would seek revenge on her enemy and his brethren, and retake her throne," Ye-Seul finished quietly. Her eyes gleamed as she appraised Violet and Miles. "I see you know your history well."

"It's the first thing anyone with magic learns," Violet confessed in a heavy tone, her expression gaunt.

"So, the first witch's name was Ran Soyun?" Miles asked in a strained voice.

"Indeed," Ye-Seul said sagely. "And her husband's name was Azazel?"

"He was a fallen angel and the Third Leader of the Grigori." Miles hesitated. "He was said to be the most skilled at magic in all of the Heavens."

Blood rushed in Mae's head, a pounding that filled her world. She recalled the vision she had witnessed that tragic night, when the crimson storm had torn through her.

"I saw it." Her nails bit into her palms. "The army of monsters that destroyed that kingdom. I saw the memories of that—that child!"

Violet's eyes rounded. "What? You never mentioned this before!"

Mae bit her lip. "I thought—I was losing my mind."

Tense silence befell them.

Ye-Seul laid a hand on Mae's clenched knuckles. "What did you see?"

Mae's stomach churned. She took a deep breath and spoke falteringly of what she had experienced that night in the autopsy lab.

"I saw Azazel and Ran Soyun," she confessed past the heavy lump in her throat. "I'm pretty sure it was them. I—" She paused and swallowed. "I could tell how much they loved their daughter and what they sacrificed to try and save her." She looked unseeingly at the floor, the images of the massacre she had witnessed playing before her eyes once more. Pressure weighed her down, so thick she feared it would crush her heart. Her tone grew in strength and fury. *"I saw my kingdom burn and my people die!"*

Violet's alarmed shout tore across the room. "Mae!"

Mae blinked. She froze, awareness returning, the voice that had left her lips echoing inside her skull.

A crimson haze had filled the bedroom, the air shivering violently as if in the grip of a storm. Every object that wasn't nailed down had levitated into the air, including her grandmother and sister, Violet and Miles, and the three familiars.

Brimstone air-walked down onto her lap, his orange eyes aglow with power and his expression calm. He touched his forehead against hers, the pentagram pendant warming their flesh where it pressed between their bodies.

Breathe.

Mae gasped, the burning sensation in her lungs abating as she finally drew air. The red mist vanished. Ye-Seul and Ryu bounced down on the bed as it thumped onto the floor. The chair Violet had been sitting on clattered to the ground. The rest of the furniture crashed noisily around them.

There was a moment of stunned silence. A yell came from downstairs.

"Everything okay up there?"

It was Yoo-Mi.

Ryu flinched. "Yeah! Sorry, I dropped something!"

"Well, be more careful," Yoo-Mi grumbled.

Mae pressed a trembling hand to her mouth. "What —what did I just do?!"

Her panicked gaze landed on Violet and Miles.

"You scared the shit out of us is what you did." Miles dropped shakily to the floor with his cousin. "I almost crapped my pants."

Sweat beaded Violet's forehead. "You lost control of your powers."

"Wow," Ryu mumbled. "That was something else."

Violet's face grew pinched at her awed voice.

"What?" Ryu said defensively. "Okay, it was scary, but you gotta admit, also super cool."

"It kinda was," Miles agreed reluctantly, admiration replacing the unease in his eyes.

"That was an expression of your rage." Ye-Seul lifted a hand to Mae's cheek, her voice surprisingly serene. "And rightly so. But you must learn to control it, child. Or else it will destroy you and everyone you love."

Mae shuddered, the pieces of the puzzle finally coming together.

"I'm her, aren't I? I'm Azazel and Ran Soyun's daughter."

A sad light danced in Ye-Seul's eyes.

"I had a dream, the night before we left South Korea, all those years ago," Mae's grandmother confessed. "In it, I saw a beautiful woman who told me to take the stupa from the Hwangs' family shrine. I woke your grandfather there and then and insisted he take me to the temple that very hour. The priest was waiting for us when we got to the shrine. He had had the same dream. Though we never spoke of it, I just knew in my bones. He handed me the stupa all wrapped up in sacred clothing and sent us on our way."

She gazed at the stone bowl and the pile of ash that had miraculously survived Mae's unintentional levitation spell. "On the day your mother went into labor, the stupa started glowing crimson. I was the only one who saw the light it emitted and felt the power of the soul who had inhabited it for thousands of years. Though the only thing that had sustained her existence was the prayers of our ancestors, and the passage of time had weakened her, she remained determined to see her promise through. At the moment of your birth, the soul of that child left her hiding place and entered her reborn body. And all that was left of the stupa was glowing ash. Luckily, the priest and I foresaw this and he gave me a second stupa to replace the original."

Mae felt an echo of the otherwordly heartbeat from that night once more. She pressed a hand to her chest. Heat scorched her palm.

"Na Ri." She met the others' stares. "Her name was...Na Ri."

CHAPTER EIGHTEEN

Light flitted warmly across Violet's eyelids. She stirred, rolled over, and blinked. A dark, triangular face with orange eyes filled her vision. Violet yelped and bolted upright, heart pounding and magic at hand.

Brimstone studied her calmly from where he'd been watching her sleep on the inflatable mattress on Mae's bedroom floor. He ignored the purple disks of power around her wrists, raised his head, and licked her nose.

Violet's breath shuddered out of her as the fox's hot tongue rasped her skin. "That kind of wake-up call is freaky. Don't do it again." She retracted her magic. "I could have hurt you."

Brimstone gave her a somewhat condescending look. Violet looked at the rabbit snoozing under the covers by her legs.

"Fat lot of good you are," she muttered.

Brimstone sniffed the familiar before licking one of her ears. Trixie woke up, froze when she saw the fox, and bolted into Violet's arms. Brimstone whined, face drooping.

He really is like a kid. Then again, he did just reincarnate.

"Don't take it personally," Violet told the fox. "It's a prey-predator thing."

Trixie lifted her head from where she'd burrowed her face in the crook of Violet's elbow. She shuffled around guiltily and twitched her nose at Brimstone. The fox came over slowly and pressed his snout against hers. A low rumble left Trixie. Her ears perked up.

Brimstone looked pleased.

"Oh. You're awake."

Violet looked around. Mae had come through from the bathroom, a towel around her shoulders.

"Yeah."

Violet rubbed a hand down her face, embarrassed at how well she'd slept. She looked over to where Miles snored gently, face down in his sleeping bag and Millie coiled on his back.

Ryu and Ye-Seul had insisted they spend the night instead of returning to Mae's apartment. Mae had agreed. She'd gone on to surprise Violet and Miles further by inviting them to attend Rose's funeral.

"Are you sure?" Violet had asked hesitantly.

She knew how much the loss of her best friend still ate at Mae. And she'd started to feel increasingly guilty about all she had yet to reveal to the newly awakened witch regarding her and Miles's presence in New York.

"Yes," Mae had replied. "Besides, I need you to take care of Brimstone until the ceremony is over."

Miles had grimaced at that. "So, you're basically using us as a familiar baby-sitting service, huh?"

"I don't want him digging up bones in the cemetery," Mae had said firmly.

From the guilty look that had shot across Brimstone's face, the fox had been entertaining precisely that idea.

"I see those two are bonding," Mae said presently. She indicated Brimstone and Trixie. "By the way, what do familiars eat?"

Violet shrugged. "Pretty much what their physical nature demands."

They observed the fox and the rabbit.

"Don't eat her," Mae warned Brimstone.

The fox looked offended. Trixie gulped.

"Or any other familiars for that matter," Violet added.

Brimstone huffed out a put-upon sigh. Miles snorted and mumbled something in his sleep.

"He's a heavy sleeper," Mae observed.

"Sometimes, Aunt Carmen has to use magic to rouse him," Violet said wryly.

Carmen Nolan was Miles's mother and the cousin of the Head Priestess of the Chicago coven.

Mae looked over at Brimstone. "Wake him up."

The fox lowered his front body with an expression of pure mischief, wagged his bushy tail, and pounced on the sleeping sorcerer.

Miles yelped. Millie shot up into the air and landed on the floor with a splat. A wheezing sound left the fox where he sat on Miles, his mouth open on a smile. Mae chuckled.

"That was not funny," Miles grumbled.

Millie hissed, annoyed.

Violet grinned. "Yeah, it was."

They freshened up and went downstairs. Ryu and her mother were laying breakfast out in the kitchen. Ye-Seul was watching the TV on the counter.

"I didn't hear your friends arrive this morning," Yoo-Mi told Mae half-accusingly.

Ryu had evidently sold her the story they'd cooked up last night to explain Violet and Miles's presence at the house.

"They were as quiet as mice," Mae lied.

She introduced Violet and Miles. Yoo-Mi greeted them graciously, oblivious to the familiars wandering curiously around her kitchen. Ye-Seul had told Mae the magic in their bloodline often skipped a generation. Violet and Miles had confirmed this was the same for the rest of the magic world. Not every child born to a witch or a sorcerer inherited their powers.

Breakfast was a lively affair. Violet could tell how close-knit Mae's family was from their easy banter. It reminded her of her own household back in Chicago and the coven she and Miles belonged to. Another family came to her mind, this one as unorthodox as they came and full of fantastical beings and creatures straight out of mythology.

A soft smile tugged at Violet's lips.

It's been a while since we visited those idiots.

Miles made a face.

"What?" Violet said.

"You're smiling."

"Yeah. So?"

"Stop." Miles shuddered. "It's creeping me out."

Violet scowled.

They surreptitiously fed the familiars under the table while Mae and Ryu kept Yoo-Mi distracted.

"What time is the funeral?" Mae's mother asked as she started clearing the table.

"One o'clock."

The mood in the kitchen grew somber. It didn't get any better after Mae went upstairs and changed into a black pant suit and scarf.

"Are you sure you don't want us to come?" Yoo-Mi asked anxiously as they prepared to leave a while later. "We should pay our respects."

Mae grimaced. "I'll break down completely if you guys are there."

Yoo-Mi sniffed. "Okay. Do give Rose's family my condolences."

"You could have at least let me drive you there," Ryu murmured.

Their cab had just pulled up to the curb.

"I need to go somewhere with Violet and Miles afterward."

Mae hadn't seemed too surprised when Violet had told her Bryony Cross wanted to meet her. Considering everything that had happened in the last week, Violet knew the Witch Queen had a lot of questions she wanted answers to.

"By the way, do you guys have a car?" Mae asked Violet and Miles as they got in the cab.

"No," Violet replied. "It's too much of a bother in this city."

"How do you get around?" Mae asked curiously.

Miles cleared his throat. "You know—"

He glanced at the cab driver and flapped his elbows.

"You do the chicken dance?" Mae said dully.

Violet bit her lip.

"I mean we fly!" Miles snapped.

The driver stared at them in the rearview mirror. Mae waited until he was looking at the road again.

"Like, out in plain sight?!" she hissed out the corner of her mouth.

"We can shield our presence to an extent with an illusion," Violet explained reluctantly. "So people don't pay any attention to us."

The cab driver's eyes rounded.

"Like an invisibility cloak," Miles added.

The driver's foot slipped off the accelerator. They jerked forward against their seatbelts. Brimstone growled in the footwell.

It took twenty minutes to get from Flushing to South Ridgewood, the cab keeping above the speed limit and taking the corners without slowing down. By the time they got out of the car, Miles and Millie were slightly green.

They parted ways outside the gates of the Jewish

cemetery, Mae joining the queue of mourners heading for the chapel. Brimstone sat by Violet's feet and watched her leave with a forlorn expression.

"She'll be back soon."

Brimstone whined softly.

CHAPTER NINETEEN

Muted voices rose around Mae as she exited the building with the rest of the congregation an hour later. Rose's family walked on ahead, her father and mother shaking with silent sobs while her elder brother Stuart draped his arms around their shoulders, his own eyes raw from crying.

Rose's sister-in-law trailed behind them, her young son at her side.

"When is Aunt Rose coming?" the little boy asked his mother brightly as he skipped along the path. "I miss her!"

Mae clenched her jaw. Rose had doted on her nephew from the moment he was born. She could guess how crushed the little boy would be once he realized he wouldn't be seeing his favorite aunt ever again.

Stuart's wife gently hushed their son, her face drawn.

Mae's chest tightened when she spotted the plain

wooden casket being carried to the graveside where Rose would be laid to rest. Except there was no body inside it to bury.

How she'd stopped herself from screaming out in denial and rage when she'd seen the coffin, Mae didn't know. Everything that had happened that night on the rooftop of the surgical block had played inside her head over and over again as she'd listened to the eulogy, her light mood from that morning a thing of the past and her subconscious seemingly determined to torture her for failing her friend.

Now that she was aware of the power she wielded and her pitiful lack of control over it, Mae knew she couldn't allow herself to give in to her anger. Not when doing so might hurt the people around her.

She'd spoken to Rose's parents briefly before the ceremony, her heart heavy with grief and guilt. The fact that she couldn't tell them the truth about what had happened to their daughter ate at her, an insidious darkness that choked her insides. Rose's mother had brightened briefly when she'd seen Mae, only for sorrow to overwhelm her all over again when she realized Mae had survived the attack on Grandview when her own daughter hadn't. Mae had hugged the older woman tightly to her chest as her knees folded, the familiar scent of jasmine drifting from her skin reminding her of her best friend.

The rabbi's voice drifted gently over them once they gathered around the freshly dug grave. It was a beautiful, clear day, the kind Rose loved. Mae raised her face to the sky, sunlight warming her skin as she listened to the prayers being read out. Tears blurred her vision. She let them fall, the trickles cooling her hot cheeks.

The conviction that had been growing inside her since the day she woke up and realized Rose wasn't at her side crystallized into a cold certainty.

I will find him. I swear to you on this false grave. I will find the devil who killed you and rip his heart from his chest.

The sound of dirt hitting the casket echoed in Mae's ears as the funeral drew to a close. She clenched her fist around the handful of earth she was given before gently letting go, the dust spiraling down onto the empty coffin with a finality that made her breath lodge in her throat.

She moved aside for the next mourner, her steps heavy.

The hairs rose on the back of her neck as she joined the rest of the congregation where they huddled on the other side of the grave. Mae turned and saw a flash of movement to the north. Her heart stuttered. She caught a glimpse of blonde hair in the shadows under the tree line, some hundred feet up the incline.

Rose!

Nikolai stood stiffly in a coppice east of where Rose Blake was being buried.

His gaze remained locked on Mae's lonely figure where she stood by the graveside, amidst her lost friend's relatives and acquaintances. She was wearing a black pant suit and scarf, her eyes hidden behind sunglasses. He could tell she'd been crying from her pinched expression and cracked lips.

Alastair cocked his head where he perched on Nikolai's shoulder, his eyes shining shrewdly. Nikolai swallowed a sigh. There was no hiding his interest in the woman they had come to New York to save.

The way his pulse quickened and his belly grew hot were surefire signs he'd formed some kind of physical attraction to the Witch Queen.

Nikolai's face tightened. Not that he intended to act on it. There was no time to indulge in foolish feelings. Not when the fate of the world was at stake.

He'd kept away from Grandview in the aftermath of the attack that had followed Mae's awakening, seeking refuge in the few places he knew the long arm of the Dark Council couldn't reach. From the rumors circulating in the magic underworld, Oscar and his henchmen were still in town.

Nikolai knew they were watching Mae's every move. Now that her soul had been roused, they could not act recklessly like before; even though she didn't have full control of her powers yet, the Witch Queen was still a formidable foe. Hence why he'd decided to keep a close eye on her since she'd left the hospital.

He'd been relieved to see Violet and Miles Nolan visit her last night, even though he'd found it strange that they'd sneaked in and out of a second-floor window to do so. It hadn't taken him long to find out their names, nor that they belonged to the Chicago coven and not the New York one like he'd originally thought. As for the fox he'd spotted with them, he was pretty sure it was the creature who'd fallen out of the portal above the hospital two nights ago.

He was debating the best time to make contact with them when a voice rose behind him.

"You know stalking is illegal, right?"

Nikolai closed his eyes briefly and sighed. He turned and met Violet Nolan's cool stare. "You guys really need to stop creeping up on me. What if I'd blasted you with my magic?"

"Oh, please," Miles Nolan scoffed. "You couldn't take both of us on."

Nikolai decided to overlook that statement.

His gaze dropped to the fox staring intently at him and Alastair. "Is that her familiar?"

"Yeah." Violet relaxed slightly when she realized he wasn't a threat. The witch hesitated. "She named him Brimstone."

The fox surprised everyone by sitting on his haunches and grinning at Nikolai, bushy tail thumping the ground in lazy swings.

"That's new," Miles said dully. "Why didn't he do that the first time he met us?"

"What'd he do the first time he met you?" Nikolai asked.

"He maimed us," the sorcerer said glumly.

His boa constrictor bobbed her head in agreement. Nikolai bit back a smile.

"He likes you," Violet murmured.

Nikolai squatted and reached a hand out to the familiar. "I'm a likable guy."

Brimstone inched forward and sniffed his fingers before giving them a careful lick.

The power inside the creature washed across Nikolai, a crimson tide that resembled his mistress's magic. Alastair flew down from his shoulder and landed next to the fox. The two familiars studied each other solemnly before gently bumping heads.

"I gave you half my pizza," Miles told Brimstone accusingly.

The fox huffed. He suddenly stiffened.

They followed his gaze as he rose on all fours, his hackles rising and a growl that sounded too loud for his body rumbling from his chest.

Mae was running up the slope toward the tree line north of the burial site.

CHAPTER TWENTY

Mae's pulse thumped loudly in her ears as she bolted into the shadows beneath the trees, her gaze locked on the figure darting between the trunks up ahead.

It was Rose. She was sure of it.

Branches and leaves snagged at her hair and clothes as she dashed through the undergrowth. She ignored the scratches on her skin and the tears in her suit, her mind full of questions and her heart singing with relief.

She's alive! Rose is alive!

The outlook opened up after some eighty feet.

Mae darted out into the sunlight and staggered to a stop in the middle of a clearing framed by mausoleums and headstones. She whirled around, her gaze frantically scanning the area for Rose. A flicker above drew her gaze. Her stomach dropped.

Rose was floating some twenty feet in the air. "Hi, Mae."

She drifted down and landed smoothly on top of a tombstone.

A chill raced down Mae's spine.

An aura of corruption was swelling around her best friend.

Rose watched her with cold detachment. The gaping hole in her chest had disappeared and she looked alive and healthy. Except Mae knew the voice that had just come from her lips. Would remember it forever more.

Rose's pupils flared crimson, her expression amused. "I see you already know the truth, witch."

Fury sent heat bubbling through Mae's veins. She clenched her fists, knowing she was close to losing control again and not caring. Not when the monster she intended to kill stood before her wearing her best friend's body.

"What have you done with Rose?!"

The devil studied her blankly before bursting out laughing. Rose cackled and wheezed until tears streamed down her face, the wild sounds she made ringing painfully in Mae's ears.

"Oh my!" the creature finally managed in between chuckles. She dropped to the ground and wiped at her cheeks. "What an inane question. What have I done with her?" She spread her arms in a welcoming gesture, her eyes mocking. "Why, she is right here, standing before you." She cocked her head to the side. "I have to admit, I like this body."

Fire filled Mae's mind. *"Get out of her, you bastard!"*

The air turned red, her magic exploding in a wave

that shook the trees and cracked headstones. The pendant inside her shirt whirred angrily.

The devil grinned, satisfaction lighting up its hateful pupils. Rose raised a hand in the air. *"Now!"*

Dark-clad figures appeared from all around the clearing, magic flickering around them and their familiars in sickening, inky auras. Their voices rose in a susurration that raised goosebumps on Mae's flesh. Dread churned her gut, the unknown spell they were chanting tugging at something deep inside her.

She hadn't sensed their presence at all.

Her gaze found the devil who'd taken Rose's form.

Wait. Is that because of—?!

Pressure dropped down on her, an invisible hammer that drew a cry from her throat and made her legs buckle. A black tempest detonated across the clearing. Light faded, the dark currents obscuring the sky and the sun.

Mae choked as she collapsed onto one knee. The air had turned thick and heavy, so much so she felt like she was breathing under water. The pendant shuddered, magic faltering.

What—what is this?!

She could feel something binding her power even as she tried to let it loose. Something evil and insidious. Her ears popped. The shadows around her started to pulse with a crimson glow. The stench of sulfur drenched the clearing.

The weight bearing down on her intensified. Mae found herself on her hands and knees, fingers sinking into the ground and body bowing under the invisible force holding her captive. She gritted her teeth, twisted her head sideways, and stole a look at the sky. Her eyes rounded.

Fear turned her blood to ice.

A portal had formed above her. One that looked identical to the one Brimstone had fallen out of two nights ago.

The devil appeared from amidst the storm.

"That's right," Rose said gleefully. "That's a doorway to Hell, little girl. We think a trip there would do you some good."

"Come now, demon, you should be kinder to my future spouse," someone drawled on Mae's left.

She looked around stiffly, the muscles and tendons in her neck screaming in protest as she fought the wicked energy immobilizing her.

A man with red hair and a hungry look in his gray eyes walked out of the shadows, a tawny lynx at his side. He closed the distance to her, stopped, and lowered himself on his haunches opposite her.

The stranger studied Mae like a scientist would an insect.

"I'm going to enjoy taming you, witch."

His loathsome gaze dropped to her mouth. He grabbed her chin in a painful grip, yanked her forward, and kissed her brutally. Mae gagged at the corrupt magic he breathed into her lungs.

The man stared into her eyes, his own full of madness and a lust that would not be quenched. He forced his way inside her mouth. She fisted her hands in the dirt, bit his tongue, and headbutted him with a vicious roar, breaking free from his kiss.

The man fell back, surprise widening his eyes. They turned ugly in the next instant.

He rose and lifted his arm to strike her. "Why you—!"

"Get away from her!"

A bright bolt of magic carved the gloom on her right. It glanced off the red-haired man's shoulder as he jumped out of the way, striking the sorcerer behind him instead. The dark-robed figure cried out and fell to the ground, a broken rib protruding through the bloodied cavity in his chest.

The lynx hissed angrily at the red-haired man's feet. Their hateful gazes locked on the figures materializing out of the tempest.

Violet and Miles approached, magic burning at their hands, their familiars' eyes aglow with power. A man with a crow on his shoulder and a double-ended spear in his hand led them, along with Brimstone.

Mae stared dazedly at the pale light on the stranger's hands and weapon before looking at his face. It was the guy who had stopped her from completely losing control, that night on the rooftop. The one Violet said had brought her the pentagram pendant.

It was his magic that had just stopped the red-haired man from hitting her.

Some of the pressure driving her into the ground abated. Mae glimpsed bodies on the ground behind Violet and Miles. They had already incapacitated several of the witches and sorcerers chanting the incantation crippling her.

The man with the crow stopped beside her and offered her a hand, his gaze and that of his familiar still on the enemy. "Are you okay?"

Heat scorched Mae's skin when she placed her hand in his. If he noticed it, he didn't say anything. She swayed as he helped her up, the mantle forcing her down ever present.

How come he and the others are moving freely?!

He glanced at her with a frown and answered her silent question. "This spell is intended to seal your powers alone. It is magic only my father, the Sorcerer King, should be able to wield." A muscle jumped in his jawline as he glared at the red-haired man where the latter had fallen back to join the devil in Rose's form. "He taught you the binding ritual, didn't he?"

Mae startled. *Wait. The Sorcerer King? The one who killed Na Ri all those years back? The Sorcerer King is this guy's father?!*

CHAPTER TWENTY-ONE

A SAVAGE EXPRESSION TWISTED OSCAR'S FACE. "ARE YOU jealous, little brother?"

Nikolai sensed Mae's surprise.

The ruby ring on Oscar's finger shifted into a sword quivering with a black aura, the precious stone settling in the ornate hilt. The power emanating from it stank of the Sorcerer King's dark will.

Nikolai clenched his teeth. "If you think I envy you, then you are gravely mistaken."

Oscar looked at Mae and smirked. "Even though I have taken the Witch Queen's first kiss?"

Fury surged through Nikolai at his mocking words. His knuckles whitened on his spear, his anger tainted with a jealousy he could not deny.

He kissed her?!

Mae glared at Oscar. "First kiss? What is this, a Harlequin novel? And FYI, your breath stinks, asshole!"

Oscar's smile faded. Violet tried hard not to grin. Miles snickered.

Brimstone bared his teeth where he stood in front of his mistress, hackles rising in a faint crimson aura. Nikolai observed the fox worriedly. He could tell the familiar was also under the influence of the Sorcerer King's binding spell, as was the pendant glowing weakly on Mae's chest.

I have to set them free!

His mouth grew dry as he thought of the spell he'd been working on secretly for the last few years, the one he'd come up with for exactly this kind of occasion. He still hadn't recovered from the powerful rituals he'd invoked in the past week and his magic reserves were at an all-time low. His fingers tightened on his spear.

Still, I have no choice but to try. Even if I only lift the seal for a moment, it might give her and the fox enough time to unleash their powers.

Nikolai turned to Violet and Miles, determination lending an edge to his voice. "Cover me. I'm going to break the binding spell."

"Break the spell?" Oscar scoffed. "Have you finally gone insane, little brother?!"

Nikolai ignored him.

Violet held Nikolai's gaze, her eyes unreadable. "You sure you know what you're doing?"

Nikolai nodded. "I do."

Violet pinched her lips together. "Okay. But we need to have a serious talk after this." She looked at Miles. "Together."

Miles dipped his chin, his face full of resolve.

The sneer on Oscar's face slipped as the pair squatted and pressed their palms against the ground, brows furrowed in concentration and magic flaring around them.

"Attack," the devil in the form of Rose Blake barked. "*Now!*"

Oscar moved toward them along with the remaining Dark Council witches and sorcerers.

Violet and Miles's familiars twined around each other, eyes glowing with power. The magic around the four of them exploded, a gold and purple haze that sparked and sizzled.

"*Shield!*" Violet growled.

The bubble solidified, forming a translucent dome some fifteen feet wide and high. Black spheres crashed into the shimmering wall as it settled into the earth.

The Dark Council's magic never reached them.

Oscar cursed and swung his sword. Sparks erupted when the blade met the wall. The barrier held.

Nikolai paused where he'd started etching out the first circle that would break the spell binding the Witch Queen. He could feel an otherwordly energy in the shield around them. One that didn't feel like magic at all.

"What is that?!" Mae shouted as the wind picked up.

Violet smiled fiercely. "Oh, just a little trick some friends of ours taught us. They did something like this in Rome once."

The storm outside the bubble intensified as Oscar reinforced the Sorcerer King's spell. Mae clutched her chest, pain leeching the color from her face. The pendant whined shrilly between her fingers. Brimstone swayed at her feet, his eyes and fur losing their shine.

Nikolai rapidly drew the spell in the dirt with his spear, his heart racing. Alastair stayed still on his shoulder, the familiar's feathers fluttering slightly as he focused their magic through his core.

The devil transformed into his true form, horns sprouting from Rose's forehead and dark wings unfurling from her back. A crimson-tinged portal formed next to the beast as he shot up into the air. He drew a jagged, black broadsword from within it and raised his hand to the sky, his expression furious.

Black lightning flashed high above. It arrowed down from the Heavens and crashed onto the weapon, drenching it in dark electricity. Nikolai's pulse thrummed wildly as the devil brought the sparking blade down on the shield with a vicious roar.

The wall wavered, violent currents rippling across it.

"Whatever you're planning to do, you better do it soon!" Violet warned.

Sweat beaded Nikolai's forehead as he finished drawing the complex symbols linking three circles. He dropped on one knee just as the devil struck the barrier again, Oscar and the Dark Council helping with their dark spell bombs.

A crack appeared in the shield.

"Shit!" Miles cursed. *"Hurry!"*

The Latin incantation left Nikolai's lips in a smooth flow, the words a means for him to focus his and Alastair's magic in a new way. Heat bloomed inside him as power poured out of their souls and into the runes. Nikolai's vision flickered, his consciousness wavering as all his strength was sucked out of him.

Dammit! I was right. We don't have enough magic!

Alastair lurched weakly on his shoulder.

Someone steadied them both. The hand that grasped Nikolai's shoulder scorched his skin through his shirt, the strength of the Witch Queen's magic pulsing weakly through him. He looked up and saw the steely resolve in Mae and Brimstone's eyes as they glowered at Oscar and the devil.

Their power was all Nikolai and Alastair needed to complete the spell. The runes ignited, filling the space inside the barrier with blinding light.

A section of the shield caved in under their enemy's next strike.

WIND ROARED, CURRENTS OF BLACK MAGIC POURING through the breach in the shield to engulf those inside.

They crashed into an expanding crimson orb.

Mae shuddered, the air clear enough to breathe once more. She inhaled raggedly, her attention focused on stopping the red-haired man and the devil's advance, the sphere that had left her hands whining as it blocked their attack.

Whatever the man with the crow had done had worked. She could feel magic flowing freely through her veins once more. The scarlet aura around Brimstone throbbed as he growled, his hairs rising and his power echoing her heartbeat.

The devil screamed in fury. Black lightning pierced the crimson sphere and struck the ground at Mae's feet. She startled as clods of dirt exploded around her. The magic orb wavered.

Violet and Miles deflected the deadly bolts that slipped through her defense with their magic. The corrupt spell bombs detonated over the trees next to them, scorching the branches and turning the leaves to ash.

"Center your magic!" the man with the crow told Mae. He was on his feet and at her side, his hand supporting her arm. He met her panicked stare. "You need the power of three to do this!"

"What do you mean?" Mae yelled, heart slamming against her ribs.

Violet shot up to engage a witch and a sorcerer, her arming sword and magic flashing through the air as she blocked their attacks. "Use your weapon, Mae!"

Mae looked wildly at the man with the crow. "How?!"

He clenched his jaw, his knuckles whitening on his spear. His brother was headed for them, murder in his gray eyes.

"Say its name, Mae. Look inside yourself and find the answer!"

He moved to block the sorcerer.

Movement ahead drew Mae's startled gaze. The devil was coming for her, pupils full of the fires of Hell and broadsword carving a lazy line in the dirt, an insane smile splitting his mouth.

Shit!

Mae swallowed and clutched the pentagram pendant. She couldn't let fear overpower her.

Her pulse thumped in her ears as she closed her eyes and focused inward, to the source of the magic inside her. Darkness filled her mind. Deep within it, as if at the bottom of a vast, inky well, something pulsed faintly.

Mae gritted her teeth. *Help me!*

A weight pressed against her leg. It was Brimstone. His presence warmed her cold flesh.

The red pulsing inside her grew brighter. A shape took form in the bottomless depths of her soul. One that had been dormant for thousands of years, waiting patiently for her body to be reborn. A weapon meant for her and her alone.

Mae clenched the medallion hard enough to cut her skin.

Please.

She felt the pendant absorb the smear of blood on her palm and heard the pleased sound that left it. A name danced through her consciousness, the weapon's low growl filled with menace.

"*Hellreaver,*" Mae whispered.

Fire surged in her blood as the weapon's power fused with hers and Brimstone's. The world slowed. Sound faded.

Mae thought she heard someone scream her name.

Power erupted inside her, so glorious and heady it filled every corner of her body with searing, crimson light. Strength flooded her, turning her bones and muscles to steel. Magic infused her every cell and pore, to the point she didn't know where it started and where she ended.

Her eyes snapped open in time to see the devil's lightning-wreathed blade dropping toward her.

Mae spun the fifty-inch, dark, curved dagger in her

hands, fingers clutching the central hilt with its knuckle-duster guard with practiced ease.

Sparks exploded as Hellreaver blocked the devil's sword, the sound of the impact booming across the clearing. The dagger's double-bladed edges morphed into serrated teeth that chomped down on the black blade, metal grinding hungrily on metal.

A vicious smile twisted Mae's mouth, Hellreaver's beastly energy bolstering her core.

Someone gasped behind her.

The devil swore and yanked his sword out of the weapon's jaws. His eyes bulged, his gaze locked on something past Mae. He retreated a few feet, dark wings spreading behind him as if readying for flight.

The Dark Council witches and sorcerers fell back with horrified cries. Even the red-haired man stumbled and withdrew several steps, head tilting.

A shadow fell over Mae. She looked around. And up.

Her stomach lurched.

Brimstone towered over her, his body now some fifteen feet of brawn and potent magic. Flecks of drool dripped from his giant muzzle. His gleaming teeth and claws were as long as her forearm and his fur a mix of rich midnight black and dazzling hellfire red. Mae's gaze rose past his glowing eyes to the powerful nine tails sprouting from his tail bone, each one vibrating with immense energy.

That's his true form?!

"I see you are as deceitful as ever, demon," the fox growled at the devil.

Mae's mouth fell open.

"*He can talk?!*" Miles sputtered at Violet.

"Damn fox!" the devil spat. "I wish Azazel had never saved you from your fate. You deserved the death that was promised to you!"

The nine-tailed beast lowered his head and glared at him, pupils dilating and constricting.

"*I may have been born evil, but I atoned for my sins,*" he hissed. "*Which is more than I can say for you, demon. Does your hatred for Azazel linger, that you would help a mere human? You, who used to lead Heavens' troops?*"

The devil's expression turned ugly. "Do not speak of sins and atonement, you foul spirit! Azazel is the biggest sinner of them all. He taught mankind magic, a wicked deed for which he was rightly punished. The Sorcerer King will help reverse his lack of good judgment!"

Brimstone straightened, his eyes full of ancient wisdom. "*So much time has passed, yet you still do not see the motivation for my master's actions. There is no hope for you, fiend. I wanted to reason with you, but I see there is no point.*" He stole a look at Mae before pawing angrily at the ground, his claws raking deep grooves in the dirt. "*You have chosen to make an enemy of my bond; hence, you are now my enemy too.*"

"Stop talking and attack them, dammit!" the red-haired man roared at the demon, spit peppering his chin in his rage. "You promised my father you would fight them!"

The devil's expression turned icy. "That was before

their awakening. Now that all three of them are roused, it will be difficult to overpower them."

"You coward! I'll tell my father of your betrayal!"

The red-haired man headed for Mae. The man with the crow stepped in his path. The red-haired man blasted him with a black orb and sent him flying to the ground.

Anger burned Mae.

"No! Stop, you *fool!*" the devil shouted.

Hellreaver left Mae's hand without her volition, her subconscious barking out the command before the thought fully formed in her mind. The weapon flashed across the clearing and pierced the red-haired man's right flank with a wet thunk. He froze, stunned.

His scream of agony rent the air as the dagger sank vicious teeth into his flesh, a famished sound rumbling out from the weapon.

"Hellreaver!" Mae barked. The weapon shot out of the sorcerer and returned to her hold, blood dripping from its jagged edges. She met the devil's gaze, her chin tilting defiantly. "Tell your Sorcerer King that I am coming for him." Her brow furrowed as her gaze swept over the red-haired man and the Dark Council witches and sorcerers. "For all of you." Her magic throbbed the air with a crimson haze, her fury growing as she recalled the misery and heartache her enemy had wrought upon her family and her people during her previous existence, and all that had happened in the past few days. "*I will have my revenge and retake my throne!*"

The devil's eyes flared at the voice underscoring Mae's words. His face turned grim. "Retreat."

"Our father's magic will consume your soul, Oscar!" the man with the crow shouted at his brother. "Leave him, before it's too late!"

The red-haired man glared at him, a sorcerer propping him up with an arm around his waist. A portal appeared behind them. They vanished inside it along with the devil and the remaining Dark Council witches and sorcerers.

The storm abated. The clouds cleared. Sunlight filled the clearing, along with a deafening silence.

Mae sagged to her knees, suddenly weak. Hellreaver transformed back into the pendant and fell into her hands. Brimstone shook himself out before shrinking back to his smaller self. He climbed onto Mae's lap, curled into a ball, and promptly fell asleep.

The man with the crow climbed unsteadily to his feet and came over, his face pale.

Mae stared at the fox.

"I can't believe I rubbed his belly," she said leadenly.

"I can't believe he spoke," Violet muttered as she and Miles joined them.

"I can't believe that thing has *teeth*." Miles indicated the pendant with an accusing finger.

Mae looked up at the man with the crow. "Who are you?"

CHAPTER TWENTY-THREE

THE CONVOY OF SUVS PULLED UP OUTSIDE A HIGH-RISE on Madison Avenue, on the Upper East Side. Their dark tinted windows drew the eyes of the crowd navigating the busy boulevard.

Mae stepped out of the second vehicle with Nikolai, the clamor of traffic and chatter around them sounding oddly surreal to her ears after everything that had just happened at the cemetery in Ridgewood. Violet and Miles emerged from the SUV behind them. Unease flitted through her as she studied the suited figures who surrounded the four of them, a vanguard fit for a king.

Or a queen.

Mae grimaced at that thought. She still hadn't gotten over the fact that she was meant to be some kind of magic sovereign. The curious stares from the people on the sidewalk burned her face as they were escorted toward the entrance of the cream stone building towering above them.

She wanted nothing more than to crawl into a hole in the ground right now.

Her gaze moved to the fox walking beside her, invisible to all but those who possessed magic in their souls. Brimstone had woken up on the drive here. So far, the fox had remained silent, as if he were waiting for the right occasion to answer the dozens of questions storming her mind.

Mae stole a look at the other figure of mystery next to her. Nikolai Stanisic had introduced himself and his crow familiar Alastair moments before the four SUVs had pulled up outside the rear cemetery gates in response to Violet's call to the New York coven.

He didn't deny it when I asked him if he was truly the Sorcerer King's son. But he wouldn't tell me more either. Mae chewed her lip. *It's a good thing Ryu isn't here. He's totally her type.*

She ignored the wry voice inside her head that told her he was very much her type too.

An expectant silence fell in the lobby when they entered it. Mae found herself the focus of dozens of awestruck stares.

"Better get used to it," Violet told her wryly. "You are the famed Witch Queen every magic user learns about when they're growing up."

"Great," Mae muttered. "Does that mean I get some kind of rider?"

One of the sorcerers guarding them heard her and looked over. "If there is anything you require to make your visit more comfortable, please say so, my queen.

Just so you know, we have prepared lunch upstairs for all of you."

Mae waved her hands weakly. "Honestly, I was kidding."

I want meat.

Mae jerked to a stop. The gravelly words reverberating inside her skull drew her gaze to the pendant hanging around her neck. She was certain they had come from the weapon. But that wasn't the strangest thing.

Hellreaver sounded as if he were made up of hundreds of voices.

Her pulse quickened.

A loud rumbling left the medallion, this one clearly audible. Their escort paled. Hellreaver flashed crimson, his hunger echoing through her. Mae grabbed her stomach as it growled in sympathy, suddenly starving herself.

Nikolai, Violet, and Miles looked from her to the pendant and back.

"Did that come from you or—?" Miles swallowed and indicated Hellreaver.

Mae made a face. "Sorry, it seems he's hungry."

"He?" Nikolai repeated dully.

The head of their escort looked like he was about to faint. "Hungry for what, exactly?"

Meat, the weapon repeated firmly. *Your blood and that foul sorcerer's sated some of my hunger, but I am still ravenous.*

Mae blinked rapidly. *So he really did drink my blood!*

Fear not, my bond. Hellreaver's tone turned smug. *As*

long as you bring me the blood and flesh of our enemy, I shall be full.

Mae grimaced. She looked up into a sea of stares. "Hmm, he says he wants meat."

Gurgles escaped some of the witches and sorcerers.

Mae registered their terror with an awkward smile. "I'm sure he doesn't mean human meat." She squinted at Hellreaver. "You don't, right?"

The weapon's sheepish silence told her she'd been right on the money. Mae cursed silently.

Brimstone sat down, limpid eyes flaring. *I would like meat too. And rest assured, I have no wish to consume human flesh.*

A look of distaste flashed across his face.

Mae wasn't sure if she should be pleased or offended. "What kind of meat do you guys want?"

Their escort watched them with bated breath.

Hellreaver spoke. *The leg of a gryphon.*

Mae narrowed her eyes. "I'm pretty sure New York doesn't have gryphons."

A dejected hum vibrated off Hellreaver.

Nikolai raised an eyebrow. "He wants a gryphon?"

Alastair the crow ruffled his feathers uneasily.

Hellreaver perked up. *How about the rump of a minotaur?*

Mae's frown deepened. "You're out of luck. The last minotaur left New York centuries ago."

The scoundrel! The weapon sounded deeply offended.

"Jeez," Miles mumbled, his tone wavering between disgust and admiration. "Your weapon is sick."

Mae sighed. She suddenly knew what it felt like to have kids.

"How does beef sound?"

Hellreaver hesitated. *You mean, those weak domesticated bovines that graze on grass?*

Brimstone pitched in.

They taste nice. Especially with fermented bean paste.

"That will be an order of prime steak and a beef in black bean sauce," Mae told the head sorcerer briskly before either of them could change their minds.

Brimstone nudged her leg.

"Make that several portions of beef in black bean sauce." She looked down at the fox. "You want rice or noodles with that?"

Brimstone appeared horrified at her suggestion.

Mae rolled her eyes. "Hold the rice and noodles."

The sorcerer hastily dispatched a couple of his associates to fulfill the unexpected order before ushering them across the hall. Several famous company names stood out to Mae when they passed a signboard. She arched a questioning eyebrow at Violet.

"Yeah, the New York coven is one of the wealthiest covens in the world," Violet confessed.

"We're talking Richie Rich," Miles added.

CHAPTER TWENTY-FOUR

Their guards guided them to a private elevator at the rear of the foyer. They were whisked to the higher floors of the building in seconds and came out in a lobby lined with dark paneling. The rich, wine-red carpet swallowed their footsteps as they advanced across the semi-circular space.

The magic Mae had sensed since she'd walked across the threshold of the high-rise intensified, a wave that pressed solidly against her skin. She sensed no ill intent from it. If anything, it bore a faint resemblance to her own power, as if it were a diluted version of it.

The sorcerer sitting behind the reception desk rose and bowed. "Welcome, my queen."

Everyone looked at Mae.

"Thank you." She arched an eyebrow, her tone uncertain. "Hmm. At ease?"

Violet's lips twitched. The sorcerer relaxed and straightened before turning to escort them down the hallway behind the reception. Thick, wooden doors swarming with glowing runes appeared at the end. Mae appraised them with a faint frown.

Though she couldn't read what they said, she seemed to know their meaning and potency inherently, as if her very DNA was coded with magic. The witches guarding the entrance bowed respectfully to her before retracting the spells.

Mae swallowed a sigh.

I'm gonna have to do something about this kowtowing business.

Brimstone spoke to her. *They do it out of respect for you.*

"Yeah, well, it gets old fast," she murmured under her breath.

Nikolai gave her a curious glance.

I bet his eyes smolder when he's turned on.

Mae flinched, shocked at the illicit thought that had just danced through her mind.

A sympathetic rumble left Brimstone. *You are in heat.*

"I am *not!*" she scolded the fox.

"You're not what?" Violet asked, puzzled.

"Nothing," Mae muttered.

She gave the fox a warning look.

He grinned and wheezed, laughing.

You must gird your loins, witch. Now is not the time to indulge in pleasures of the flesh.

The doors swung on silent hinges before Mae could come up with a scathing riposte. They revealed a sumptuous room some forty feet long and wide.

Panoramic views of the Metropolitan Museum of

Art and Central Park stretched out beyond the floor-to-ceiling glass wall at the far end. A conference table dominated the area to the right, the waxed wood gleaming under the row of crystal chandeliers suspended from the ornate ceiling. A formal dining space dressed with gleaming China and shiny cutlery occupied the section to the left, along with an extensive seating area dotted with brightly colored Chesterfield sofas and chairs. The dark paneling theme continued inside the room, the upper sections of the walls studded with portraits of solemn women.

"They're the previous High Priestesses of the New York coven," Violet told Mae in a low voice.

"Oh."

Mae glimpsed an office through a doorway to the left and what looked like private stairs leading to a penthouse. Her gaze skimmed the curious mix of expensive, vintage and modern decor before landing on the woman standing at the head of the conference table, a retinue of three sorcerers and four witches at her side.

Bryony Cross looked to be in her early sixties and sported a regal air that matched her station. Her gray eyes glimmered shrewdly in her sharp face and her ash-white hair was piled in an elegant bun at the back of her head. A black cat with intelligent green eyes lay on the table in front of her.

The familiar rose when he spotted the creatures who'd entered the chamber. A curious meow left him. He stared at Brimstone.

"I think he will take offense if you do that for too long, Penley," Bryony told her cat drily.

The familiar hesitated before leaping down from the table and padding over to Brimstone. He stopped in front of the fox, sat down on his haunches, and looked up at him. Mae bit her lip.

A low growl left Brimstone. He bared his fangs.

The room seemed to hold its breath.

Penley blinked, dropped to the floor, and presented his belly to the fox.

Brimstone huffed, pleased. He pressed a gentle paw on the cat's stomach, acknowledging the deference to his status.

Violet blew out a sigh.

"You thought there was gonna be bloodshed too?" Mae said out the corner of her mouth.

Violet gave her a look. "You realize he's *your* familiar, right?"

"He and Hellreaver are like kids on steroids," Mae admitted glumly.

"That bad, huh? Well, you're just gonna have to show them who's boss."

"At this stage, I'm not even sure who *is* the boss."

Miles studied Bryony expectantly.

The High Priestess furrowed her brow. "What?"

Miles grinned. "Just wondering if you're gonna roll over and present your belly to Mae too."

Mae sucked in air. The atmosphere in the chamber turned glacial.

"Wow," Nikolai murmured.

The sorcerer next to Bryony took a step forward, a

scowl darkening his face and his hand dropping to the pommel of the dagger at his waist. "You really have a death wish, don't you, kid?!"

Bryony pinched the bridge of her nose. "It's alright, Abraham. I know them from way back. Besides, Barbara will tan my hide if any of us raise a finger to her niece and nephew." She lowered her hand, met Mae's gaze, and bowed. "Welcome, my queen. I am Bryony Cross, the High Priestess of the New York coven. My people and I are yours to command."

Mae grimaced. "Can I make a request?"

Bryony paused, a guarded expression flashing in her eyes. "Anything, my queen."

Mae waved a hand. "Can we stop with all this queen nonsense and kowtowing? It makes me uncomfortable."

Nikolai smiled.

Bryony blinked slowly, as if she didn't understand the request.

"But—you're our queen, as decreed by the prophecy," she protested. "As such, you deserve the honor of being called our supreme leader."

Mae narrowed her eyes. *Prophecy?*

"Supreme leader sounds even worse." She sighed. "Look, I'm just a chick from Koreatown who likes beer and cutting people up, not some exalted figurehead. Up until a few days ago, I had no idea magic even existed."

She observed Bryony's fallen expression with an internal groan.

CHAPTER TWENTY-FIVE

Tradition is obviously important to this woman.

An idea came to her. She brightened. "How about this? As your queen, I can make decrees, right?"

Bryony nodded glumly at her question.

"Decree number one is this," Mae commanded in a resolute voice. "No more calling me queen or bowing to me."

Bryony opened her mouth to protest.

"Just take it as a win, Aunt Bryony," Violet advised. "Bad things tend to happen when she gets upset."

The other sorcerers and witches exchanged uneasy glances.

"What kind of bad things?" Nikolai asked Violet curiously. He waved a vague hand. "I mean, besides tearing apart a city."

Mae pursed her lips guiltily.

Violet wrinkled her nose. "Everything around her kinda levitates and she absorbs the magic in the area."

Mae's mouth went dry. "I do?"

Violet pursed her lips. "Yeah. Miles and I thought you had enough going on without telling you what happened."

Mae recalled their worn expressions last night.

I can absorb other people's magic?!

She wasn't sure if this realization pleased her or scared the hell out of her.

Mae realized everyone was staring at her expectantly. "Let's start over." She offered her hand to Bryony. "Hi, I'm Mae Jin. You can call me Mae."

The older woman hesitated before accepting her hand, her grip firm. "Hello...Mae." Her shrewd gaze shifted to Violet, Miles, and Nikolai. "Now, how about we all sit down and you tell us what happened today?"

The High Priestess and her advisors listened attentively as the four of them recounted the deadly turn of events at the cemetery in Ridgewood.

"The fox transformed into a giant beast?" Abraham said skeptically after they finished.

From his appearance and demeanor, Mae gathered the sorcerer was Bryony's aide and bodyguard. His familiar was an owl with limpid, yellow eyes.

"Yes," Violet replied, unfazed.

"You should have seen her weapon." Miles's eyes gleamed with worrying enthusiasm. "That thing is wicked."

Hellreaver vibrated against Mae's chest, annoyed.

Why does that human keep using derogatory terms to describe me?

Mae remembered what Miles had said in the foyer.

"They're not derogatory terms," she murmured. "He means you're cool."

Nikolai looked at her with a faint frown.

Cool? Hellreaver sounded puzzled. *But I was forged in the fires of Hell.* He paused. *Is that man an imbecile?*

Mae sighed. "Cool is the same as amazing."

Oh. Hellreaver sniffed, pleased. *And so it should be. I am the most wondrous thing in this world, after all.*

Brimstone smirked.

I can see your mocking smile, fox.

Brimstone's grin widened.

Oh, really? What are you going to do about it?

A crimson haze trembled around Mae as the weapon and the fox faced off against one another.

She looked skyward.

Dear Lord, please give me the patience not to strike these fools.

We heard that! Hellreaver snapped.

Mae realized everyone in the room bar Nikolai, Violet, and Miles was staring at her warily.

"Who are you talking to?" Bryony asked carefully as the red aura faded.

Mae indicated the pendant and the fox. "Hellreaver and Brimstone."

"You mean to tell us you can commune with your weapon and your familiar?" a witch asked in disbelief.

"That's preposterous!" Abraham scoffed. He turned to Bryony. "I know you want us to accept this woman as the Witch Queen of prophecy, but there are limits to the claims she and her friends are making!"

"Are you accusing us of lying?" Violet said in a dangerous voice.

Nikolai looked at Mae, his expression resigned. "This might go faster if you just show them."

"Yeah," Miles concurred, scowling at Abraham.

Mae hesitated. *They're right.*

She rose from the table and headed to the middle of the room, Brimstone padding beside her.

"What's she doing?" Abraham asked suspiciously.

"Giving herself space," Nikolai replied curtly.

Mae stopped in the center of the chamber. She raised a hand to the pendant, reached for the ever-present points of heat in her heart and belly, and unleashed her magic, careful to control the flow of power pouring from her core. She didn't want her first official visit to a coven to end with the building collapsing around her.

The air turned red. Glass vibrated, the crystal chandeliers and wine glasses trembling under the magic washing over them. A shudder shook Brimstone as he transformed into the nine-tailed fox. His claws clinked on the wooden floor, his massive head brushing the ceiling when he was forced to crouch. Hellreaver morphed into his dark, double-bladed, curved-dagger form, the knuckle duster on his hilt guard gleaming where it fit snuggly atop her hand.

Abraham jumped up, his chair clattering behind him and his owl flying off his shoulder in alarm. "What the—?!"

Blood drained from his face as he looked up at Brimstone's monstrous form. Bryony and the rest of the coven members rose shakily to their feet, their expressions similarly stunned and their familiars frozen beside them.

The chamber doors opened. The sorcerer who had escorted them to the coven headquarters appeared, two of his acolytes wheeling in a pair of large, silver service carts loaded with fresh steak and beef in black bean sauce.

"We have prepared the meat you requested, my qu—"

He froze when he registered Mae's magic and the beast and weapon in the center of the room.

Meat! Hellreaver growled.

He left Mae's hold, flew across the chamber, and sank into a steak like knife through butter. The edges of his blades transformed into jagged teeth. He chomped down.

The sorcerer and his subordinates fell back with horrified cries.

Hellreaver ignored them, a happy hum leaving him as he siphoned blood out of the thick slice with a grizzly sound.

Brimstone padded over, lay on the floor, and carefully skewered a piece of beef with a giant claw. He opened his jaws and dropped it down his gullet, swallowing it whole.

"*Thank you,*" he growled at the ashen-faced guards, a wicked tooth gleaming.

Bryony and her coven startled as his voice boomed across the chamber.

Brimstone glanced at Hellreaver. "*I apologize for my*

friend's lack of manners. He is a savage through and through."

Hellreaver glared at Brimstone and stole a piece of his beef. Brimstone's hackles rose, his magic filling the room with pure menace.

"I swear to God, I will ground your sorry asses if you fight in here!" Mae snapped.

Brimstone's aura abated. He and Hellreaver carefully avoided looking at one another as they wolfed down their meal. Mae rubbed the back of her neck, a headache throbbing between her temples.

She returned to the table. "Sorry about that."

Violet and Miles were grinning, their expressions vindicated. Nikolai sighed. Bryony and the rest of her coven slowly took their seats, their faces pale.

"That is the first time I've heard of a sentient weapon and a familiar who can talk," the High Priestess confessed after a short silence, color gradually returning to her cheeks. "The prophecy did not mention it."

Mae couldn't help feeling guilty.

Bryony noticed her expression. "You have nothing to reproach yourself for. You cannot help who you are or the power you wield."

Mae found herself liking the older woman more and more. A thought came to her.

"By the way, what's this prophecy everyone keeps talking about?"

Bryony arched an eyebrow at Violet and Miles. "You didn't tell her?"

Violet shook her head. "We thought it best coming

from you." The witch made a face and cocked a thumb at Mae. "Besides, there's no way in hell she would have come here if we'd told her about it."

Mae squinted, suspicion dawning.

Bryony took a breath. *"Upon the day the world becomes shrouded in a storm of fire and ash, a woman with white and dark magic will bring about an age of justice and the fall of a false god. She is the rightful Witch Queen and shall govern the world of magic henceforth."*

Her words echoed in Mae's ears, bringing with it a wave of dizziness.

"That's the main gist of the prophecy," the High Priestess said. "It also mentions your awakening but doesn't go into details." She hesitated. "Can you tell us about it? It would be good to understand how it happened."

Bryony looked at her advisors. They mumbled their agreement, even the ashen-faced Abraham.

Mae traded a glance with the others, the words of the prophecy still ringing in her head and making her heart thump. They dipped their chins.

She inhaled raggedly and told Bryony and her coven about the events that had unfolded in the autopsy lab at Grandview on the night of the attack, up to the time she fainted on the rooftop. She didn't tell them what Ye-Seul had revealed to her and Ryu the night before, regarding Ran Soyun and the Jee family. Somehow, she sensed it would only put her family in the limelight and expose them to danger.

The guarded looks Violet and Miles gave her told Mae they would keep her secret. Relief filled Mae. She trusted the witch and the sorcerer with her life, especially after everything that had happened in the last couple of days. It felt good to have allies she could rely on in this mad world she found herself thrust into.

Mae became aware of a beady stare and met Alastair's eyes. The crow seemed to be telling her she could trust him and his master too.

Bryony drummed her fingers on the table. "I see." Her eyebrows drew together as she studied Nikolai. "We've been aware of the Dark Council's movements escalating in Europe and across the world over the last two weeks. Were the incidents in Budapest and Stuttgart of your making?"

Mae cut her eyes to Nikolai. *Budapest and Stuttgart?*

"Yes," the sorcerer said quietly. "The Dark Council tracked me there and I fought them."

Bryony arched an eyebrow. "I heard you bested some of the Sorcerer King's most proficient guard dogs."

"You heard correctly."

The High Priestess regarded Nikolai steadily. "Does this mean you have chosen your side in the upcoming war?"

CHAPTER TWENTY-SIX

NIKOLAI MET BRYONY'S SHREWD GAZE UNFLINCHINGLY. He knew the High Priestess of the New York coven already knew the answer to her own question. He clenched his jaw.

She's testing me.

Alastair squawked irritably on his shoulder, feathers rustling.

Nikolai raised a hand and settled him. "It's okay, Al."

He could feel Mae's stare boring into his face.

"There was never a side to choose. My father's madness must be stopped."

One of Bryony advisors made a doubtful sound. "Are you really expecting us to believe you have willingly left the Sorcerer King's side to ally yourself with our cause? You, one of the strongest sorcerers in the Dark Council?"

"This is probably just another dirty trick his father's put him up to," Abraham told Bryony scathingly. "I bet he's here to spy on us."

Nikolai's nails bit into his palms under the table. He could not deny that he'd carried out the orders of the Sorcerer King for many years, nor that his hands were stained with the blood of the innocent. He couldn't expect them to believe that it had all been so he could survive long enough to fulfill the promise he'd made to his mother and to himself the night she died. Still, he had to try.

Nikolai tilted his chin. "Do you know how Oscar and I were chosen as the heirs to the Sorcerer King's throne?"

Bryony's mouth pressed to a thin line. "You know as well as I do that the affairs of your father's court and the Dark Council are shrouded in secrecy."

"It was by the Trial of Blood."

His declaration made Bryony stiffen and drew shocked gasps from her advisors.

"Wait." Violet frowned. "The Trial of Blood?"

Miles's confused gaze swung from Violet to Bryony. "Wasn't that barbaric practice banned centuries ago?"

"What's the Trial of Blood?" Mae said blankly.

Nikolai met her puzzled stare. "It's a battle to the death between the Sorcerer King's children to assess their magical abilities and bloodlust. They have no choice in the matter. To refuse means instant execution."

"The first Sorcerer King instituted the custom thousands of years ago," Bryony explained at Mae's horrified expression. "The practice eventually fell out of favor and was formally outlawed after the fourth Sorcerer King came to power."

Mae's eyes rounded. "Wait. The fourth Sorcerer King? You mean, there have been *several* of them?!"

"Yes." A heavy sigh left Bryony. "As you've no doubt surmised from your brief involvement in our world, not everyone yields to the men who have proclaimed themselves our leaders as successive Sorcerer Kings. There have been many wars over the millennia between the Sorcerer Kings and the humans gifted with the knowledge of magic. The most brutal skirmish took place during the Middle Ages and ended with the Treaty of Argentheim, when a truce was reached between the leaders of the other magic councils and the Dark Council, to stop the massacre of thousands of magic users."

"The accord was tested on a few occasions in the centuries that followed, the most prominent incidents being the witch trials of the 16th and 17th centuries," one of Bryony's advisors continued somberly. "For the most part, the High Council and the Councils of the Moon and the Sun have been forced to overlook the worst of the Sorcerer King and the Dark Council's transgressions, in exchange for the fragile peace that has lasted to this day."

Nikolai couldn't help the bitterness that surged through him at their words. He knew the rest of the magic world had been powerless in the face of his father and the Dark Council's overwhelming strength and dominance. Still, it infuriated him that he and his fallen half brothers and sisters had been left to suffer at the Sorcerer King's hands, while they averted their eyes and lived in their ivory towers.

"Vedran resurrected the Trial of Blood fourteen years ago," he said coldly. "At the time, he had twenty children. All of us were forced to participate in the selection competition, despite previous Sorcerer Kings keeping the entry age to fifteen years. The youngest to perish during the trial was only ten years old."

Several of the coven members swore. A muscle jumped in Bryony's jawline.

"Vedran?" Mae repeated.

Nikolai ground his teeth. "Vedran Borojevic is the name of my father, the sixth and current Sorcerer King."

He looked down at the table, the memories from those two dreadful days and nights searing his mind all over again. He had been sixteen at the time and had had no idea on the morning his father gathered all his concubines and children in the amphitheater at the top of his palace that his hands would be drenched with the blood of his siblings by dusk.

"I was surprised he even allowed me to participate in the trial. Of all of my father's children, I was the only one who could not use black magic. It was a flaw for which my mother and I were often whipped and beaten, for as long as I can remember." His jaw ached as he spoke, his words choking in his throat. "I would have had two more brothers and a sister had the Sorcerer King not killed them while they were still in my mother's womb. It seems his distaste for her white magic was matched only by his lust for her body, hence why he always saved her from death. So he could violate her all over again."

A hand landed gently on his knee. Nikolai turned his head and met Mae's gaze. Anger burned in her eyes, as well as a wealth of compassion. Her touch gave him the strength he needed to continue.

"By the time night fell on the second day and the moon shone down on the arena where the trials took place, only Oscar and I were left standing," Nikolai said in a haggard voice. "Though we were on an equal footing fighting skills wise, his magic was more powerful than mine. Sensing my imminent defeat, my mother begged the Sorcerer King to spare me. Oscar —" He stopped and swallowed convulsively, his heart twisting with a fresh wave of agony. "Oscar killed her with a single blow to the head. He claimed she had distracted him. Though he was livid, our father agreed to overlook his transgression, even though trial participants were officially forbidden from harming spectators."

Nikolai shuddered as he recalled the jeers of the Dark Council and the insane look in his father's eyes that night. It was as if the Sorcerer King had been trying to push him past his breaking point. To see his rage explode and know his true feelings.

To test if he truly had the potential to be his heir, even if it cost him his favorite concubine's life.

CHAPTER TWENTY-SEVEN

NIKOLAI TOOK A PAINFUL BREATH. "I DON'T REMEMBER much else after that. When I woke up in my room, I realized that instead of letting Oscar finish me off, the Sorcerer King had spared me. It was only later that I found out that had been his plan all along." A bitter chuckle left him. "He needed two successors, in case one ever fell to his enemies. With Oscar and I the last of his children standing, he always intended to stop the fight before one of us killed the other."

"That man is a monster," Mae growled.

Nikolai blinked and met her furious scowl. Something lightened inside him then. Though he had made allies who had helped him survive the Sorcerer King's court and his life as one of the Dark Council's minions over the years, he had never had friends before. True friends. Men and women who would stand by him through thick and thin.

He had a feeling Mae, Violet, and Miles would be that kind of people.

That's if Mae ever forgives me for what I did. Guilt left a sour taste in his mouth at the thought of the secrets he had yet to reveal to her. Resolve filled him. *I'll just have to make her understand the reason for my actions.*

"I made a vow the night Oscar killed my mother." Nikolai frowned. "That I would not only find a way to avenge her death, but that I would stop Oscar and my father. Even if it meant selling my soul to the devil." He met Bryony's stare squarely. "So, I kept my head down and I waited for the right opportunity to strike."

The New York coven High Priestess watched him impassively in the taut silence that followed.

She stole a glance at Violet and Miles. "An…ally of ours warned us something was going to happen in New York. And that it likely had to do with the Witch Queen's prophesized awakening. How did you and the Dark Council find out this would not only happen, but that it would take place in my city?"

An ally? Nikolai cut his eyes to Violet and Miles. *She must be talking about someone they know.* Understanding dawned. He stiffened. *So, that's why they were ready for the fight that night!*

Nikolai decided now was not the time to question them or Bryony about their source.

"Two weeks ago, one of my father's Seers experienced a vision of the Witch Queen's awakening. The details were blurry at best. All she could make out was that it would happen in a city, under a gibbous moon. New York wasn't the only place the Dark Council sent reinforcements to."

Surprise flashed on the faces of the coven members.

"So, that's why their activities increased in every major metropolis in the world," Abraham said grimly.

Mae arched an eyebrow at Violet and Miles. "Really?"

The cousins nodded.

"Then, how did *you* know the Witch Queen would awaken in New York?" Bryony asked Nikolai, her jaw set in a hard line.

Mae studied him with a faint frown, equally curious. Remorse flooded him all over again. He knew what he was about to disclose would cause her pain.

"I performed a scrying ritual to search for her soul."

"A scrying ritual?" Miles repeated blankly.

"Wait." Consternation clouded Bryony's face. "The only scrying ritual that can locate a lost soul is—"

"*The Aura of the Moon!*" Violet's eyes bulged. "But—you'd need several sorcerers and witches to carry out a rite that powerful. Especially one intended to search for a soul gone astray! And the chances of success are—"

"Less than one percent," Bryony said in a flinty voice.

Disbelief washed across Abraham's face. He scowled.

"Are you saying you executed that spell on your own?"

The other coven members looked equally skeptical.

"I haven't exactly been sitting on my ass the last fourteen years," Nikolai said stiffly. "As one of the Sorcerer King's heirs, not only did I regularly spar with some of the most powerful sorcerers and witches in the Dark Council, I also had access to their library and a private training room. Though the stakes may be high, that rite can be performed by a single person. The trick is to find the perfect location and the right phase of the moon."

"High?!" Bryony snapped. "You could have surrendered your soul to Hell!"

Mae recoiled. A stilted hush followed.

Nikolai could tell his revelation had done little to inspire the trust of the sorcerers and witches in the room.

"So, you saw Mae's awakening?" Bryony said tensely once she'd calmed down.

Nikolai hesitated. *Here we go.*

"Not exactly. I knew the Witch Queen would awaken somewhere in New York. I just didn't know whose body she would arise in."

Bryony narrowed her eyes. "I don't understand."

"I forced her awakening before Oscar and the Dark Council could find her."

Shocked silence descended around them.

Bryony blinked slowly. "Pardon?"

"The magic explosion," Violet mumbled, color draining from her face. "The spell you unleashed that night, on that high-rise. *That's* what that was for? To force Mae's soul to awaken?!"

"*Soul Storm,*" Bryony said glassily. "You carried out *Soul—*"

Magic flooded the room, a red mist of fury.

Nikolai grunted as Mae grabbed him by the throat and lifted him into the air, everything and everyone except for Brimstone and Hellreaver levitating helplessly around them under the influence of her rage.

His stomach dropped. He could sense his and Alastair's magic being sucked away by Mae.

Violet was right!

"You're the one who caused all that destruction?!" Mae roared, her pupils a pure vermilion. *"You're the reason Rose and all those people died?!"*

Nikolai grabbed her wrist and met her wrathful glare, Alastair fluttering weakly around his head. He was hardly surprised by her reaction. Still, he hadn't thought she would try to kill him in such a spectacular fashion.

"I had to!" he choked out. "It was the only way!"

Mae's hold tightened on his neck. Black spots swarmed Nikolai's vision.

Bryony and Violet shouted at Mae to stop, magic flaring around them as they tried to resist the Witch Queen's formidable power. Abraham and Miles were the only other magic users still conscious, the other coven members having passed out. Brimstone and Hellreaver rocked up to Mae's side, torn between supporting her and calming her deadly rage.

The doors opened at the far end of the chamber.

Nikolai turned his head a fraction.

A blond man with reddish-brown eyes walked in, a white Bengal tiger by his side. He wore an expensive tailor-made suit, black-diamond ear studs, and dark nail polish.

Mae's gaze locked on him. She flinched when she saw that he could move in the face of her magic.

The stranger walked calmly over to her and pressed a finger to her forehead. His pupils and those of the tiger flashed crimson.

"Sleep."

Mae blinked. Her eyelids fluttered closed, her grip loosening on Nikolai as her magic faded. He dropped to the ground and coughed fitfully, air wheezing through his swollen windpipe.

The blond man caught Mae in his arms as she fainted.

CHAPTER TWENTY-EIGHT

"You know that guy?!" Violet Nolan whispered to Bryony Cross.

The New York coven High Priestess glowered at Vlad. "Yes, for my sins."

Vlad Vissarion smiled, undeterred. "Oh, come now. Is that any way to greet an old friend?"

His familiar Tarang yawned where he lay curled around his feet, exposing shiny, sharp fangs. The tiger propped his head on his giant paws, his eyes shrinking to half slits as he snoozed, unconcerned by the other familiars eyeing him warily from around the chamber.

Bryony's advisors and guards studied his beast with equal caution.

"An old friend would have sent a message," Bryony grated out. "Especially considering the current circumstances."

Vlad stretched his arms casually atop the back seat of the Chesterfield sofa, careful not to disturb the precious cargo on his lap.

"You guys made quite a mess of that situation." He made a show of examining his manicured nails. "I doubt the Sorcerer King will forgive your transgressions." He paused, a thin smile playing on his lips. "Then again, it was hardly your fault."

His gaze found Nikolai Stanisic. He'd caught glimpses of Vedran Borojevic's second son in the past, during dealings his family had had with the Dark Council. Stanisic was by far a more pleasant prospect for the Sorcerer King's throne than Oscar Beneventi, his older brother and now likely sole heir to Vedran's legacy.

Vlad suppressed a grimace.

And what a king he'll make. That guy is nuts.

Considering his own savage reputation in the criminal underworld, that was saying something.

"We're not planning to ask for his forgiveness," Bryony said coolly. "Now that the Witch Queen has awakened, the rest of the magic world will support her claim to his throne."

Vlad stared, not sure if she was being serious. He snorted when he realized she was.

"Surely, you don't believe the Sorcerer King and the Dark Council will just roll over and play dead now that the Witch Queen is back in the land of the living?"

"Of course not." Bryony pinched the bridge of her nose. "Why are you here, Vlad? As you can see, we're a bit busy right now."

She indicated the sleeping woman lying on the sofa, her head on his lap.

Vlad caressed Mae Jin's cheek with a gentle finger.

"I need to talk with my queen. I believe she has answers to some of my questions."

"Don't touch her!" Nikolai snarled.

Vlad met his stormy stare. "Or what, mongrel?" His tone turned mocking. "You should challenge me when you can suppress her powers like I just did. Otherwise, shut up and stay put."

Frustration flashed in Nikolai's eyes. Vlad smirked, aware his words had rung too close to home for the other man.

"How *did* you suppress her powers?" Violet asked stiffly.

She was slightly flushed, as were most of the witches in the room bar Bryony. It took experience to resist his allure. Still, Vlad could tell Violet's magic was almost strong enough to withstand the call of his blood.

Impressive. The Chicago coven has some powerful witches.

"That's for me to know and for you to find out, little girl."

Violet's expression turned deadly. Vlad's smile widened.

Mae stirred on his lap.

He stilled, his cold heart fluttering a little. Tarang looked at him curiously, no doubt sensing the rare emotion dancing through his soul.

It had been decades since someone had piqued his interest as much as the woman who was currently waking up as if she were the proverbial sleeping beauty. Desire warmed Vlad's blood.

I can't wait to make her mine.

MAE CAME AROUND TO THE SOUND OF LOW VOICES. HER head felt fuzzy, as if she hadn't slept in days. Something warm pressed on her chest. She blinked.

Brimstone was curled up on her where she lay on a red Chesterfield sofa. He raised his head when he felt her rouse and licked her chin, his face sad. Hellreaver hummed anxiously against her breastbone, the weapon back in his pendant form.

Mae's magic throbbed across her bond with them, a hot connection that seemed to bring them both comfort. She looked carefully to the right.

Bryony, Nikolai, and the others were sitting on the chairs and couches opposite. They were frowning and talking in an urgent tone. She couldn't make out their words past the buzzing in her ears.

Mae's stomach twisted with remorse when she saw the bruises on Nikolai's throat.

Damn it. I lost control again.

She recalled what he'd said before her rage had swallowed her whole.

He must have a good reason for what he did. He wouldn't have helped me otherwise, that night or today.

Rose's face flashed before her eyes. Mae clenched her jaw.

She had a choice to make. She could either continue to blame Nikolai for her best friend's death or she could elect to hold the circumstances and the people who had brought him to New York responsible for the horror that had been visited on Grandview the night he seemingly forced her soul awakening.

Judging by what he'd revealed about his awful past, the sorcerer must have known he was signing his own death warrant when he chose to oppose the Sorcerer King's orders. That he had risked his own life to save hers was something she couldn't ignore.

Brimstone's gaze moved to something above her. He growled, exposing his fangs.

"Hi there," someone said quietly.

Mae looked up, surprised. Her heart throbbed.

Even though the man smiling at her was upside down, she could tell he was drop-dead gorgeous. His reddish-brown eyes twinkled warmly as he met her stare, his hair a luxurious flaxen color where it framed his charismatic face in overlong strands.

Mae realized her head was on his thighs. Not that she cared. Her gaze moved to his lips. They were full and perfectly formed. She realized she was dying to kiss him.

The stranger's eyes flared, pupils flashing crimson.

Lust made her pulse skitter. She reached up and tugged him down, his nape scorching her fingers where they touched.

"That's enough!"

Mae flinched and froze. *Wait! What the hell was I just about to do?!*

She snatched her hand away, shocked at her wanton behavior.

Nikolai was on his feet, his expression furious.

The blond man sighed and straightened. "My queen and I were just about to share our first kiss." He raised an eyebrow at Nikolai, his eyes cold. "I would be grateful if you could refrain from interrupting us, mongrel."

Mae bolted upright and shifted from the stranger's side, the pull of attraction she was feeling for him still present, if somewhat moderated by her magic. She shuffled to the opposite end of the sofa and clutched Brimstone defensively against her chest.

The fox's growl intensified.

The stranger ignored the familiar and stretched a hand toward her, an alluring smile curving his beautiful lips. "It's alright, my queen. You can stay by my side."

His pupils glowed with fire.

Desire slammed into Mae. She leaned toward him.

Brimstone spat at the blond, hackles rising. *What you are experiencing is not real, Mae. He has incubus blood flowing through him!*

Mae blinked and stilled. "Incubus? Those things exist?"

The blond man's eyes flared in surprise. His gaze dropped to the fox.

An angry snarl erupted at his feet.

Mae registered the white tiger who'd been sleeping on the floor. The beast had raised his head and was baring his teeth at Brimstone, the challenge on his face clear. She swallowed and looked at the stranger.

They're the ones who stopped me!

"How did you do that?" she mumbled. "How did you curb my powers?!"

The blond sat back and sighed, looking a little hurt that she'd chosen not to take his hand. "My magic and yours are similar."

Mae stared, nonplussed. "Come again?"

A sinful smile stretched his lips, his eyelids drooping as he focused on her mouth. "I would love for both of us to experience that as soon as possible, but we have company." He popped the first button on his shirt, his voice dropping an octave. "Unless you don't mind some hedonistic voyeurism, in which case I'll be happy to oblige."

Mae flushed, her gaze locking on his fingers and the tantalizing glimpse of muscular, toned chest he was threatening to bare. She gulped.

Gird your loins, my bond, Hellreaver warned. *You must resist his bewitching charms!*

The weapon's magic and Brimstone's power flooded her, dampening her lust.

"You know as well as I do that's not what I meant," she said between gritted teeth when she could speak again, fighting his glamor as best she could.

"He's a cambion," Bryony stated sourly.

Mae squinted. "A cambion?"

The blond smiled. "The offspring of an incubus and a human. My father was a demon and my mother a witch. My name is Vlad Vissarion." His pupils flashed crimson. "You and I are the same, my queen."

CHAPTER TWENTY-NINE

Mae's heart thundered violently against her ribs at his claim.

"I do not know the name of the one who sired me," Vlad drawled. "But my power is comparable to yours."

He raised his right index finger. A small, crimson ball flashed into life above it.

Mae's eyes widened. *That's—*

Brimstone's voice sounded in her head. *Demonic magic. And powerful, at that.* The fox's tone turned thoughtful. *His father must be a formidable incubus and his mother an equally impressive witch.*

Mae studied the blond guardedly. She wasn't sure how she felt about him yet.

"Vlad is also the heir of the leader of *Chernyye D'Yavoly*, or the *Black Devils* as they're more commonly known," Bryony explained. "My coven and the High Council have had dealings with them in the past."

Mae's stomach flip-flopped. She could see her shock reflected on Nikolai's face. The *Black Devils* were the biggest Russian crime syndicate not just on the East Coast, but in the whole of the U.S. They were equal to the original *Bratvas* of Europe.

"We know each other from way back." Vlad grinned at Bryony. "Don't we, my dear?"

The witch murmured something rude under her breath.

A lightheaded feeling came over Mae. So much had happened already that day and she was struggling to process it all.

"Why don't we get some lunch while we talk?" Bryony suggested. "It's going to get cold."

Mae noted the carts and serving staff by the dining table. She met the older witch's sympathetic gaze, grateful for the distraction.

It wasn't until they sat down and she found herself squashed between Vlad and Nikolai that she realized she'd just leapt from the pan into the fire. The animosity between the two men practically made the air sizzle as the waiters started dishing out the food.

Violet smirked at her from across the way.

Mae narrowed her eyes. "You're enjoying this, aren't you?"

Violet's smug smile widened. "You gotta admit, that's quite a catch you've got there." She cocked her head to the side. "A demon to the right. A sorcerer to the left. It's like a sandwich of sin and debauchery."

Miles chortled and stabbed his beef with his knife and fork.

Vlad and Nikolai eyed them coldly.

"I'm sure Mae doesn't feel that way." Bryony tucked

her napkin on her lap, her expression disapproving. "Why don't you two hotheads back off and give her some space?" she told Vlad and Nikolai gruffly. "The poor girl is probably starving."

Mae's stomach grumbled loudly on cue. It had been several hours since breakfast. The tension between Vlad and Nikolai abated as they settled down and everyone tucked into their lunch.

Mae noted the other familiars keeping well away from the floor space to the right while she ate. Brimstone and Tarang had reached an uneasy truce where they sat chowing on the meat the coven staff had brought them, Hellreaver wolfing his steaks between them like he hadn't just consumed a cartful load of the stuff a mere hour ago.

What a glutton.

Hellreaver shot a shameless look her way.

Mae sneaked a peek at Vlad. He'd barely batted an eyelid when the medallion had shifted to his true form a short while back.

This guy really has nerves of steel.

She finished her plate and eyed the food carts.

"Would you like some more?" Vlad asked with a charming smile.

Mae pursed her lips. She didn't want to look like a pig, but damn if using her magic didn't make her famished. "Yes, please."

And you're calling me a glutton, Hellreaver mocked.

Mae ignored him. Vlad got up to serve her. So did Nikolai.

Her stomach sank as more and more food piled up

in front of her. "Hmm, you guys, I don't think I'm gonna be able to finish all of this."

The two men ignored her, their attention focused on besting one another in some kind of futile one-upmanship. Bryony sighed. Mae was about to tell them off when Hellreaver came to her rescue.

Vlad and Nikolai froze as the weapon rocked up to the table and gobbled half the contents of her plate.

"That was for your mistress, you foul fiend!" Vlad said sharply.

Nikolai scowled. "He's right. You shouldn't eat Mae's food."

Hellreaver bared his teeth at them.

"That's enough, all of you!" Mae snapped. She narrowed her eyes at Vlad and Nikolai while Hellreaver grumpily returned to his own meal. "Let me make one thing clear. Men who throw temper tantrums do not appeal to me. So, whatever this thing is between you, get over it!"

She stabbed a piece of chicken violently with a fork and shoved it in her mouth.

Violet choked on a chuckle. Miles chewed slowly on a carrot, his fascinated gaze swinging between the two men and Mae.

Bryony sniffed. "Well said."

Vlad and Nikolai took their seats, their faces stiff.

Miles pointed his knife at the pair framing Mae, his expression innocent. "Does that mean you're actually interested in both of them?"

Magic fluttered around Mae. The table trembled.

"Jesus, read the room!" Abraham hissed at Miles.

It wasn't until they retired to the lounge area for coffee that Mae finally got to voice some of the burning questions at the forefront of her mind.

"Does your presence here have anything to do with *Oniks* and Alexei Antonovich?" she asked Vlad.

The others looked surprised.

"Antonovich?" Bryony repeated.

Mae didn't look away from Vlad. "It's the name of the guy I was performing an autopsy on, the night of the attack."

Nikolai shared a confused glance with Violet and Miles.

Vlad's lips stretched in a smile that didn't quite meet his eyes. "I'm...a little shocked you made the connection so quickly."

"Don't be. It was the NYPD detective and the FBI agent who interviewed me yesterday who first hinted at a possible connection between Antonovich and the attack on Grandview."

Vlad leaned forward, his elbows on his knees. "I take it you're referring to Lieutenant Dickson and Special Agent Calvarro?"

Mae dipped her chin.

A far away look came over Vlad. "Those two are... interesting." He steepled his hands under his chin, his red-brown gaze growing focused as it bored into her. "Do you believe there *is* a connection?"

Mae's scalp prickled. *What does he mean, interesting?*

She hadn't detected any magic or danger when Dickson and Calvarro had visited her yesterday. She decided to overlook Vlad's words for now and recalled the creature who had possessed Antonovich.

"Yes. But not in the way the cops think there is."

This time, Vlad's smile was genuine. "You would be right. And, before you ask, Antonovich died at the hands of one of my men."

Though Mae had begun to suspect that was the case, she still drew a sharp breath.

Bryony pinched her lips together. "Should you really be confessing to a crime in front of so many witnesses?"

For some reason, Mae sensed she was more upset about the fact that he'd admitted to ordering the murder of a man in a roomful of people than the act itself.

Vlad shrugged, nonchalant. "Antonovich was possessed by a powerful demon under the direct control of the Sorcerer King. He had lost his humanity a long while back." He gazed at Mae. "The reason I was tailing him was to find out just how many of those demons had infiltrated *Oniks*."

A sour taste filled Mae's mouth. "Is that why he didn't die as easily as the other demons I killed that night? Because the Sorcerer King was controlling him?"

"Correct." Vlad's expression turned brooding. "He's a new kind of demon. One I haven't encountered before." He grimaced. "One that's a serious pain in the ass to kill."

"You're telling me," Mae muttered. "I literally had to cut his head off."

"His demon went dormant after we shot him." Vlad eyed her pensively. "Your awakening must have roused him."

Bryony shifted in her chair, her eyes dark with unease.

"You're saying this man was directly controlled by the Sorcerer King and was almost impossible to kill as a consequence?"

"Yes," Vlad said curtly.

Mae chewed her lip. "Is that why the *Black Devils* chose to overlook *Oniks* for so long, even though they've been operating in your territory? Because of the Sorcerer King's involvement with them?"

Vlad dipped his chin. "Indeed. I warned our group not to interfere with them lightly when I detected they were under the protection of powerful black magic. I was tracking Antonovich's movements the night he died. Unfortunately, somebody got in my way and I ended up having to take…extreme measures."

The strange slug Mae had extracted from Antonovich's brain flashed through her mind. "The bullet I found in his head. I've never seen anything like it before." She hesitated. "Was it…imbued with magic?"

Vlad smiled faintly. "You really do surprise me, my queen. I didn't think you'd connect the dots so fast." He rubbed his jaw. "Yes, that bullet and the gun my sniper used were infused with magic. It was the only way Antonovich was going to stay down once we shot him. Now, if you don't mind, it's my turn to ask questions. What did you find when you examined his body?"

Mae pursed her lips. "What makes you think I found something?"

"Because of the transcript of the audio recording from the autopsy."

Mae's eyes widened. "What? But I thought everything in the lab got trashed by the demons who invaded the hospital!"

"Your notes were already saved on the offsite server before they destroyed the computer," Vlad said with a dismissive wave. "It's why the cops and the FBI are sniffing around you. They don't know anything about your awakening or that you're the Witch Queen, but they sure as hell are interested in why Antonovich's body vanished from that lab."

CHAPTER THIRTY

Nikolai observed Vlad's confident face with a frown. It seemed clear the mobster knew more about his father's dealings in New York than Nikolai's own informants. He'd had no idea about the Dark Council's involvement with a new Russian crime gang in the city or that Vedran had placed fiends he could control amongst them until the mobster had revealed this just now. He wondered if Oscar was in on the Sorcerer King's plans.

A chill danced down his spine.

What are they trying to do? I thought their main purpose in New York was to capture Mae before her awakening.

"It was an enlarged pineal gland," Mae admitted reluctantly.

Nikolai blinked slowly. *Pineal gland?*

"It's an endocrine gland found in the midbrain," she explained at their blank stares. "It produces melatonin, the hormone that controls our sleep cycle, and is thought to regulate the pituitary in some way. Its functions have long eluded science."

"Isn't the pineal gland where Descartes thought the human soul lived?" Vlad said curiously.

Lines furrowed Mae's brow. "You know your philosophy."

The smile the incubus gave Mae had Nikolai's hackles rising.

"I'll be happy to discuss philosophy and anything else you want to talk about over dinner, my queen."

Mae bit her lip. "You're really coming on strong, aren't you?"

Vlad's smile widened. "Would you like me to dial it down?"

"A little bit."

He chuckled, the sound and the flare of incubus power that burst from him causing several witches to flush.

"I've been meaning to ask you." Mae studied Vlad warily, the faint color on her cheekbones telling Nikolai she wasn't completely immune to his charms either. "What you did to me when you restrained my magic. Was it similar to the binding ritual Oscar Beneventi used on me?"

Vlad stilled.

He narrowed his eyes at Nikolai. "She's already crossed paths with Oscar?"

Nikolai nodded grimly. "This morning. Oscar and the Dark Council ambushed us at the cemetery where Mae's best friend was being buried."

"Except Rose isn't really gone." Mae's expression

grew flinty. "A devil stole her body the night my soul awakened. He took her form and attacked us today."

Vlad's forehead wrinkled. "A devil?"

Mae dipped her chin jerkily. "Big guy, eight feet tall, with horns and black wings. His pupils were crimson, like yours and mine."

"That means he's a high-level demon." Vlad tightened his hands to fists. "Possibly an Archduke of Hell." He paused. "No, I didn't bind your magic. I just overwhelmed you with my incubus energy. Lust and rage are two sides of the same coin." His scowl faded to a small, saccharine smirk. "I just flipped yours."

The sexual connotation of his words didn't escape anyone in the room.

"That's sick," Violet said, her tone half contempt, half admiration.

Mae bit her lip, color flooding her cheeks.

Nikolai spoke, determined to cut the electric tension between them. "I think that devil is the reason my father can call forth fiends from Hell and force them to do his bidding."

Vlad's smile vanished. Mae sobered.

"What?" one of Bryony's advisors said, eyes bulging.

Bryony glared. "We suspected as much from the demons we fought at the hospital. You're saying this—devil has granted the Sorcerer King the power to raise those monsters at will?"

"All Sorcerer Kings boast that ability, to an extent," Nikolai explained. "It's how the first Sorcerer King gathered a demonic army and killed the child born of Azazel and the first witch."

Mae's hands clenched on her lap.

"I only became aware of his existence recently," Nikolai confessed grudgingly. "From our fight today, it looks like Oscar knew about him already. Which makes me wonder how long that demon has been around." He finally voiced the suspicion that had been brewing inside him since he first discovered his father's alliance with the devil. "And whether the reason the first Sorcerer King grew so powerful and could control monsters from Hell was as much to do with his influence as it was with Azazel's teachings."

A fraught hush followed.

It was broken by a wave of powerful magic as Brimstone shook himself out into his nine-tailed-beast form. Tarang's ears flicked back, the tiger leaping to his feet with a startled hiss. He froze when Brimstone lowered his enormous head and huffed gently in his face.

"I mean your master no harm, cat."

Tarang shrank back on himself. He looked at Vlad. The incubus motioned him over. The tiger practically ran to Vlad's side and let out an embarrassed rumble when his master petted his head.

"What's wrong?" Mae asked Brimstone in a strained voice.

Vlad observed the beast warily.

The nine-tailed fox crouched next to Mae's chair and looked into her eyes, his own filled with a wisdom as old as time.

"The devil the son of the Sorcerer King speaks of is Barquiel. He is the ninth leader of the Grigori and a fallen

angel who once bore the name Lightning of God. He is an Archduke of Hell, as the incubus scion correctly postulated. His dislike for Azazel was legendary even before Satanael and his followers were banished from the Heavens by the divine army led by the Archangel Michael."

A heavy feeling settled in the pit of Nikolai's stomach.

That devil is a fallen angel?!

"The Grigori?" Vlad said with a calculating look. "As in the Watchers who fell from Heaven because they lay with humans?"

"Indeed."

Mae paled. "Wait. You mean—all that Bible stuff is *real?!"*

"Yes." Bryony cleared her throat and stole a glance at Violet and Miles. "We met several of those fallen angels a few years ago."

"You did?" Nikolai said dully.

The three of them nodded grimly.

Brimstone studied Mae with a brooding look in his orange eyes.

"I believe Barquiel is the one who gave the current Sorcerer King the power to create the binding ritual that locked our magic. I could smell a trace of his demonic energy in the spell."

Nikolai stared blindly at the floor, the horrifying revelation made by Mae's familiar reverberating through his very bones.

That would make sense!

He looked up, jaw clenching. "That power. They weren't just planning to bind you with it before you awakened. They were going to break you, body and mind."

Mae paled. "What do you mean?"

"I came to New York to force your soul awakening because of what I uncovered about the Sorcerer King's plans concerning you."

Nikolai swallowed heavily, unsure how to voice the dreadful scheme he'd chanced upon the night he went to his father's study to inform him of the results of his latest mission and overheard the latter's conversation with Oscar. Alastair fluttered onto his shoulder and pressed his body against his cheek, seeking to comfort him. He raised a hand and stroked the bird, grateful for his presence.

Nikolai took a shallow breath and met Mae's gaze squarely. "Vedran wants to force your union with one of his heirs, namely Oscar."

Bryony recoiled. Fury lit Vlad's pupils crimson.

"The Sorcerer King wishes to impose a *Marriage of Magic* on Mae?" the incubus growled.

"Yes."

"He wants me to hook up with that asshole?" Mae's lips curled. "What the hell would that achieve?!"

Nikolai's lifeless words echoed in the fraught silence. "It would give him and Oscar control over your powers."

"What?" Mae jumped to her feet, magic pulsing off her in a faint, angry wave. "How?!"

Brimstone nudged her with his head. *"Calm yourself, my witch. Let us listen to him."*

Mae's nostrils flared. She sat down, her mouth a thin line. Bryony and Vlad shared a taut glance.

"A *Marriage of Magic* is a ritual that allows one person of magical persuasion to command the power of another," Bryony said. "It is a sacred rite, one rarely performed these days. Most who went through it in the past did so to share their magic equally with their partner."

"Which is obviously not what Vedran and Oscar intend," Vlad said sourly.

Mae ran a hand through her hair, a heavy sigh blowing out of her. "But wouldn't that mean I would have an equal chance to overpower Oscar?"

"No," Nikolai said in a hard voice. "They were planning to bind your soul before you awakened and torture you into submitting to them. Without access to your magic, you would have been helpless to defend yourself." Outrage filled him when he recalled the ghastly details he'd gleaned of his father and Oscar's awful ploy. "It wasn't just physical torture they were entertaining. What they intended to put you through would have shattered your sanity. Had you continued to resist, I suspect the devil would have stepped in and brought you to heel."

The sound that left Brimstone made the glass wall overlooking Central Park vibrate. The fox's hackles rose, flecks of drool dripping from his jaws as he grasped Nikolai's unspoken words.

"They plotted to go that far?!"

Hellreaver hummed angrily where he hung from Mae's neck, silver glowing red.

Mae touched the pendant and the familiar, quieting their wrath. "It's okay." She met Nikolai's gaze, her own filling with deadly resolve. "It seems I have you to thank for saving me from that grim fate." She faltered. "I may not be able to forgive you for Rose's death right now, but know that I acknowledge the reason for your actions."

CHAPTER THIRTY-ONE

THE RELIEF THAT FLOODED NIKOLAI'S FACE HAD MAE'S gut twisting with regret. Though what she'd said was the honest truth, it was clear to her how much the consequences of Nikolai's acts weighed on his conscience.

He may represent the bloodline of the sorcerer who robbed Na Ri of her past happiness and destiny, but he is no monster.

Brimstone's low huff and Hellreaver's rumble indicated the familiar and the weapon shared her feelings on this subject.

"By the way, something puzzles me about your encounter with Oscar." Vlad tilted his head to the side as he studied Mae. "If he used a binding ritual the Sorcerer King and Barquiel himself came up with, how did you escape it?"

Mae exchanged a cautious look with Violet and Miles before indicating Nikolai. "He broke the spell."

Bryony inhaled sharply.

Guilt darted through Mae. They hadn't revealed that aspect of their fight yet.

Vlad's eyes flared with grudging admiration. "You undid magic created by an Archduke of Hell?"

Nikolai looked very much like he wanted to sink into a hole in the ground. "It was only for a moment."

"Still, not many can claim to be able to do something like that," Bryony said sternly.

Newfound respect shone in her advisors' eyes as they observed the sorcerer.

Nikolai examined his hands, his face growing unfocused. "It was my mother's magic. Vedran and Oscar don't know it, but I've been refining my white magic on the side for years."

Mae's heart twinged at his haunted expression.

"Your mother was one of a small group of humans able to wield magic similar to the first witch's powers," Bryony told Nikolai gravely. "All the councils who opposed the Sorcerer King were devastated when she caught his eye and he forced her to leave the Council of the Moon to join his court. I know you likely harbor bitterness toward us for abandoning your mother to her fate, but I for one am glad she passed on her powers to you."

A muscle twitched in Nikolai's cheek. He dipped his head wordlessly, emotion darkening his eyes.

Mae turned to Vlad, unwilling to explore what she was feeling for the man who had rescued her from a fate worse than death itself. "What do you think the Sorcerer King is trying to do with *Oniks?*"

Vlad rubbed the back of his neck. "I have a vague

suspicion, but my syndicate and the ones helping us gather this information abroad are reluctant to accept it. They don't believe in demons and magic, despite many of them knowing what I can do."

"You mean, it's not just the criminal underworld here in New York?" Bryony's shoulders slumped. "The Dark Council are involved with other international crime syndicates too?!"

Vlad waved a hand vaguely. "All the major crime families have had something to do with the Dark Council at one point or another in the last century, from the Yakuza all the way to the Cosa Nostra. Most don't know the true identities and abilities behind the faces of the Dark Council representatives they've dealt with, but they all share the same interests. Narcotics and illegal firearms trade, money laundering and sex trafficking, you name it, the Dark Council has a hand in it."

Bryony's stiff gaze locked on Nikolai. "Is that true?"

He nodded, his expression pained.

"No wonder they have so much wealth and influence," Abraham said glumly.

Bryony rubbed her temples. "We've long suspected them of being involved in shady dealings. But to think they are so heavily invested in the criminal world is pretty damning. We should have kept a closer eye on their activities." She clenched her jaw. "I'll have to report this to our High Council."

Mae focused on Vlad again. "What is it you suspect?"

"This is just my theory," Vlad warned.

"Spill it."

Vlad smiled at her commanding tone. She chewed her lip.

Darn it, why the hell is he so sexy?

Vlad grew serious. "The human trafficking business in New York boomed around the time *Oniks's* influence started growing in the city. It's the same with the other cities I've been investigating." He paused. "I think they are providing experimental subjects to the Dark Council."

A perplexed hush ensued.

"Experimental subjects?" Violet repeated.

Mae curled her hands into fists, the truth in Vlad's eyes all too clear. "You mean, lab rats?"

Shocked murmurs rippled across the room.

Vlad dipped his chin. "I believe Vedran and the Dark Council intend to raise a new army. One made of modified demons. I think they're buying human slaves for that purpose."

Mae's pulse stuttered. Bryony froze.

"Why?" Miles mumbled. "What would he need an army for?"

Nikolai grew ashen, as if he'd just grasped an awful truth. He looked at Vlad.

"What would you do if you were a tyrant who controlled the most powerful witch on Earth and had a legion of demons at your disposal?" he said in a stilted tone.

Vlad's eyes blazed, understanding flashing on his face. "You would conquer the world."

Violet scowled. "Shit."

Mae's nails dug into her palms. *This is insane!*

She swallowed heavily. "But—wouldn't he need a helluva lot of demons to do that?"

Brimstone spoke. *"He already has the means to obtain demons."*

Vlad's face tightened. "Barquiel."

Brimstone growled his assent. *"Hell has an endless supply of fiends."*

Mae's heart beat sluggishly as she digested this. "I wonder if that's why there are so many demons in New York." She realized everyone was staring at her. "What?"

Bryony lowered her brows. "What do you mean?"

Mae stared. "There are demons in New York. Like, hundreds of them."

"What?!" Abraham gasped.

"You can detect humans who bear demons inside them?" Nikolai asked urgently.

"Yes." She indicated the area above her head. "They have that whole dark aura thing going on and the odd flash of yellow in their pupils?"

Mae paused when she registered their shocked expressions.

"I can just about feel them out when they're close," Vlad admitted with a frown. "Like a sixth sense. You mean to say you can actually *see* them while they are still in their human form?"

"Uh, yeah." Mae scratched her cheek awkwardly. "Looks like I'm the only one, huh?"

Bryony looked questioningly at Violet and Miles,

her expression grim. The cousins hesitated before dipping their heads, as if granting her permission.

"You're not the only one who can see demons in their human flesh," the New York coven Head Priestess confessed. "Remember how I said we met some fallen angels a while back? The ones who fought and defeated them can see them too."

"They are our friends," Violet said. "Allies and divine beasts who have literally been to Hell and back. And not all fallen angels are our enemies. There are some who stand firmly by mankind, like Azazel once did."

Blood pounded in Mae's ears, this revelation yet another bombshell that rocked her once normal world.

"Divine beasts?" she repeated numbly.

"Yes." Violet made a face, as if she'd recalled something unpleasant. "There are seven of them, along with the ones they have bonded with."

Mae looked jerkily at Brimstone. *Divine beast? Is he one too?!*

The fox heard her questions.

"I was originally a spirit your father once saved from death," he said gravely. *"The first* kumiho *upon which all nine-tailed-fox legends are based. I swore my fealty to him after he nurtured me back to health. When Azazel was seeking a familiar for his unborn daughter, I was one of many hellbeasts and powerful spirits who offered to serve her. Azazel chose me in the end."* He licked Mae's cheek carefully and ended up soaking her entire head with drool. *"I am glad he did."*

Mae grabbed a napkin and dabbed her face and

hair, still dazed. "Any idea what Hellreaver originally was?"

Brimstone eyed the pendant with a beady stare. *"That fool is made of the souls of a thousand demons. He was forged in the fires of Hell by a fallen angel who was once the greatest metalsmith in the Heavens."*

Hellreaver hummed smugly, evidently choosing to ignore the 'fool' comment.

Mae grimaced. "A thousand demons, huh? No wonder he's tiresome."

Hellreaver sulked and grew heavy around her neck. Mae wondered if she should reveal what else she had sensed yesterday.

"I gather from what I've seen of Violet and Miles in action that sorcerers and witches can feel out each other's magic?" she said carefully.

"Not everyone can," Bryony replied. "It takes practice and experience for most who do develop that skill. Some are naturally born with the ability to do so."

Violet squinted at Mae. "Why?"

Mae swallowed a sigh.

Best not tell them I can kinda see a map of New York in my head with all their locations.

"Nothing," she mumbled. "It's just…I think I can detect other people's magic too." Something came to her mind, causing her to frown. "Although, truth be told, the Dark Council sorcerers and witches who ambushed us this morning did surprise me. I couldn't pick up on their magic at all, including Oscar's."

"That's because my father forced a spell upon us that can shield our abilities, especially in combat situations," Nikolai confessed. "It's magic that all Dark Council members bear, including his children."

"That's one spell we truly wish never existed," Bryony said with a sour expression.

A memory flitted through Mae's mind. Of the vast army who had destroyed Azazel and Ran Soyun's city and palace.

I wonder if that's the reason my father didn't see the enemy coming.

A fluttery feeling swarmed her belly. It was the first time she'd unconsciously referred to Azazel as her father. It should have felt wrong. Except...it didn't. She sobered in the next instant.

The first Sorcerer King must have been truly powerful to mask such an extensive force from Azazel.

"I'm going to get to the point." Vlad studied Mae and Bryony with a piercing look. "I want you to help me stop *Oniks* and those demons."

CHAPTER THIRTY-TWO

RELIEF FILLED MAE AS SHE WALKED THROUGH THE FRONT door of her apartment.

Home sweet home.

Nikolai, Violet, and Miles piled into the foyer behind her. Mae eyed them with a jaundiced air as she dropped her keys on the console table in the hallway.

"I told you guys I'd be okay," she repeated for the tenth time.

"And like we said, you can never be too safe," Nikolai replied.

He moved past her and crossed the open-plan living area to the windows. He checked the street outside before tugging the curtains closed.

"Oscar and the Dark Council are still out there," Violet said sternly. "We should stick with you until things die down."

Miles dropped the overnight bags he and Violet had picked up from their penthouse in Midtown in the middle of the living room.

Mae sighed.

Great. Now I know what it feels like to be in a witness protection program.

Luckily, her place was just about big enough to accommodate all four of them. Located above the oldest cinema in Ridgewood, her apartment was a nine-hundred-square-feet, two-bedroom unit. The building itself stood at a five-way intersection on Forest Avenue and made up the cornerstone of two adjoining streets of flat, front-brick rowhouses. Though Mae could afford a place closer to her family home in Flushing or where Rose had lived in Long Island City, she loved the quaint feel of this area of Queens with its historic architecture and eclectic community.

Most people would have shied away from renting an apartment above a cinema. Mae, however, had fallen in love with the building the first time she saw it, when her father had brought them to watch one of Ye-Seul's favorite movies, on her sixty-fifth birthday. It had become their favorite place for special family outings after that.

It was Ryu who'd alerted her that Mr. Seong was looking for a reliable tenant for the two-bed unit above the cinema; the old couple who'd lived there had relocated to Kansas to be closer to their daughter and her family. Mae had taken one look at the exposed-brick walls, parquet floors, and tin ceiling that characterized so many of the early 20th century brownstone properties in Ridgewood and signed the lease that day.

The apartment had a crooked layout due to its location, which only added to its charm. The hallway was long and cut across the unit diagonally, the two bedrooms and main bathroom opening off it. The rest of the floor was taken up by the living space, the once narrow galley kitchen given a breath of life after the previous tenants knocked down a wall when they refurbished the place. The large windows let in light from the north and the east and a small balcony outside her bedroom gave rise to a fire escape that led to a private rooftop garden. It was Mae's oasis in her hectic life and somewhere she and Rose often had barbecues.

Mae's chest ached as she thought of her best friend. She still hadn't come to terms with the fact that Barquiel now possessed Rose's physical form and was walking around New York doing God knew what with her body. She clenched her teeth.

The sooner I accept she's gone, the better it will be for me when I have to deal with her again.

Mae didn't doubt that their paths would cross in the future. With the Dark Council seemingly determined to capture her, and Barquiel supporting Oscar and the Sorcerer King, it was inevitable.

Vlad's request flitted through her mind.

"You want us to do what?" Bryony had said flintily.

"I want Mae and your coven to stop Vedran's influence in the New York underworld," he'd stated succinctly. "It's in your best interests that you do so." He'd tilted his head at Mae. "They are going to keep coming after our queen."

Mae couldn't help but shiver as she recalled the smoldering heat in his eyes. In need of a distraction, she headed into the kitchen, opened the refrigerator to grab a drink, and stopped dead in her tracks.

The shelves were empty bar three bottles of beer, a carton of milk, and a jar of pickled gherkins.

Mae closed the refrigerator and eyeballed Violet and Miles. "I could have sworn this was full of food the last time I was here."

They met her accusing stare with shrugs.

"Hey, don't blame us," Violet said. "Your familiar is a pig."

"We even had to order pizza on top of everything he ate," Miles complained.

Intuition had Mae checking her cupboards. They were bereft of edible contents, as if a Hunger Fairy had swept through the apartment and swooped up everything fit for human consumption.

The 'Hunger Fairy' returned from where he'd been proudly showing his new domain to Trixie, Millie, and Alastair.

He sat on his haunches, his tail swishing languidly across the parquet floor, and looked expectantly at Mae.

What is for dinner?

Mae swallowed a curse.

"Is there a problem?" Nikolai asked curiously.

He was back from checking the apartment.

"Yeah. I'm gonna need to get a third job to feed the fox and the demonic weapon."

Violet raised an eyebrow. "You can always ask the New York coven to take care of your expenses."

Mae brightened. "I can?"

Nikolai pursed his lips. "Is that how you guys landed that penthouse in Midtown?"

Miles shrugged. "Nah, we paid for that ourselves."

Mae narrowed her eyes at the cousins. "By the way, I never asked, but what do you guys do for a living?"

"I'm an Engineering major at UChicago," Violet replied guilelessly. "Miles is in the family realtor business. He's also an MBA student at Harvard Business School."

Mae and Nikolai traded a look of commiseration.

"So, you're just stinking rich," Mae muttered.

"Hey, he's loaded too," Miles protested, cocking a thumb at Nikolai.

Nikolai narrowed his eyes. "I don't rent penthouses in Midtown. Besides, my father never believed in showering his kids with money *or* affection."

A stilted silence befell them. Brimstone huffed at the change in the mood. A knock came at the front door.

They froze.

"You expecting anyone?" Nikolai asked tensely, magic flaring at his fingertips.

Mae frowned. "No. And put that magic away before you hurt someone."

A frail voice carried through the apartment from the landing outside. "Mae?"

Mae relaxed. "It's okay. It's just my landlord."

She strode down the hall and opened the door, ignoring their hissed protests.

Mr. Seong blinked up at her, a liver-spotted hand clutching his walking stick and the other holding a carrier bag. Old age and osteoporosis had shrunk his once prime five-foot-four frame to a more demure five foot two. The wisps of receding gray hair covering his scalp just about reached her chin.

"Hi, Mr. Seong."

"Hi, Mae. It's good to see you again." Her landlord fidgeted. "Are you okay? Mrs. Son-Ha called and said you got dropped off by some strange men in suits."

Mae masked a grimace. Bryony had insisted the New York coven give them a ride home when they'd parted ways. Had she known this would involve two swanky SUVs pulling up outside her place and her escort practically rolling out a red carpet as they walked her to the door of the building, she would have called a cab. She sobered.

Mrs. Son-Ha's spy network is scary.

"Yeah, I'm okay. Thanks for taking care of the place while I was in the hospital."

"It's no problem." Mr. Seong handed her the bag. "Here, I made *bulgogi* and *japchae*. There's some *kimchi* on the side." His face fell when he noticed the figures crowding the hall behind her. "I didn't realize you had friends over. I would have brought more."

"Thank you. And it's okay to ignore them."

This was proving to be a hard thing for either of them to do considering the *sotto voce* conversation taking place in the foyer.

"What if he's a sorcerer in disguise?" Violet muttered darkly.

"If he is, that's a damn good cover-up." Miles's tone remained skeptical. "Never saw a fake sorcerer with a walking stick before."

"Guys, I really think he's just her landlord," Nikolai murmured.

Mae cut her eyes to them. They stopped talking.

Something rumbled hungrily. Mr. Seong's gaze dropped to Hellreaver.

"Sorry about that," Mae said brightly. She rubbed her belly, a fake smile on her face. "Looks like I'm ready for dinner."

"Oh." Mr. Seong blinked. "Well, I best leave you to it." He turned, stopped, and looked over his shoulder. "I'm glad you're safe, Mae. It would have broken your family's heart if something had happened to you."

Emotion clogged Mae's throat. "Thank you, Mr. Seong."

The old man nodded and smiled. He headed slowly down the stairs, one hand gripping the banister firmly. Mae waited until she heard the door close at the bottom before heading back inside the apartment with the others.

Brimstone came out of her bedroom and dropped a purple, rubber object at her feet.

What is this curious chew toy?

Mae grabbed the vibrator, strode across the living room, yanked a window up, and hurled it outside.

Brakes squealed. There was a bang followed by distant cursing.

Mae closed the window and tugged the curtains together guiltily.

"Was that a—?" Violet started.

"No, it wasn't."

They ended up ordering takeout to satisfy Brimstone and Hellreaver's bottomless appetites and feed the other familiars. They'd just finished stuffing their faces when a cell phone rang. It took a few seconds for Mae to realize it was the one Vlad had given her when she'd left the New York coven headquarters that afternoon. The way he'd slipped it into her back pocket had been downright illegal and nearly caused Nikolai to have some kind of fit.

She fished the phone out and took the call. "Hello?"

"Hi, Princess," Vlad drawled.

His voice sent a delicious shiver down her spine.

Wait. Does his incubus power travel across phone lines?

She asked him the question.

Vlad chuckled. "No, it doesn't.'

"Oh." Mae scratched her cheek and did her best to avoid Nikolai's cold stare. "So, hmm, why are you calling?"

There was a short silence. "Can't I just call to say hi to my queen?"

The way Vlad dropped his tone an octave did all kinds of crazy things to Mae's pulse. She swallowed, turned away from the others, and clutched the phone to her face.

"Stop kidding around and tell me what you want!" she whispered fiercely, trying her best to sound admonishing. "I have two trigger-happy sorcerers and a witch in my apartment right now and this little game of yours isn't helping the situation!"

She could feel Vlad grinning at the other end of the line.

"You got a pen and paper?"

"Wait. Let me grab them." Mae rose, went into the kitchen, and took the shopping list pad off the refrigerator. "Okay, I'm ready."

"Meet me at this address downtown in two hours. We have work to do." He paused. "There's a dress code. I'll send some clothes over."

CHAPTER THIRTY-THREE

NIKOLAI's face grew frosty as their cab pulled up outside an exclusive strip club near an intersection off West Broadway.

"Why didn't we take the car the coven gave you?" Miles grumbled when he alighted from the vehicle.

Mae dragged her distracted gaze from the glitzy facade before them.

"Because I don't want to owe them anything," she told the sorcerer firmly. "Not until I know where I stand with them."

Bryony had had her people deliver a brand-spanking-new SUV to her address just as they were headed out. It even came with car insurance and additional extras.

"They only mean to help," Violet protested.

"I'm not one to look a gift horse in the mouth, but I doubt that favor came with no strings attached."

From Nikolai's expression, he agreed.

Mae became conscious of a battery of stares. The

line of people outside the strip club was ogling her. She grimaced.

Have I got something on my face?

She realized their interest had been captured by something behind her. The women's cheeks bloomed with color, their expressions growing hungry.

"I see you're wearing the outfit I chose for you."

Mae turned. Vlad was strolling down the sidewalk, a group of hulking bodyguards framing him. He wore a black, tailor-made suit and vest, the red buttons and jewel cufflinks matching his silk shirt and leather brogues.

The incubus looked like sin and smelled like heaven.

Vlad raked her figure with his gaze, his eyes telling her he liked what he saw. Mae told her libido to calm the heck down.

Great, now we look like a couple.

She sneaked a peek at Nikolai from under her lashes. The sorcerer was studying Vlad like he was making notes of vital points to sink a knife in later.

The outfits Vlad had dispatched for their outing had arrived courtesy of two somber-faced men who wouldn't have looked out of place on an FBI crime watchlist. Mae fervently hoped Mrs. Son-Ha's spies hadn't seen them pay her a visit.

The red leather pants, black jacket, and dark sequin top she'd found inside the garment carrier intended for her had had Mae pursing her lips and wondering if Vlad's powers included reading her measurements. The outfit fitted her like a dream and accentuated her slender curves in ways that made her appear more voluptuous than she was.

Even Violet's trendy jeans and top and Miles's casual-chic suit were a perfect match. As for Nikolai, Vlad's choice made him look like some brooding, Wall Street king, his navy suit with its silver accents and cufflinks showing off his athletic frame and the matching boutonniere accentuating his eyes.

"Thanks for the gift," Mae murmured.

Vlad ignored Nikolai's icy stare and captured a handful of her hair. Her breath froze when he lifted it to his lips.

"Did you like the lingerie I sent you?"

Mae swore several women and even a few men in the line swooned. She bit her lip and flushed, recalling the racy items Vlad had included in her package.

Yoo-Mi would definitely faint if she saw those.

"Wait," Violet whispered in her ear. *"He gave you lingerie?!"*

"Wow, this guy moves fast," Miles muttered.

The cousins peeped at Nikolai. The sorcerer was clenching his jaw so hard Mae was surprised he hadn't bitten his tongue.

Tarang smirked where he sat by Vlad, invisible to everyone but them. It was clear the tiger was proud of his handsome master. The creature tensed a little when Brimstone stepped out from behind Mae. Tarang lowered his head in deference to the beast.

Vlad smiled thinly at Nikolai before deliberately turning his back on the sorcerer and hooking Mae's arm through his elbow. "Shall we step inside, Princess?"

"It's Mae."

Vlad gave her a puzzled look as he guided her to the entrance of the strip club.

"Call me Mae. Princess and queen make me uncomfortable."

"But you *are* my princess *and* my queen."

The way he said the words made Mae feel like she was being worshipped.

Vlad's gaze skimmed Nikolai. He leaned in close, his eyelids drooping as he focused on her mouth. "And, if you let me, I will make it so that you never look at another man."

Mae's pulse stuttered. His breath where it washed across her lips held a promise of sex and pleasure so intense it would likely make her faint. Heat flooded her body in places she hadn't felt in a long time. She stared into his eyes and read desire.

There was something else there. Something that should have scared her but didn't. A darkness that threatened to eat her whole and spit out her bones.

Mae shivered.

He's dangerous.

Vlad straightened, his expression growing shuttered.

The doormen moved aside, the cautious looks they cast at Vlad and his bodyguards indicating they knew who he was. They entered a sumptuous lobby area and were escorted through a beaded curtain by a hostess. Music thumped across Mae's skin as they entered the club. She looked around the crowded interior, her eyes adapting to the low, neon lighting.

A bar ran along the east wall of the main floor. The suited men and women behind the counter wore professional smiles as they attended to customers, the spotlights above them highlighting well-stocked shelves gleaming with expensive liquor and champagne bottles. Cocktail servers in elegant vests over white shirts and dark slacks circulated the room, along with VIP hostesses tending to the private areas and lounges hugging the west and rear walls.

Artfully lit stages dotted the club, showcasing the dancers working silver and gold poles. The women were all stunningly beautiful, their lithe bodies toned and spray-tanned to perfection, their outfits doing little to hide their assets as they writhed and undulated.

It was clear from the decor and the clientele that this place carried a hefty price tag for its services.

Vlad was looking at them with an amused expression. "Is this your first time at a strip club?"

"Yeah," Mae murmured.

"I'm only twenty-one," Violet said defensively.

Miles's wide eyes indicated this was new for him too.

Nikolai remained tactfully silent.

He must have frequented these kinds of places as a member of the Dark Council.

For some reason, that thought irritated Mae.

Brimstone spoke.

What are those females doing?

Mae looked down at the fox. He was staring at the strippers with a puzzled expression. Tarang rumbled something to him.

Really? Brimstone looked up Mae. *Please assure me that you shall not be indulging in this kind of activity to satisfy the desires of the incubus and the sorcerer. Just because you are in heat does not mean you should bring shame to our status.*

Tarang and Hellreaver snickered. Trixie and Millie blushed.

Alastair ruffled his feathers, beady stare cold as he observed the weapon and the familiars haughtily.

"Are you okay?" Violet asked Mae. "There's a vein throbbing in your temple."

"I'm fine," Mae said between gritted teeth. She eyeballed Vlad. "Don't you think it's about time you told us why we're here?"

CHAPTER THIRTY-FOUR

Nikolai ground his teeth. He shot a heated look at Vlad before observing the group across the way.

They were in a private area, in the basement of the club. Seated at the tables beyond a corded-off section opposite them, hands busy stuffing dollar bills in the G-strings of the strippers performing on their stage, were members of *Oniks*.

The group numbered sixteen men. Their loud jeers and raucous laughter echoed around the underground room as they drank and smoked cigars, fingers merrily groping the entertainers dancing on their laps and the hostesses serving them.

Nikolai could tell the women were uncomfortable.

The security guy and waiters manning the floor were ignoring their subtle distress signals, their gazes skimming the rowdy gang as if they were invisible. Most other patrons had vacated the basement. The only parties remaining were Vlad's, *Oniks*, and a group of drunk frat guys who seemed oblivious to the fear steeping the room.

Nikolai's gaze strayed to a man with a scar running vertically down his right eye and cheek. He sat apart from the rest of *Oniks*, the space around him a buffer no one dared cross. He was the only one who looked stone sober, his disinterest in the women servicing the other men plain to see. The strippers all kept away from him and the hostesses averted their gazes from his chilly eyes.

The guy's name was Emil Sobol. He was the second *Oniks* member Vlad had been shadowing besides Antonovich and one of the gang's most ruthless generals. Vlad suspected Sobol's recent rise in the ranks was a direct result of working with the Dark Council.

The fact that they were in an enclosed space with people who could be harboring demons and sorcerers was making Nikolai twitchy. It didn't help that Sobol had been openly staring at them for the last five minutes.

Shit. Does he know who we are?

Vlad and Mae were ignoring the guy, the pair sipping their drinks and whispering in each other's ears like they were lovers, much to Nikolai's ire. Miles and Violet were chatting to their hostess, Vlad's bodyguards towering next to them. Despite their relaxed demeanor, he knew they were on edge too.

Alastair shifted on Nikolai's shoulder, his eyes and those of the other familiars focused on the gang members opposite them. Animals could sense a lot more than humans and it was clear the familiars considered *Oniks* dangerous.

Movement to the left drew Nikolai's gaze a moment later.

A man with a hulking physique had walked into the basement, an entourage of suited guys around him. They looked South American, the bulges under their armpits indicating they were carrying. Sobol's gaze shifted to them.

The man smiled at the *Oniks* general, his snake-like eyes cool. He walked over and sat opposite Sobol, his escort falling back slightly. Some of Sobol's men sobered and straightened in their chairs when they registered the other guards' presence.

Nikolai frowned.

Not so drunk after all.

"That's Vasco Gomez," Vlad said in a low voice. "He's the linchpin of the *Bacatá Cartel* operations in the U.S."

Nikolai's stomach sank. The *Bacatá Cartel* was one of the most vicious gangs in Colombia and the whole of South America. Their brutality was the stuff of horror stories and their gut-churning deeds had made headlines all over the world. It was patent they were aiming to be as influential as the *Medelin* and *Cali Cartels*.

The faint frown Vlad sported made it clear he hadn't been expecting the Colombian.

"You think they're the ones providing slaves to *Oniks*?" Mae asked.

"The deteriorating geopolitical situation in

Colombia and the rest of South America means human trafficking is on the rise again. It's now a prime money maker for the gangs that dominate the landscapes in those countries. The *Bacatá Cartel* was the first to seize the opportunity when it arose and has been riding the high for a while. Securing a supply line with *Oniks* will not only be a notch on their bedpost that will solidify their position on the continent, it will also open up the doors for trade with other prominent gangs in Europe."

He paused when he noticed their blank stares.

"So, you're not just a pretty face, huh?" Violet said.

Their hostess had gone off to fetch more drinks.

Vlad smiled. "You don't become the future heir to the *Chernyye D'Yavoly* by batting your eyelashes at your enemies."

Nikolai realized Gomez was looking at them over his shoulder. He stiffened. Sobol had just said something to the *Bacatá Cartel* mobster. The Colombian rose and came over to their table, almost strutting in his arrogance.

"Vlad Vissarion?"

Vlad observed Gomez with a bored expression. "And you would be?"

Something ugly flashed in the Colombian's eyes. He evidently didn't like being baited. "I'm Vasco Gomez, of the *Bacatá Cartel*."

Vlad cocked his head to the side, pensive.

"*Bacatá. Bacatá,*" he murmured. "Hmm, I'm afraid I don't know a cartel by that name."

The tension in the room ratcheted up a couple of notches.

Nikolai clenched his teeth, his gaze moving carefully from Gomez to Vlad.

This guy has a death wish.

The lazy smile playing on Vlad's lips suggested he knew exactly what he was doing. Nikolai recalled his words from earlier.

"A shipment of slaves came into New York yesterday from South America. The final deal is being closed here, tonight. There's a place somewhere nearby where the goods are being kept. I want to stop *Oniks* and capture the parties involved."

Mae had observed Vlad with an incredulous expression. "You want to stop the deal? How?"

"By creating a diversion." He'd shrugged at Mae's confused look. "It's the perfect opportunity to put a wrench in *Oniks's* and the Dark Council's plans. It will also give me a chance to interrogate them and find out what they're intending to do in the city."

"Interrogate?" Mae had asked sharply. "You mean, you're going to kidnap members of *Oniks* and torture them?"

Vlad had shrugged. "Something like that."

"You realize that if there are any Dark Council members among them, they might recognize Mae and me?" Nikolai had growled.

"That's kind of what I'm counting on. But I doubt all Dark Council members are aware of Mae's exact physical description. The same applies to you. Oscar has been the face of the Dark Council for the last ten years, while you were relegated to the shadows. It seems to me the only ones likely to recognize the two of you are the core group of sorcerers and witches working with Oscar and Barquiel to capture Mae."

That Vlad knew so much about the inner workings of the Dark Council would have irritated Nikolai in the past. Now, he was just relieved for the other man's insight.

Say what you want about the bastard, he is *clever.*

Nikolai had cause to doubt his own judgment as he watched Gomez's face turn red.

"I see the heir to the *Black Devils* is as proud as the rumors say," the Columbian growled.

Vlad's smile filled his face. "Why, thank you."

"Hey, how about you give us a lap dance?" someone said to Nikolai's right.

His head swiveled round. He bit back a curse.

One of the frat guys had come up to their table and was leering at Mae, his beer breath fogging the air. Gomez examined him as if he were an insect.

"I think it would be best if you left," Violet warned Frat Boy.

Frat Boy sneered at her. "I ain't talking to you, Pancake Chest."

Violet narrowed her eyes and made to rise.

Miles grabbed her arm, his expression flinty. "He's not worth it, Vi."

"He seriously isn't," Nikolai muttered.

Mae stood and leaned her hands on the table, her jaw set in a hard line.

"Leave," she told the guy in a deadly voice. "Your breath stinks and you're being rude to my friends."

Nikolai realized she was giving the fool a chance to escape certain death. Gomez regarded her with fresh interest.

"Or what?" Frat Boy lifted his chin defiantly. "Whatcha gonna do, bitch?"

Nikolai swore under his breath. The kid's friends were coming over, some of them swaying under the influence of alcohol.

These assholes are going to get themselves killed!

The security guy at the far side of the room motioned to a hostess, a muscle twitching in his cheek. She slipped out of the basement, no doubt on her way to get help. Nikolai had a feeling it would be too late to prevent bloodshed.

The room was already filling with a murderous aura.

Frat Boy chortled at his friends, clueless when it came to the men watching them with menacing intent. "Hey, maybe she'll do some kind of karate move and beat us up?"

He raised one knee in the air and started making shrill battle cries while waving his arms in a parody of martial arts moves.

Vlad's smile faded. Brimstone growled under the table.

Frat Boy bumped into Gomez. "Oh. Sorry, I didn't see you there, Big—"

Mae reacted so fast Nikolai barely caught her

movement. Frat Boy's head smashed face down onto the table. His nose broke in a burst of blood.

Nikolai blinked.

Did she just use magic?!

"Hey! What the fuck—?" One of the guy's friends surged forward, fist rising to strike Mae as she held the kid by his head.

He froze. Vlad's bodyguard was pressing the muzzle of a gun against his temple. Fear leeched the color from the group's faces as they registered the weapon.

The dancers and hostesses fled the basement with shrill cries. *Oniks* and the Colombians paid close attention, Sobol's interest in Vlad's reaction all too evident.

"Oh," Vlad drawled. He crossed his legs, tucked his hands in his pockets, and leaned back in his seat, his expression relaxed. "That *Bacatá Cartel.*"

CHAPTER THIRTY-FIVE

Mae let go of the frat boy. The kid slumped to the floor, semi-conscious.

"Take him and go," she told his friends coldly.

Her pulse thrummed rapidly as she watched them leave with their comatose companion. The atmosphere in the basement was so fraught a single wrong move would have turned the place into a blood bath.

Frat Boy's head lolled lifelessly as his friends dragged him out of the room. A twinge of guilt shot through Mae.

He'll thank me later.

She'd been careful to cushion his skull with a layer of magic when she'd grabbed his head and smacked his face on the table. She only wanted him to suffer a broken nose, not a cracked eye socket or a cranial fracture.

"I see your lady friend knows how to stand up for herself," Gomez told Vlad with a grunt.

"Thank you." The proprietary look Vlad gave Mae

raised goosebumps on her over-hot skin. "Although, truth be told, she could probably kick my ass."

Gomez smiled, plainly disbelieving the Russian's words. "Why don't you join us for a drink?"

A few minutes later found them sitting at *Oniks's* tables, several gang members vacating their seats to make way for Vlad's party. One of them had gone upstairs to have a word with management. A slew of ashen-faced strippers and hostesses were making their way back down into the basement, their eyes dark with fear.

Mae could hardly blame them.

"So, what brings you to this part of our fair city?" Gomez asked Vlad as a hostess poured their drinks.

"My girlfriend wanted to see the best strip club in New York."

A muscle twitched in Nikolai's cheek.

Gomez and Sobol studied Mae.

She kept a straight face by sheer willpower.

Girlfriend?!

Mae smiled coolly at Sobol and Gomez and carefully pressed a heel on Vlad's foot. Considering she was wearing stilettos, it had to hurt. He touched her knee and squeezed lightly. The message was clear.

Play along.

"I'm new in town," she said grudgingly.

Vlad's hand remained on her thigh, his touch burning her flesh.

"Really?" Sobol murmured. "You have a Queens accent."

She met his stare unflinchingly. "I grew up here and just moved back."

Other men in Sobol's position would have been vexed by her open impudence. Sobol just watched her with an inscrutable expression.

"Come now, Emil," Gomez said amiably. "Everyone has a backstory."

"True." Sobol's gaze moved to Nikolai. "What about you? What's your backstory?"

"Vlad and I know each other," Nikolai told Sobol in a neutral voice.

"We were college buddies in Paris," Vlad drawled, the lie falling from his lips with practiced ease. "You could say we're brothers in arms."

Though he didn't show it, Mae felt Nikolai's twitch. His reaction seemed to amuse Vlad.

She swallowed a sigh.

He's such a goddamn tease.

Vlad's eyes twinkled, as if he'd read her mind.

A thin smile played on Sobol's lips. His gaze swung between Nikolai and Vlad. *"Vous n'avez pas l'air de gens qui sont allé à la fac à Paris."*

Mae stiffened.

He speaks French?!

"Et tu n'as pas l'air du genre de gars qui parle français," Nikolai said fluently just as Vlad opened his mouth to reply.

"Touché," Sobol murmured.

Mae sensed Brimstone's restlessness where he sat under the table. To be fair, she was feeling pretty on edge too. The faint aura of corruption she'd detected above Sobol's head was now fully evident, the ochre light in the depths of his dark pupils as he observed them a surefire sign he was possessed by a demon.

He wasn't the only one. There were four other demons and six sorcerers in the room, all part of *Oniks*. A bitter tang of black magic came off the sorcerers; they hadn't bothered to shield their powers, no doubt confident in their abilities to overcome any foe who crossed their path. As for Sobol, it seemed he was able to suppress his demonic energy to an extent.

Her hands fisted on her lap.

Does that mean he's more powerful than Antonovich was?

Brimstone spoke. *From your memories, I would say yes.*

Mae masked a frown. *Think you can take him on, Hellreaver?*

The pendant answered with a smug hum. *Of course.*

Two of Sobol's men started talking to one another in low voices, brows furrowing. They were staring at Nikolai. The tension winding through Mae intensified.

The pair were sorcerers.

Dammit! Have they recognized him?

Nikolai's fingers strayed to his watch. Violet and Miles braced themselves where they sat at the next table.

"Oops, sorry about that," Vlad observed, not sounding the least bit contrite. He shot a glance at Nikolai. "Looks like I was wrong."

Nikolai gave him a dirty look. Gomez stared, puzzled. One of the sorcerers whispered in Sobol's ear.

"Vasco?" Vlad said calmly.

"Yeah?"

"This isn't personal."

Vlad grabbed Gomez's arm and hurled him to the far side of the room with superhuman force. The mobster crashed into the wall and slumped to the floor, stunned. Mae blinked.

Vlad hadn't used his magic to throw the guy.

There was a moment of breathless stillness. The *Bacatá Cartel* members jumped to their feet and drew their guns, expressions furious.

The four *Oniks* members hosting demons in their souls transformed, their eyes going midnight black and their pupils flaring ochre. The Colombians cursed and backed away hastily as the monsters grew in size, shirts and suits ripping over bulging muscles and nails lengthening to ugly claws.

The terrified strip club staff screamed and legged it to the exit, several stumbling and falling in their haste to get away.

"Take Gomez and go," Vlad told the *Bacatá Cartel* gang coldly. "Tell him I'll be in touch after this is over. You don't want to be here for what's about to go down."

He joined Mae where she'd moved to the middle of the basement, Nikolai at her side and Violet and Miles covering their backs with Vlad's bodyguards.

Magic flared on Violet and Miles's hands. The ring and bracelet transformed into the arming sword and saber, Trixie and Millie focusing their powers where they sat at their feet. Alastair squawked threateningly on Nikolai's shoulder as the sorcerer unleashed his spear, white magic dancing on his fingers and in the crow's eyes.

The studs in Vlad's ears dropped into his hands and changed into two black swords with gleaming, diamond edges, his power a red light blazing in his pupils and dancing on his blades.

The Colombians stared, looked at one another, and left hurriedly. Gomez groaned between them as he started to regain consciousness. Vlad eyed one of his men. The bodyguard dipped his head and vanished after the Colombians.

Sobol pressed his hands on the table and rose to his feet.

"My men tell me you are the Dark Council traitor the Sorcerer King is seeking to capture," he told Nikolai, his voice deepening to an inhuman growl.

Capture? Mae's chest tightened. *I thought they were trying to kill Nikolai!*

Nikolai tilted his chin defiantly. "Yes, I am Vedran's son."

His words seemed to infuriate the sorcerers with *Oniks*.

Sobol let his demon free.

Mae swallowed, head angling to take in the *Oniks* general's monstrous, seven-foot frame as his shadow fell over them. Some of his men staggered away, their fear all too apparent. Though they didn't leave, it was evident they were human through and through, unlike some of their peers.

"That's one fugly son of a bitch," Vlad remarked as

he studied Sobol. "He must be a modified demon, like Antonovich."

Tarang snarled beside him.

"Brim?" Mae said stiffly.

Yes?

"Don't transform down here. We need to be careful with our magic or we'll wreck the place."

The fox huffed, irritated. *I will lend you my powers as much as I can.*

"Thanks."

Hellreaver changed into his dagger form. Sobol's gaze locked on the weapon. The human *Oniks* gang members swore and recoiled. Several of the sorcerers frowned heavily, recognition dawning in their eyes.

It seemed news of Hellreaver had reached their ears.

The weapon spoke. *Can I consume their flesh?!*

Mae made a face at Hellreaver's eager voice. "You wanna eat them?"

The *Oniks* members blanched.

Yessss!

"We had dinner three hours ago," she reminded him.

Hellreaver's tone turned into that of a petulant teenager.

That only satisfied a fraction of my demons.

Mae sighed. "Alright. But don't be messy. I don't want to ruin these clothes."

Black magic shot across the chamber. Vlad and Nikolai deflected the spell bombs before they reached Mae. The orbs smashed into the ceiling. Plaster dust rained down on them. Mae stared at the craters before eyeballing the two men with a piercing frown.

Vlad shrugged. "What?"

"I said mind the building!" she snapped.

Nikolai grunted and engaged a demon, his spear blocking the claws headed for his eyes.

"Is she always like this when she fights?" Vlad asked the sorcerer, his swords slashing two *Oniks* members nearly in half as he advanced toward Sobol.

"Like what?"

"Too nice for her own good?"

Nikolai blasted a sorcerer with magic and swooped beneath the demon's next attack. "Yeah!"

He stabbed the monster in the foot with the spear, pinning him to the floor.

"It's called not being a destructive asshole!" Mae snarled.

She smashed Hellreaver's knuckle duster into a demon's face. The creature screamed, his nose coming away from his skull. The weapon chomped down on the flesh and cartilage he'd bitten off.

"That's gross," Violet said dully.

The *Oniks* gang members fired their guns. Hellreaver left Mae's hands, blurred through the air, and ate all the bullets. The men gurgled in terror as the weapon chewed the slugs with sounds of contentment.

"He's *so* sick," Miles muttered, his voice full of admiration.

CHAPTER THIRTY-SIX

A SAVAGE THRILL MADE VLAD'S BLOOD THRUM AS HE ducked beneath Sobol's fist. He jumped, propelled himself off a wall, and twisted in the air as he rose.

The demon blocked his kick and his swords, the diamond blades cutting an inch-deep line into the monster's palms. Sobol snarled when Hellreaver sank his teeth in his shoulder from behind. An aggrieved rumble left the weapon as he tried and failed to tear off a chunk off the demon.

Sobol moved. Mae leaned back in mid-air where she hovered behind him and narrowly avoided the punch meant for her head. She somersaulted, landed on Sobol's arm, and roundhouse kicked him in the face. Her foot barely dented the demon's cheek. An irritated light flashed in her eyes, her pupils crimson with subdued power.

Vlad shivered, his heart racing with excitement and desire.

She's beautiful!

Sobol bared his fangs and brought his hands together to crush Mae. She jumped, braced a hand on the snarling demon's skull, and pivoted over his giant body. She landed nimbly beside Vlad, her breathing steady and not a hair out of place.

"I see what you mean about being difficult to kill." She noticed his faint smile. "What?"

"I kinda wanna kiss you right now."

Color blossomed on Mae's cheeks. Her eyes shrank to slits. "You're a sick bastard, you know that?"

Vlad grinned. "And you like it."

They looked over to where Nikolai, Violet, and Miles had engaged the remaining demons and sorcerers, their familiars at their sides.

"Shall we, Princess?"

Mae dipped her chin. They launched themselves at Sobol, their movements perfectly synchronized.

The pressure in the room plummeted. Vlad's ears popped. He dropped down beside Tarang, his scalp prickling. The familiar growled in alarm.

Mae halted and looked up, pupils flaring.

Vlad followed her gaze.

Black clouds had burst into life above Sobol, eddies swirling in the grip of a violent storm. A crimson light pulsing with evil wreathed the currents.

"Shit!" Vlad cursed.

Even he recognized the hellish energy gathering in the room. It made his incubus blood boil, the darkness inside him responding to the mayhem and madness it promised. He gritted his teeth.

He had given in to the evil that lurked inside his

bones once before. He never wanted a repeat of that experience.

Static flashed in the inky currents.

"That's Barquiel's power!" Mae spat.

Sobol pushed his hands into the tempest, withdrew a black-lightning-wreathed ball of magic, and hurled it at them. Mae and Vlad jumped out of the way. The demonic spell bomb crashed into the wall behind them, carving out a six-foot hole underneath the building.

Cold fingers brushed Vlad's spine as he observed the twisted steelwork framing the jagged opening and the tunnel beyond it. Bedrock sizzled and metal tinkled as they started to cool, their redness fading to black scorch marks.

A train screeched in the distance.

"Dammit!" Nikolai swore from across the way. "Did that reach the closest subway line?!"

Mae's mouth flattened to a thin line. "It sure looks like it." She met Vlad's hard stare. "We need to stop him!"

He gripped his blades. "Agreed."

Tarang came over from where he'd been mauling an *Oniks* member. Power flooded Vlad as their magic fused, the tiger's life force warming his soul.

Mae leapt first, Hellreaver spinning in her hands. She back-kicked Sobol in the jaw, blasted his face with a sphere of crimson magic, and sliced quick lines across his torso as he swung for her. Vlad blocked the demon's fist inches from Mae's head, his swords trembling as he resisted the monster's overwhelming strength.

Sobol's pupils flared with a sickening yellow light. He snarled and forced Vlad down. The ground caved where Vlad landed. His feet sank into the concrete. He bared his teeth and pushed back.

A volley of black spell bombs flashed toward him from the right. Mae raised a hand to cast her magic. Her eyes widened when she realized she was going to be a fraction of a second too late to block all of them.

Three of the explosive spells detonated into her crimson spheres. A double-bladed spear streaked across the basement and pierced the last one before it could reach Vlad. The spell bomb exploded, heat washing across Vlad in waves that were too close for comfort. The spear stabbed the ground an inch from his right foot and vibrated slowly to a stop.

Nikolai came over and retrieved his weapon, his crow's eyes bright with magic. "You owe me one."

Vlad frowned.

Nikolai looked past him to Mae. "Can you guys handle him?"

He glanced over to where Violet and Miles were keeping two demons and a sorcerer at bay with a shield, the air shimmering purple and gold with magic.

Mae's face tightened as she studied Sobol. "Yes. Go help them."

Vlad's mouth went dry at the fierce light in her pupils. His queen was everything he could have imagined and more.

"Brim! Come!" Mae roared.

The fox leapt onto her shoulder, the creature managing to balance himself perfectly. Magic exploded across the basement, a crimson haze that made the air vibrate.

Mae rose, her hair fluttering wildly in the tempest that was her power.

"Wind Fury!"

Surprise shot through Vlad a second before the spell ignited. The force of Mae's magic made his eardrums throb and pushed him back a couple of feet.

A red and black tornado wrapped around Sobol. The demon roared as he was lifted bodily off the ground, arms and legs secured flush against his monstrous body. Mae raised a hand. The whirlwind responded to her will.

Sobol smashed through the ceiling and kept on rising. She followed, Brimstone perched atop her shoulder and Hellreaver cackling in her hand.

Wind Fury carved a hole straight through the upper levels of the club all the way to the rooftop, the spell casting anyone in the way aside to safety under her command.

Mae's heart pounded as she and Sobol emerged under the night sky, the demon struggling in the grips of the conjuration that had come to her out of the blue, very much like *Devour* and *Eclipse* had during the attack on Grandview. It was as if a repository of dangerous spells resided deep in her hindbrain, the magic only revealing itself when she needed it most.

Plaster and concrete dust fluttered free from her

body where she hovered in mid-air. She cocked her head to the side and appraised Sobol for a moment before curling her fingers into a fist.

Wind Fury wrapped ever tighter around Sobol, magic cutting into his flesh. He screamed, a sound of rage and pain.

Mae had to remind herself that Vlad needed him alive to interrogate him. She moved closer to the demon.

"Submit."

Sobol glared at her and struggled violently against the black and red bands binding him.

"Never, witch!"

Mae narrowed her eyes. Sobol grunted as Hellreaver sliced into his left flank and out his back. Shock widened his ochre eyes.

"That's right," Mae hissed in the demon's face. "You're inside my magic, monster. I can weaken your flesh and tear you asunder!"

Untamed power blazed through her as she watched Sobol squirm, the demon desperate to escape Hellreaver's vicious bite. Mae took a ragged breath and shifted back a little, conscious her wrath was close to overwhelming her again.

The pressure dropped around her. Mae stiffened and scanned the area warily. A flicker of movement caught her eye. Her stomach lurched.

A portal had appeared silently beneath Sobol. The demon bared his teeth in a triumphant snarl and dropped into it.

Mae ended *Wind Fury*, alarmed. "Hellreaver!"

The weapon ripped from Sobol's flesh and darted toward her. His blades skimmed the boundaries of the closing portal as he returned to her hand, too close for comfort. The gateway vanished with an anticlimactic 'pop.'

Silence rang in her ears for a couple of heartbeats. It was replaced by the drone of New York traffic.

"Was that Barquiel's doing?" Mae asked Brimstone stiffly.

Yes. The fox jumped to the ground as she alighted on the rooftop. He turned and watched her, his expression pleased. *You are getting better at controlling your power, my bond.*

Hellreaver spoke. *Did I do well?!*

The weapon waited expectantly, like a puppy hoping for a pat on the head.

A smile tugged at Mae's mouth despite their circumstances. "Yes, you did. I almost lost you there. I'm sorry."

She stroked him. Hellreaver rumbled happily. He shifted back into the pendant and returned to her neck, still humming.

Ambulances and patrol cars were pulling up outside the strip club, sirens screaming and flashing lightbars sending red and blue pulsing against the facade of the nearby buildings. By the time Mae and Brimstone took the service stairs and returned to the basement, Vlad, Nikolai, Violet, and Miles were surrounded by armed officers.

"Ms. Jin," someone said behind Mae as an array of guns swung to cover her. "We meet again."

Mae raised her hands and looked carefully over her shoulder. Dickson and Calvarro had strolled inside the chamber. The NYPD lieutenant and the FBI agent wore tactical vests and grim frowns.

Mae met their irate stares and swallowed a sigh.

Great.

CHAPTER THIRTY-SEVEN

THE 17TH PRECINCT WAS LOCATED ON EAST 51ST Street, in Midtown. Despite the late hour, the station was busy. The perps waiting to be processed eyed Mae and the others curiously as they were marched straight through reception to a secure door leading to the back offices. Vlad had already been divested of his gun. To Mae's surprise, Nikolai had also been packing, the handgun strapped to his leg small enough to avoid detection by curious eyes when they'd been at the club. They were escorted to separate interview rooms that stretched along two intersecting corridors.

"We should contact Bryony," Miles told Violet as he and Vlad were led down the passage to the left.

"Don't worry, Princess," Vlad called out to Mae, his bored face drawing the ire of the cops beside him. "I'll have my lawyers get us out of here soon."

"Move!" a detective snapped.

He pushed Vlad.

Vlad stopped and eyed the man coolly. "Mind the suit, monkey-face."

Tarang's growl was audible only to Mae and the others. The tiger rose on his hind legs and snarled, his deadly claws and teeth inches from the unsuspecting cop's throat. The familiar paused and looked at Vlad, answering his silent command. A disgruntled huff left him as he dropped onto all fours.

Mae chewed her lip. *To think he and other familiars like him have been wandering around New York without anyone being the wiser.* She wondered if there were any animals bigger than Tarang out there. A grimace twisted her mouth at that thought. *And now I have acid.*

Mae, Nikolai, and Violet were guided into the opposite corridor. Mae watched the other two disappear into rooms a few doors down from hers. The officers led her inside the chamber they'd assigned to her interrogation, told her to sit, and left.

"Hey, don't I get a phone call?"

The door slammed closed in her face. She cursed under her breath, glanced at the cameras on the ceiling, and headed over to the metal chair and table.

Mom is going to kill me if she finds out about this.

Mae drummed her fingers on the armrest. *Ryu and Ye-Seul on the other hand would want every sordid detail.*

Dickson and Calvarro left her to stew for two hours. Mae spent that time mulling over what had happened at the club, Brimstone snoozing at her feet and Hellreaver similarly napping where he hung around her neck. Though she felt hungry, it wasn't the famished feeling she'd experienced after her fight with

Oscar and the devil at the cemetery. She looked at her hands.

Are my powers starting to stabilize?

The cores of magic in her heart and belly seemed more focused than before. Mae frowned. The only thing that remained was making sure she didn't lose control in the heat of battle. Sobol's monstrous form appeared before her mind's eye. She clenched her teeth.

The difference between Sobol and Antonovich had been worryingly clear. Even if Antonovich had not been disadvantaged by the fact that he'd been dead and divested of most of his organs when he'd attacked Mae, he still would not have been as devastatingly strong as the demon she and Vlad had faced tonight.

The thought of an army of such creatures roaming New York made her shudder. They had to stop *Oniks* and the Sorcerer King, come what may.

By the time Dickson and Calvarro walked into the interrogation room, Mae was entertaining asking Brimstone and Hellreaver to help her find the others and smash their way out of the building. She couldn't help but feel that time was running out and that the window of opportunity to put an end to whatever scheme their enemy was concocting was fast closing.

Brimstone stirred where he'd coiled his tail around her legs, his orange eyes focusing on the pair who'd just entered the room.

Mae registered his curious interest. *What is it?*

Hmm. The incubus was right.

Mae was about to ask him what he meant by that when Dickson spoke.

"Would you like a drink, Ms. Jin?"

She observed the cop as he took the seat opposite her, his tone affable. Calvarro leaned against the wall to Mae's right and crossed her arms and ankles.

"You should switch it up some time," Mae said.

Dickson gave her a puzzled look.

Mae cocked a thumb at Calvarro. "You should play bad cop and let her play good cop."

The pair's expressions grew a fraction chillier.

"You appear pretty relaxed for someone who could be facing murder charges," Calvarro said thinly.

"Really?" Mae sat back in her chair, her hands lying slack on the table. "And whom, pray tell, are you accusing me of killing?"

She was surprised at how calm she felt considering the situation. There was a good chance this could lead to her losing not only her job, but her medical license as well. Still, something told her it would not go that far.

This had more to do with what Brimstone and Vlad had implied regarding Dickson and Calvarro than her newfound powers and the status she hadn't even been aware of a week ago. Even though she was supposed to be the prophesied queen of the magic world, she still didn't feel that way.

Dickson and Calvarro's silence only added to her impression that they weren't who they said they were.

"We've heard from Vlad Vissarion and your other friends," Dickson said stiffly. "Care to tell us what happened tonight?"

"We went to a club. Two gangs clashed. A fight ensued."

Dickson's brows drew together.

"Funny," Calvarro said silkily. "That's exactly what the others stated too."

Some of the tension left Mae.

Good. They stuck to the story.

It was Vlad who'd told them what to say if they got arrested tonight, before they'd ventured into the basement of the strip club and come face to face with *Oniks*. By the sounds of it, it was a tale the incubus was used to spinning.

Dickson changed tactics. "Would you happen to know anything about the people we found in a building a few hundred feet from the club?"

The lieutenant had dropped his good cop act and was watching her with steely eyes.

Mae studied them blankly, genuine for once. "What people?"

Dickson and Calvarro traded a guarded glance. Calvarro nodded.

"We had word a shipment of humans trafficked out of South America was arriving in the city tonight," Dickson said. "NYPD got a tip-off on their whereabouts shortly before we were called to the disturbance at the club."

Mae's pulse quickened. *Vlad's bodyguard!*

It seemed the incubus had helped free the slaves intended for the Dark Council before *Oniks* could get their hands on them. A warm feeling filled her chest.

That guy isn't anywhere near as bad as he makes himself out to be. Him or his tiger.

"I'm afraid I don't know anything about that," Mae lied.

Dickson and Calvarro looked unconvinced.

"We didn't know you were Vlad Vissarion's girlfriend," Dickson said.

Mae squinted. *Strike that. That guy's an asshole.*

"We are more acquaintances than boyfriend and girlfriend," she muttered, unable to hide her sullen undertone.

"That's not what he said." Calvarro raised an eyebrow. "He claimed you were gonna get engaged."

The table trembled slightly. Dickson and Calvarro stared at it.

Mae unclenched her teeth and suppressed the burst of magic that had escaped her.

I'm gonna kill that red-eyed bastard!

Brimstone was similarly aggrieved. *I shall assist you!*

"You hang around in dangerous circles, Ms. Jin," Dickson remarked.

Mae met his gaze unflinchingly. "These are dangerous times, lieutenant."

Her words made a strange expression dart across Dickson and Calvarro's faces. The door opened because Mae could ask them who they really were.

A woman in a smart business suit walked in with two identically dressed men. They ignored the detective protesting in their steps and stopped by the table.

"Ms. Jin?" the woman said briskly.

"Yes?" Mae said warily.

"My name is Piper Bennett. I am an attorney with Benson and Benson. I will be representing you and your party. These are my associates."

The men beside her dipped their chins in greeting. Mae stared. Benson and Benson was one of the biggest law firms in the city.

"I work for Bryony Cross," Bennett added at Mae's blank expression.

"Oh."

Mae studied the three lawyers closely. She couldn't feel any magic from them.

Bennett's cool gaze landed on Dickson and Calvarro. "My client has a right to counsel. As of now, I'm advising her not to say a single word to NYPD. This interrogation is over."

Dickson narrowed his eyes. Calvarro's face turned stony.

To Mae's surprise, the lieutenant assented to Bennett's request without raising a fight. He asked the detective who'd accompanied the attorneys to prepare Mae and the others' discharge paperwork, his tone stiff.

"Vissarion's lawyers are here too," the man told Dickson grimly. "They're demanding the same thing."

"Let him go," Dickson said dismissively. He sighed at the detective's pinched expression. "All we'll end up with is a pile of paperwork and a headache if we try to fight those guys."

The look on Bennett's face said she agreed. Mae

rose to follow the attorney, Brimstone padding silently by her side.

"Ms. Jin?" Calvarro called out.

Mae stopped and turned to the agent.

"What did you find during Antonovich's autopsy?"

Bennett frowned. "Don't answer that."

Mae contemplated Calvarro and Dickson thoughtfully. "It's okay."

Brimstone spoke, his tone pensive. *They are not our enemies.*

His words convinced her to disclose the truth hovering on her lips.

"It was an enlarged pineal gland."

Confusion clouded Dickson and Calvarro's faces.

"An enlarged pineal gland?" Dickson repeated slowly.

"Yes. I believe that's why he was so freakishly strong."

Mae turned and exited the interrogation room, the detective and the agent's stares boring into her back. A bolt of intuition flashed through her. Dickson and Calvarro's zealous interest in Antonovich could only mean one thing.

They knew he was more than a criminal.

And they were likely the ones that got in Vlad's way when he was tracking down Antonovich.

CHAPTER THIRTY-EIGHT

Dawn was an hour away when Mae walked through the front door of her apartment. Nikolai, Violet, and Miles trailed in behind her.

"There's bedding in the hallway closet and the spare bedroom. I'll leave you guys to decide who's sleeping where," Mae told them tiredly. "Goodnight."

They didn't argue, their faces similarly exhausted.

"Goodnight," Nikolai murmured.

Mae headed off to her room, the events of the last twenty-four hours catching up with her. Vlad's words when they'd parted in front of the police station flitted through her mind as she undressed.

The Dark Council won't let this slide. Be on your guard.

Nikolai had concurred. The sorcerer had fallen into a meditative silence shortly after and had barely exchanged a word with them while Bennett drove them home. The attorney had informed them Bryony would be expecting a visit at the Madison Avenue high-rise later that day. She'd advised they use the SUV

Mae had been gifted. Mae wondered how much the lawyer knew about her client.

Her troubled thoughts returned to Nikolai. She suspected that, out of all of them, he was the most worried about what the Dark Council would do in retaliation for messing up their plans.

That's a problem for another day.

She brushed her teeth, slid under the covers, and turned the bedside light off. The faces of the two men who had entered her life and who now seemed to occupy her every waking thought lingered before her eyes as sleep claimed her.

It felt like she'd hardly rested when a hot tongue rasped her cheek.

"It's too early, Brim," Mae mumbled.

She turned over and burrowed under the covers.

That was not me.

Her eyes snapped open. She twisted around.

Tarang sat by her bed. The tiger blew a friendly huff in her face, his blue gaze warm and his tail swinging languidly across the parquet floor. Brimstone was perched on the windowsill, eyes closed to slits as he basked in the sunlight.

Vlad was watching her from the chair opposite the bed.

Mae bolted upright, the covers sliding to her waist.

He didn't even blink when he caught the cushion she instinctively hurled at him. His gaze dropped to her nightshirt. His lips twitched.

She flushed.

"I wouldn't have put you down as a bunny girl," the incubus drawled.

Mae was acutely conscious of the pink rabbits gamboling merrily all over her chest. She tugged the nightshirt down her thighs.

"How did you get in? And it was a Christmas gift from my sister."

"Through the window."

The bedroom door slammed open. Nikolai stood on the threshold, two white orbs spinning above his palms.

He scowled when he saw Vlad. "Alastair felt something."

Mae noted that he didn't retract his magic for several seconds. Violet and Miles appeared behind Nikolai.

"What's going on?" Violet rubbed her eyes sleepily.

Miles yawned so wide he nearly dislocated his jaw.

Their familiars sauntered into the room and started exploring. Alastair fluttered down onto the bed and eyed Tarang beadily. The tiger sniffed the crow before giving him a careful lick. The bird ruffled his feathers and hesitated before bumping heads with him. Brimstone jumped down from the window and joined them, his tail brushing across their bodies as if to mark them.

Mae frowned. "What is this, a *Disney* movie?" She pointed to the door. "Everyone, out. *Now!*"

They all turned and headed out of the room, humans grumbling and familiars huffing. She narrowed her eyes.

Vlad was still sitting in the chair.

"As your boyfriend, I'm allowed to stay," the incubus said. His eyes flared as her magic levitated him out of the room and plopped him down unceremoniously in the corridor. "Don't be shy."

The door slammed shut in his grinning face.

Should I eat them?

Mae looked at Hellreaver. "Is eating the only thing ever on your mind?"

Hmm. Sexual intercourse used to be my other principal preoccupation, back in the day. Hellreaver perked up. *If you like, I can switch my interest to—*

"I'll buy you a steak dinner if you stop talking right now," Mae said hurriedly.

She walked out into the living area a short while later, her hair still damp from the shower.

"Something smells nice. What's cooking—?"

She froze when she came in view of her kitchen.

Vlad stood at her range, the bunny apron Ryu had given her tied fetchingly around his waist while he fried bacon and eggs. Nikolai, Violet, and Miles sat at the dining table stuffing their faces with the breakfast sandwiches he'd made.

"Isn't it a bit late for brunch?" Mae said.

"It's never too late for brunch," Vlad assured her, cheeks dimpling.

Mae chewed her lip as she observed the incubus. Everything he did or said somehow ended up sounding sexual.

I bet he'd look hot even if he were wearing a sack.

Vlad's smile widened knowingly. "How do you like your eggs?"

"Over easy please," Mae murmured.

She put a fresh pot of coffee on and ate leaning against the counter. She licked her fingers clean after she finished. Vlad's breakfast muffin was the best thing she'd ever tasted.

"Would you like a second one?" the incubus asked.

Her stomach rumbled before she could reply.

Vlad chuckled. "Go sit. It'll be ready in a moment."

The absurdity of the situation wasn't lost on Mae as she headed over to the dining table. There was a world-renowned mobster standing in the kitchen, making her breakfast. A man born of an incubus and a witch, with the power to smash through walls and make her commonsense waver.

"He'd make a good house husband," Violet remarked when Mae took the seat beside her. The witch waved a vague hand. "Well, except for the overflowing sex appeal and the killing."

Nikolai sipped his coffee, his expression cool.

"What's the game plan?" Mae asked after they finished eating. "Do we just sit around and wait to see what *Oniks* and the Dark Council's next move is?"

"We don't have the leisure to wait around," Nikolai said darkly. "We should track them down and stop them."

"And how do you propose we do that?" Vlad arched a disparaging eyebrow. "It took me weeks to find out about last night's little meeting at that club. You think your contacts can do better?"

Nikolai clenched his jaw. He didn't have an answer.

A stilted silence befell them. Mae was about to ask Vlad and Brimstone about Dickson and Calvarro and how the pair fitted in the picture when her cell rang. She slipped it out of her jeans. It was Yoo-Mi.

She'd given her family her new number last night, before they'd headed out to the club. Mae grimaced, finger hovering over the answer button.

Is this about being arrested? She silently cursed Mrs. Son-Ha's spies. *If it is, maybe we should ask her network about Oniks.*

She took the call. "Hi, Mom."

"Mae?!"

Mae stilled, the terror in her mother's voice turning her blood to ice. "What's wrong?"

"It's Ryu and Ye-Seul," Yoo-Mi said tremulously. "They went out this morning to visit one of Ye-Seul's friends, in that new retirement place—you know, the one near the golf course in Clearview? They haven't come back. Ryu isn't answering her phone. I just called the retirement home. They—they never made it there!"

CHAPTER THIRTY-NINE

NIKOLAI'S STOMACH PLUMMETED AS HE WATCHED COLOR drain from Mae's face. She rose to her feet, her movements jerky. Brimstone whined and paced the floor around her, his distress plain to see.

"Mae?" Vlad said tensely.

She looked at them blindly.

"Here's what I need you to do, Mom. Grab a pen and paper and write this address down. I want you to get in the car and go there right now." Mae clenched her teeth, agony and rage filling her eyes before she squeezed them shut. "Mom, stop talking and listen to me!" she snapped. "I don't have time to explain right now. I will, when this is all over. Please, just do exactly what I'm telling you to do."

The air trembled with a flash of crimson magic. Mae opened her eyes. The light in her pupils and her tone when she spoke again sent a shiver down Nikolai's spine.

"I will find Ryu and Ye-Seul. I swear it on Dad's grave."

Violet and Miles exchanged a strained look.

Nikolai met Vlad's thunderous gaze. "They've made their move."

The incubus nodded and started making calls.

Mae finished giving her mother instructions, disconnected, and phoned Bryony. "The Dark Council has my sister and my grandmother. My mom is on her way to you. Protect her with your life." She paused, a muscle twitching in her cheek. "Thanks, Bryony. I'll have Violet contact you with details once we know more."

A suffocating hush descended when Mae ended the call.

Magic exploded where she stood in the middle of the kitchen, her hands fisted at her sides and her wrathful gaze unseeing. Her hair fluttered wildly around her face, the storm focused in a two-foot radius that spared them and the rest of the apartment.

I can't believe she's able to control her rage right now.

Nikolai's chest twisted as he recalled the fateful night Oscar had killed his mother, amidst the laughter and jeers of the Dark Council. The blinding fury that had overcome him still came like flashes of a bad dream. He hadn't been aware of his scream of agony or the way he'd clumsily attacked Oscar. He never felt the cut Oscar inflicted on his back with his sword or the hot blood dripping on the ground. All he could see was the light fading from his mother's eyes while her body grew limp in his arms.

The shrill ring of Mae's cell made him jump. She looked at the display. Her jaw set in a hard line.

Nikolai knew instinctively who was calling. He thought the phone would crumble in Mae's hand she gripped it so tight. She took a ragged breath and settled her magic before answering.

"What do you want?" Mae's tendons stood out in her neck as she listened. "I'll wait for your call." The screen cracked when she jabbed the end button. She met their gazes, her own deadly. "They want me to surrender or they'll kill Ryu and Ye-Seul."

Vlad's mouth thinned. "What's our deadline?"

"Midnight. They'll call me with the location later."

Relief filled Nikolai at the fighting light in her eyes. Mae wasn't just going to roll over and obey the Dark Council.

"They probably won't give you much notice," Vlad said flatly. "I've asked my men to track down any *Oniks* member they can find and bring them to us."

Nikolai shook his head. "It'll be too late by then," he said, frustration lending an edge to his voice. "I'm certain Oscar will have asked them to lie low. The Dark Council is unlikely to leave any loose ends lying around that might lead to them."

"What do we do?" Violet asked grimly.

Mae narrowed her eyes at Vlad. "Can Dickson and Calvarro help?"

Nikolai looked between them, his puzzlement reflected on Violet and Miles's faces. "What's the cop and the FBI agent got to do with this?"

"They're not who they say they are," Mae replied bluntly.

Surprise shot through Nikolai. Vlad was silent for a moment, his face pensive.

"I'm not sure," he finally said. "All I know is they were determined to get their hands on Antonovich. And that they are not…human."

Heat flushed through Mae's body, panic and anger a maelstrom threatening to swallow her whole. She knew the devil who'd taken Rose and the Dark Council wouldn't hurt Ryu and Ye-Seul. Not badly, anyway. Not if they wanted her to cooperate.

Still, the thought of the two of them in the hands of those bastards was enough to make her see red.

She turned to Brimstone, her face tight. "You said they are not our enemy. Do you know what they are?"

The fox shook himself out into his nine-tailed form. Mae blinked. He'd made himself smaller, so he wouldn't wreck the apartment. He still had to crouch so as not to damage the ceiling.

"The woman smells of Hell and the man carries traces of angel blood."

Nikolai flinched. "What?"

"You mean, Calvarro is a demon?" Vlad frowned. "I didn't get that from her at all."

Mae clenched her fists. "Neither did I."

If Calvarro was a fiend, she was doing a damn good job of hiding her aura.

"She is not a demon," Brimstone said. *"But she* is *from Hell."*

Violet and Miles exchanged a startled look.

"It could be someone working with one of the others," Violet murmured.

Miles grimaced and rubbed the back of his head. "And angel blood might mean one of *them.*"

Nikolai's lips pinched together. "Who are you talking about?"

"Remember we said there are demons who are working against Satanael?" Violet reminded them. "Calvarro may very well be one of their people."

"There were humans gifted with the powers of an archangel, a long time ago," Miles explained. "Their descendants look like ordinary men and women, but they possess supernatural abilities."

A flush of adrenaline sent tingles through Mae's body.

"Are these the allies you referred to before?"

"Yes." Violet faltered. "We didn't want to tell you this earlier, but they're the reason we came to New York. One of them—you could say their leader—warned us what was going to happen."

Mae's stomach grew hard. *Someone else foresaw my awakening?!*

For a reason she couldn't fathom, she didn't sense much surprise from Brimstone and Hellreaver.

"Is that person a seer?" Nikolai asked sharply.

Violet's face grew guarded. "Yes. But she's not just any seer. She's been tasked with gathering everyone we're going to need."

Mae traded a mystified look with Nikolai and Vlad.

"Everyone we're going to need for what?" the incubus said carefully.

"Everyone who will stand with Heaven's army and protect mankind at the End of Days."

Deafening silence befell them in the aftermath of Violet's bombshell revelation.

"You're not joking, are you?" Vlad asked the cousins in a somber voice.

Mae had never seen the incubus look more serious. Violet and Miles shook their heads.

Hope burst into life inside Mae, making her breath catch. "Can they help us? If this seer can see things, maybe she'll know where—"

"No." Violet's face turned hard. "They can't."

Nikolai's knuckles whitened on the table. "Why not? If they want us as allies, then surely they'd want to—"

"Because this is our trial to overcome," Violet said quietly. "The people I'm telling you about? And those with the divine beasts I spoke of before? They've all suffered hardships and conquered challenges you can't even begin to imagine. This is ours." She met Miles's resolute gaze. "A test to see if we deserve to stand with Heaven's warriors."

Mae's heart sank. She knew the witch meant what she'd just said too.

"She is right."

Mae's pulse raced as she looked into Brimstone's wise gaze.

"Azazel spoke of it while we were in Hell. Of Uriel and

Michael and the others who wanted to give mankind a fighting chance against the armies of Hell."

Hellreaver hummed. *If these allies are of those angels' bloodlines, then they are soldiers worthy of our respect.*

Frustration brought a sour taste to the back of Mae's mouth.

But they won't help us. Or rather, it sounds like they can't.

Vlad drummed his fingers on the table, his brow furrowed. "If Dickson and Calvarro are part of those groups, then they must have been sent here for a purpose."

"I agree," Violet said reluctantly. "We weren't aware of their identities."

"We should call them," Mae said brusquely.

She'd just brought up the number for the 17th Precinct when Nikolai spoke.

"Before you do that, I have an idea."

CHAPTER FORTY

Ryu's stomach churned as she sneaked a look at the dark-clad figures visible through the doorway of the dilapidated room where she and Ye-Seul were being kept prisoner.

They'd been halfway to Clearview when their car had been run off the road on a secluded stretch next to a park. Ryu had barely had time to register what had happened before she and Ye-Seul were pulled out of the vehicle. They'd had hoods yanked over their heads and been hastily bundled into the back of a van before they could utter a single scream.

For a moment, Ryu had feared they had been kidnapped for ransom or were the target of gang crime, victims of mistaken identity.

The glimpse she'd caught of one of their assailants from underneath the covering obscuring her vision while her hands and feet were being tied told her the reason for the attack was wholly different and even more deadly than she'd thought.

There had been an animal with the man. A rat perched on his shoulder that the other kidnappers seemed to ignore.

A familiar.

It was only when she and Ye-Seul had reached their final destination and been greeted by the last person they'd expected to see that Ryu had realized how much trouble they were in.

She glanced to her left, fear tightening her chest.

Ye-Seul lay on her back, eyes closed and face pale. She'd knocked her head badly on the dashboard when they were driven off the road and had become increasingly drowsy in the last few hours, the blood from the gash on her forehead congealing messily on her thin skin.

Ryu bit her lip, hesitating. She took a ragged breath.

I can't be weak. Mae will come for us. I have to keep it together until then!

"Hey!" she called out. "I need some help in here!"

Silence greeted her. A man finally appeared in the doorway. He studied her coolly before turning away.

Ryu scowled. "I'm not done talking to you, asshole!"

Footsteps drew close, the clickety-clack of heeled boots echoing across a cavernous space. Ryu's mouth went dry at the sight of the figure looming in the entrance of their makeshift cell. She swallowed and met the eyes of the woman who was once as close to her as Mae.

Rose Blake smiled faintly. "Few dare raise their heads in my presence. I see the Witch Queen's family are all made from the same mold."

Ryu clenched her jaw at the inhuman voice that left Rose's lips. "Ye-Seul knocked her head when your goons ran us off the road. She needs medical attention."

Rose's gaze shifted to Ye-Seul. She came inside the room, the air around her smelling of despair and chaos. Ryu flinched when she squatted next to Ye-Seul.

"The old woman is not near death's door yet." Rose traced Ye-Seul's cheek with a light finger. "I'm sure she'll live to see us capture her beloved granddaughter."

Ryu's eyes widened. Crimson drops were blooming on the thin line Rose had scored in Ye-Seul's skin. Her face grew hot.

"Don't touch her, you bitch!"

The slap came out of nowhere. Ryu's jaw snapped sharply sideways, black spots exploding in front of her eyes. She tasted blood on her tongue as she shook her head dazedly, her ears ringing. She licked the cut on the inside of her cheek, turned, and glared at Rose.

The creature who inhabited the flesh of Mae's best friend smiled widely, eyes mocking. She froze when Ye-Seul grabbed her wrist.

Ryu stared at her grandmother, equally shocked.

Ye-Seul's eyes were open and surprisingly lucid as she observed their captor. "Ran Soyun sends her greetings, demon. Know that she watches over Na Ri from the Heavens. So too will Azazel, once he hears of their daughter's resurrection. You will not win this war. The Witch Queen will defeat you. Mae...will defeat you...all..."

Horror drenched Ryu in a cold sweat as Ye-Seul's eyes rolled back in her head. The old woman fainted.

She lunged awkwardly toward her, the ties binding her cutting into her wrists. *"Grandma!"*

The creature possessing Rose snatched her arm away from where Ye-Seul's hand still gripped it, livid finger marks slowly fading. She stood and towered above them, her face dark.

For a moment, Ryu thought she would strike them.

A commotion outside drew the demon's attention. Rose stormed out of the cell, the stench of Hell following her.

THE HELICOPTER HOVERED HIGH OVER LOWER Manhattan, rotors spinning to maintain a stationary position.

"Are you sure about this?" Mae asked Nikolai tensely.

They hunched opposite one another, feet wide apart and hands braced against the roof of the passenger cabin.

"Yes," he replied, his jaw set in a hard line.

It had taken thirty minutes to get to the East River pier where Bryony had chartered a helicopter for their use. Vlad had watched them lift off with a flinty expression, the incubus flanked by his bodyguards. He was staying back to coordinate the *Black Devils* so they'd be ready to take on *Oniks* when the time came.

Brimstone's claws sank into the seat next to Violet, the fox looking distinctly uncomfortable as he clung to the solid surface. Being this far up in the air was evidently not his thing.

Mae wet her lips and pressed a hand to Nikolai's chest. "Tell me if it hurts."

He nodded curtly, his heartbeat steady beneath her fingers. His magic was a ball of flickering white light in her mind's eye. Mae hesitated, Violet's warning echoing in her ears.

"You want her to do what?!" the witch had gasped back at the apartment, eyes wide and staring.

"I'm going to expose the spell Vedran placed inside me to obscure my magic," Nikolai had repeated. "I want Mae to try and take it apart. It might help locate the position of the Dark Council members in the city."

"Messing with your magic like that is dangerous!" Violet had protested. "It could damage your soul or even kill you."

Mae had studied Nikolai with a sick feeling. "Is that true?"

Nikolai had pressed his lips together. "It doesn't matter."

"Yes, it does!" Mae had said between gritted teeth, aghast that he would even suggest something so unsafe.

"His white magic will protect him."

They'd all turned and stared at Vlad.

The incubus had grimaced. "Trust me, nothing would make me happier than getting rid of my competition, but I honestly believe he can survive such a process."

"Thanks," Nikolai had muttered, tone half-ironic.

He'd met Mae's distressed gaze, his own reassuring. "If anyone can do this, you can."

Mae took a shallow breath and closed her eyes. Heat suffused her veins as she reached for her magic. She guided it to her fingertips. Nikolai stiffened as her power sank into his flesh.

"I'm ready," Mae said after a moment.

"Okay."

His pulse spiked a second before he engaged his father's spell. Mae flinched.

It was as if a black wall had crashed down before her, obscuring the brilliance of his soul, the ramparts so tall she could barely see the top.

She clenched her jaw. *So, this is the power of the Sorcerer King!*

She couldn't see any obvious runes or locks she could undo on the barrier. She focused, Brimstone's magic swirling inside her as he lent her his strength.

Something flashed on the wall. A point of light high up and to the left.

Mae levitated in the space inside her mind, her gaze riveted to the spot where she'd seen the flare. She drew closer to the wall, the corrupt magic it contained brushing unpleasantly against her consciousness.

There was a chink. A tiny crack in the wall Nikolai had erected.

She touched it.

Nikolai gasped. Mae's eyes snapped open.

The sorcerer swayed where he stood before her, the color draining from his face. Alastair squawked in alarm on the seat and flew onto his shoulder.

"It's okay," Nikolai mumbled through bloodless lips.

He'd addressed the words to both her and his familiar. Mae's stomach twisted. She started to retract her magic.

"*No!*" Nikolai grabbed her hand, his touch scorching her despite his clammy skin. "This is the only way for us to defeat them!"

Mae stared into his eyes and finally saw the truth. This was as much about him avenging his mother as it was about her saving Ryu and Ye-Seul.

Her throat grew tight. "I don't want to kill you."

Nikolai shuddered. "You won't."

He let go of her wrist, clasped her face, and kissed her.

Mae froze, eyes rounding.

His lips burned her, his emotions a wire that electrified her soul. She sank into him, eager for more, her mouth parting as he deepened the kiss. Some color had returned to his face by the time he finally lifted his mouth off hers, his gaze bright with a resolve she could not deny.

"Do it, Mae."

CHAPTER FORTY-ONE

Mae's vision blurred with a film of tears. She
knew what she was about to do could potentially kill
him. She wiped her tears away angrily, flattened her
palm against Nikolai's heart, and closed her eyes. She
found herself in front of the black wall once more. She
located the breach she'd identified, pressed her fingers
to it, and let her magic loose.

Nikolai's grunt of pain reached her dimly as the
sound of her own heartbeat filled her ears. Light
exploded from her fingertips and raced across the
nigh-impenetrable fortification, crimson threads that
mapped out the tainted runes making up its building
blocks.

I see it. Mae's breath stuttered. *I see the spell!*

She shot back until she could visualize the entire
wall. Awareness blossomed. Her breath caught.

She knew what she had to do.

The incantation came to her on a whisper, her
memories of the being she had once been bringing

forth a complex conjuration that solidified into a single command.

"*Nullify.*"

For a moment, nothing happened.

The wall started to tremble, bricks and mortar quaking as if under the influence of an earthquake. The tremors intensified.

The magic buried in the structure resisted, pure corruption filling the thin cracks that appeared all over it. Mae narrowed her eyes and lifted the lid off her powers a fraction more.

A muffled shout echoed distantly in her ears. She ignored the agony of the man whose soul she was about to undo and gritted her teeth so hard she tasted blood.

Crimson clashed with black, her magic and that of the Sorcerer King colliding with a force that shoved her away from the barrier. Mae roared and pushed back, the power of Azazel and Ran Soyun blazing deep within her soul.

The wall quivered violently. It exploded in the next instant, the dark blocks disintegrating to ash. And there, flickering weakly as it fell, its size greatly reduced, was Nikolai's soul magic.

Mae moved rapidly toward the glimmering orb and caught it in her hands. She pressed her lips to it and channeled the dazzling light of Ran Soyun's magic into the kiss.

The orb flared, growing in size and brightness, the steady pulsation within a reflection of the heart of the man who bore it.

Mae opened her eyes and stared into Nikolai's tear-streaked face. They were both crying where they knelt on the cabin floor, her mouth pressed to his to give him breath just as she had breathed life into his soul. Alastair swayed on Nikolai's shoulder, the familiar drained.

Mae and Nikolai caught him as he fell. The crow's pupils flared white and his feathers regained their luster, his powers returning under their combined touch.

"What the hell just happened?" Violet mumbled, ashen-faced.

"She did it." Nikolai's voice trembled as he gazed into Mae's eyes. "She broke the spell." He swallowed. "Do you think you can do it now? Do you think you can sense them?"

Mae rose, her heart hammering against her ribs.

"Oh, I can do more than that," she said grimly. She looked over at Miles where he sat in the passenger seat in the cockpit, his face pale. "Tell the pilot to brace."

He nodded shakily.

Mae tightened her fists and planted her feet wide. Magic bloomed around her.

It blasted through the cabin and out of the aircraft, a scarlet wave that spread across New York with a single beat of her heart.

"*Nullify!*" Mae growled.

The helicopter juddered and dropped altitude sharply, the aircraft whining as it tilted violently from side to side. Brimstone yelped, claws scoring deep lines in the seat as he slid sideways.

Nikolai grabbed her arm, alarmed. "Mae!"

"It's okay."

She pressed a hand against the roof and stabilized the wildly spinning aircraft with her magic, her pulse racing as she waited for the pilot to regain control. The helicopter finally straightened into a smooth hover. Everyone breathed a sigh of relief.

"I think I just crapped my pants a little," the pilot mumbled.

Mae closed her eyes and focused on the city spread out beneath them, her brow furrowing. The sources of magic she was seeking appeared in her consciousness, a congress of dark souls.

Gotcha!

Her eyes snapped open. She leaned into the cockpit, gazed out the windshield, and slipped her cell out of her pocket. She pressed a number on rapid dial. It connected in two seconds.

"Vlad?"

"Was that you just now?" the incubus asked stiffly.

"Yeah. I have their location. They're on the Brooklyn waterfront."

THE RAMSHACKLE BUILDING STOOD NEAR AN abandoned pier overlooking Upper Bay, at the end of a maze of twisted alleyways obstructed by the carcasses of burned-out vehicles and the makeshift dumping grounds that had sprouted up in what had once been a thriving commercial zone. The four-story industrial relic was open to the sky in parts, its broken windowpanes gaping maws in the fading light.

Vlad could sense the heavy presence of black magic inside the structure, as well as the corrupt energy of demons. It made the incubus in him stir with bloodlust.

Tarang shifted restlessly at his side.

Vlad stroked the tiger's head. "It's okay. You'll get to play soon."

The familiar snarled hungrily, pupils flashing crimson.

"Our men are in place," one of his bodyguards said curtly.

Vlad dipped his chin. His father and the senior *Black Devils* generals had approved his request for their men to be deployed to take down *Oniks*. Vlad was aware that his reputation as heir to the crime syndicate was on the line. If they failed to overpower *Oniks*, the blame would be placed squarely at his feet.

Not that he cared. He might be the adopted son of Yuliy Vissarion, but his power and influence in the *Black Devils* was undeniable.

The low growls of motors reached his ears. Vlad turned. A pair of sport bikes were winding their way rapidly up the shadowy alley, lights blinking off as they approached. The lead motorcycle screeched to a halt a couple of feet from him.

Mae removed her helmet and climbed off the back seat, her face tight with determination. Nikolai turned the engine off and joined her, Violet and Miles alighting from the second bike.

"That was quite some move back there," Vlad said quietly.

The magic Mae had released over New York had made him shiver as it washed over him a while ago, the potency of the spell raking at his very soul. It had unraveled the magic shielding the Dark Council members in the city and helped Mae identify their hidey-hole.

"It's a new party trick." A muscle jumped in Mae's cheek as she scrutinized the run-down factory looming against the darkening sky. "The New York coven are on their way. I don't think we can wait that long."

"Why not?"

"Because he knows we're here."

A wave of demonic energy blasted out from the building near the pier.

Cold fingers skittered down Vlad's back at the rage he sensed within it. "That's one pissed-off fiend."

"I'm going in alone."

Vlad stared at Mae, unsure he'd heard her right. "What?"

Nikolai stormed over and clutched her shoulder in a white-knuckled grip. "Are you crazy?!"

"I'm not saying I'm gonna fight them on my own." Mae met their tense stares with a calm expression. "I want to make sure Ryu and Ye-Seul are safe first."

Vlad clenched his teeth so tight his jaw ached. He exchanged a frustrated look with Nikolai and the Nolan cousins.

Mae moved past them and headed toward the factory, Brimstone at her side.

"Stay here until you get my signal," she said in a hard voice.

"What signal?" Violet called out, confused.

"You'll know when you see it."

Vlad watched the witch and the familiar disappear into the gloom, unease a heavy weight in the pit of his stomach.

CHAPTER FORTY-TWO

Dirt puffed under Mae's boots as she entered the run-down building through a loading bay. She passed files of looming, steel columns and tired, metal frameworks and soon reached the center of an immense, debris-strewn floor, the shadows around her alive with malice. She stopped and looked up.

Graffiti-covered walls and galleries of orange-rusted machinery extended to a yawning section of roof high above. A dangerous growl left Brimstone where he stood beside her.

Most of the catwalks spanning the width of the factory were impassable, as were the staircases rising to the upper levels. It hadn't stopped the small army the devil and Oscar had gathered from occupying the walkways, guns in hand and magic flaring at their fingertips as they emerged from the gloom.

"I see you came before the deadline."

Mae turned and eyed the red-haired sorcerer walking toward her from the left, a group of demons, sorcerers, and *Oniks* gang members following in his footsteps. She shuddered at Oscar's hungry expression.

I can't believe they want me to marry this asshole.

Brimstone snarled. *I should chew his balls for even entertaining the idea!*

Oscar mistook her shiver for fear. "Do not be afraid, my queen. As long as you cooperate, I shall see that no harm befalls you." He stopped in front of her and grasped a handful of her hair before raising the dark strands to his lips. "You are to be my wife, after all. And what a pretty bride you shall make."

He smiled viciously. Some of his men chortled.

Mae swallowed bile. Whereas Vlad's identical move the night before had had her blood trembling with desire, Oscar's made her want to throw up.

The sorcerer arched an eyebrow. "By the way, I am curious as to how you found us."

Mae ignored his curious words. "Where are my sister and grandmother?"

Oscar's eyes grew hooded, the sorcerer clearly displeased at her tone. "They are safe and sound."

Mae's nails bit into her palms. "If you've hurt a single hair on their heads, I swear I will—!"

Corruption filled the building, the air thickening with an oily miasma.

Mae's gaze found the devil where he hovered between the second and third floor. He was in his demon form, his horns and wings dark under the stars emerging in the night sky above him, his pupils full of hellfire.

"They are unharmed." The devil paused, his voice taunting. "Mostly."

Rage burned through Mae. She gritted her teeth and curbed her wrath.

Not yet.

Hellreaver whined on her chest, the weapon eager to release his fury and magic. The way Brimstone's hackles rose told her he felt the same way.

Mae looked from the demon to Oscar. "Take me to them."

Oscar frowned. "Not until you surrender your powers."

"For all I know, they're already dead." Mae's tone turned icy. "I would have to be the biggest fool in the world to believe the word of monsters."

"Do as she says," Barquiel ordered.

Oscar protested. "That wasn't what we—"

The devil narrowed his eyes. Pressure filled the chamber, a heaviness that bore down on *Oniks* members and sorcerers alike. Oscar's expression turned ugly.

The demon's crimson pupils flared. "Do not make me repeat myself."

The Sorcerer King's heir backed down reluctantly. He motioned to someone on his right.

To Mae's utter lack of surprise, Sobol walked out of the shadows next to a rusting oil tank, his gaze glinting with menace. The *Oniks* general was maintaining his human appearance by the barest of threads, the crown of darkness boiling above his head indicating this would not be the case for long.

Mae and Brimstone were escorted by the demon and a group of sorcerers to the fourth floor, Oscar watching them leave with cold eyes. A locker room came into view beyond a row of boilers at the north end of the building. Mae hastened her steps, hope a bright light inside her.

"That's close enough!" Sobol barked, his words underscored by a demonic growl. "You can talk to them from here."

Mae stopped a few feet shy of the threshold of the chamber, her heart thundering against her breast. "Ryu?"

Her sister's voice when it came was the sweetest thing Mae had ever heard. "Mae?!"

Relief made Mae tremble. She swallowed. "Are you okay?"

"Yes and no," Ryu replied stiffly, out of sight. "Ye-Seul hurt her head when they attacked us. She needs to go to the hospital."

Mae finally allowed her rage to escape her soul, the tide of magic that pulsed from her body making the building shake and filling the surrounding neighborhood with a crimson haze.

It was her signal to the others to make their move.

Heat blossomed inside her as she unleashed her powers. She raised a shield around the locker room just like Violet and Miles had taught her before they took off from the heliport and turned to face her enemy, Hellreaver in her hands. Brimstone shook himself out beside her, his towering, nine-tailed form casting a shadow on the ground that made the Dark Council sorcerers stumble back in trepidation, his powers amplifying hers.

Sobol released his inner demon, his hateful eyes gleaming ochre.

Mae's fingers clenched on Hellreaver. Now that Ryu and Ye-Seul were inside a protective barrier, she could finally let loose. She jumped, pushed off a nearby boiler, and side-kicked the fiend in the chest.

Sobol grunted and stumbled backward, surprise flaring on his face. Mae landed smoothly on her feet, not a hair out of place.

"That's right, assface," she sneered at the stunned demon. "We weren't at max power when we fought you that night."

An array of black-magic bombs arrowed toward her. She blocked them with a crimson sphere.

"*Devour!*"

The red globe obeyed her command and expanded, swallowing the sorcerers' spells hungrily. Mae cast her globe back at them. The men's screams filled her ears as they were thrown across the floor. The scarlet ball detonated against the east wall of the building and carved out a hole through which the sorcerers dropped.

Sobol came at her with a snarl. Mae blocked his attack, Hellreaver juddering in her hands.

The demon bared his fangs when the weapon sank his teeth into his fist. A black storm exploded above him, dark lightning agitating the red-tinged currents. Sobol growled in delight.

Brimstone bit the demon's hand off as he reached inside the tempest for Barquiel's magic.

Sobol froze. He looked blankly at the black liquid oozing from the ragged stump that was all that remained of his upper left extremity.

"Like I said." Mae levitated off the ground, her magic sending her hair and clothes fluttering wildly, her tone dropping to chilling depths. "We were not at max power when we fought that night."

She pressed a hand to Sobol's chest and focused. Sobol's eyes rounded. Black blood spurted from his lips. He looked down to where Mae had punctured his rib cage and grasped his heart. He groaned as she crushed it.

Still, he did not fall.

Mae frowned. *Just like Antonovich.*

She yanked her hand free, propelled herself off Sobol's body, and somersaulted through the air. She swung Hellreaver as she dropped upside down behind the demon, the weapon's blade and her magic carving straight across the monster's neck and slicing it in two.

By the time she landed on her feet, Sobol's head had thudded to the floor some fifteen feet away.

The *Oniks* general staggered blindly for several seconds, his one functioning hand reaching for his missing skull. Demon blood bubbled out of the raw wound at the top of his severed spine and splattered onto the floor. He fell into the dark, expanding pool, his body shrinking to his human form.

Mae cast a glance at the locker room, her heart racing.

She could feel Ryu and Ye-Seul's life forces beyond the shield. Though Ryu's felt stronger, their grandmother's was still potent despite her injury. She fisted her hands.

She had no option but to leave them there for the time being.

Brimstone nudged her with a giant leg. *"They will be safer within the barrier than out here."*

"I know." Mae turned and headed for the stairs. "Let's go."

Brimstone followed. Hellreaver hummed savagely in her hands.

Their magic exploded across the building as the first wave of sorcerers and demons reached them.

CHAPTER FORTY-THREE

NIKOLAI DUCKED BENEATH A SPELL BOMB, CAST HIS magic at the Dark Council witch to his left, and swiped the legs out from under the *Oniks* gang member to his right. He stabbed the man in the chest and kicked the gun in his hand under a boiler before looking up, his pulse pounding.

He could feel Mae's magic on the uppermost level of the factory, where she fought Oscar and Barquiel's forces.

Vlad had engaged the Sorcerer King's heir at the other end of the first floor, his crimson-tinged diamond swords clashing repeatedly against Oscar's blade. The incubus was an equal match for Nikolai's half-brother and seemed to be enjoying himself, his familiar batting away at the *Oniks* members trying to attack him while his men engaged the rest of the mobsters spread out across the building.

"Is it bad that I find that incredibly sexy?!" Violet

said to Nikolai's right. She was eyeballing Vlad's fierce smile.

Nikolai's lips curled. "It's probably the power of his incubus blood."

Alastair squawked in agreement.

"Still, I like a man who isn't afraid to face danger head on."

"Is that why you dumped Erik?" Miles asked as he blocked an attack and drove a witch into the far wall with a spell bomb.

Violet narrowed her eyes at her cousin. Trixie's pupils flashed purple.

"Who's Erik?" Nikolai said blankly.

"Erik Nox," Miles supplied, heedless of Violet's murderous glare. "He's Regina Nox's son, the High Priestess of the Vegas coven."

"Oh. Isn't he that elite sorcerer every coven is after?"

"Yeah. He's a nice guy. More of a pacifist than a warrior." Miles glanced at Vlad before meeting Violet's hot gaze. "So, you like them rough, huh?"

"No, I do *not*!" Violet snarled. The witch blasted two gang members and a sorcerer with her purple magic. "The reason we broke up is because he—" she paused and flushed, "Erik didn't want to have sex until after we got married, okay?!"

Nikolai almost tripped as he deflected an attack.

Miles's eyes rounded, as did his familiar's. "Hang on. Does that mean you're still a vir—?"

"Don't say it!" Violet growled. She punched a guy in the face and kneed another one viciously in the balls.

"A woman has needs. And I swear that asshole wears a chastity belt!"

The air inside the factory grew heavy. Nikolai's ears popped. He stiffened, startled.

"We have company!" Miles warned behind them.

Nikolai and Violet turned.

A group of demons who looked like copies of Sobol were walking out of a giant, crimson-tinged portal. Nikolai clenched his fists, gaze searching for the fiend who had unleashed them. He caught a glimpse of monstrous horns on the second-floor gallery.

Nikolai bolted for the stairs, Alastair hanging on grimly to his shoulder.

"Hey, where are you going?!" Violet shouted.

"I have to stop Barquiel!"

"Are you nuts?!" Miles yelled. "You're no match for him!"

The shadow of a modified demon fell upon the sorcerer. He jumped and narrowly missed the monster's swinging fist. Colorful spell bombs crashed down on the creature, halting his charge.

Nikolai paused, a foot on the first step. He looked up and clocked the figures hovering above. The New York coven witches and sorcerers had arrived, Abraham leading them with his owl familiar.

"We told you guys to wait for us!" Bryony's aide snapped.

"Yeah, yeah," Miles grumbled. "How about you stop bitching and help us kill some demons?"

Abraham scowled.

Relief darted through Nikolai. *They'll be okay!*

He ascended the rickety staircase rapidly.

The second floor was eerily silent when he reached the top, the sounds of the battle unfolding above and below strangely muffled. He scanned the shadows as he advanced carefully across the debris-littered ground.

Where is he?!

Heat flared on his back. Nikolai grunted and stumbled forward, the demon's spell bomb crashing into the barrier of white magic protecting his body. He gritted his teeth and turned.

Barquiel narrowed crimson eyes where he stood some fifteen feet behind Nikolai, his black-lightning-wreathed sword in hand. The devil observed the shimmering haze around Nikolai with a pinched expression.

"How is that possible?"

Nikolai gripped his spear, his chest tingling. Truth be told, he didn't know exactly how it had happened. The only thing he was certain of was that he'd felt different ever since Mae had undone the spell his father had imprinted in his body when he was still a child.

It was as if his soul could breathe again.

With the act had come power, the white magic in his blood finally set free from the shackles that had bound it.

Nikolai still wasn't certain he could take on Oscar. And he sure as hell couldn't defeat the demon who'd stolen Rose Blake's body.

But he had to try. For his mother's sake and for the

woman who had come to mean so much to him in the short time he had known her.

Has it really been less than a week since we met?!

"Never mind," the devil said dismissively. "Now, put down your weapon and come with me."

Chilled raced across Nikolai's flesh.

Sobol was right. They no longer want to kill me. But why?!

He steeled himself. No way in hell would he return to the Dark Council of his own free will.

"Over my dead body, asshole."

Barquiel's pupils flared.

His next attack slammed into Nikolai with the force of a freight train. He crashed into a piece of disused machinery with a grunt. Pain bloomed on his back despite the magic protecting him. He dropped to the ground, his legs tingling while he tried to catch his breath. Had he not shielded himself, he was certain that would have broken his spine.

Static filled the air as the demon drew on his lightning magic once more. Alastair spread his wings when the spell bomb he cast sailed toward them, the familiar's powers augmenting Nikolai's own. White magic lit up his spear. He raised it and braced, his jaw tight.

This is gonna hurt like a bitch!

There was movement to his left. A figure flashed in front of him and deflected the black-lightning sphere a second before it reached him and Alastair.

Nikolai's breathing stuttered.

Alicia Calvarro stood before him, her back straight

and her stance firm as she faced off against the devil. His eyes widened when he saw the scythe she held. It was twice her height and midnight black.

"Hello, Barquiel," Calvarro said coolly.

The fiend scowled. "*You!*"

Jared Dickson appeared behind the demon from the direction of the stairs.

"I thought I told you to wait for me, dammit!" the detective growled at the FBI agent, a broadsword in hand.

Barquiel twisted around and cast a spell bomb at the cop.

"Watch out!" Nikolai shouted.

Golden light exploded on Dickson's blade. A focused expression filled his face. He stopped, twisted to the side, and sliced the spell bomb clean in half as it shot past him.

The devil swore and lifted off the ground. "*How?!*"

Dickson arched an eyebrow. "You mean the sword or the divine power it contains?"

"Both!" the demon barked.

"Let's just say I know this metalsmith in Chicago with some pretty remarkable skills."

The air trembled around Barquiel, his fury plain to see. He ascended rapidly and smashed through the metal ceiling with ease.

Dread drenched Nikolai in a cold sweat. "He's going after Mae!"

He sprinted toward a staircase leading to the upper levels.

Dickson cursed and followed. "Wait up!"

A shape overtook them from above, casting a long shadow on the ground. Nikolai stumbled and almost fell.

Calvarro transformed as she soared up the stairs, her clothes morphing into a raven-black cloak that covered her head and fell well past her feet, the hand holding the scythe shifting to bare bones where it peeked out from beneath a sleeve.

"What—what is she?!" Nikolai stammered.

Dickson made a face. "She's a pain in my ass, is what she is." He sighed ruefully. "Her name is Thod."

"Thod?" Nikolai repeated, confused.

"The Queen of Soul Reapers." Dickson shrugged, as if he'd just commented on the weather. "Let's just say she has a bone to pick with Barquiel." He paused. "No pun intended."

"Right," Nikolai mumbled weakly.

Mae's magic detonated somewhere above them.

Nikolai's heartbeat quickened. They darted after Calvarro.

CHAPTER FORTY-FOUR

Mae spun, Hellreaver snarling in her hands and Brimstone roaring above her as they deflected the blows and spell bombs raining down on them with brute force and magic. The Dark Council had intensified their attacks once she'd gotten to the third floor, scores of sorcerers and witches appearing from the shadows to fight alongside the demons.

Oscar was still downstairs from what she sensed of his magic. As for Barquiel, it was hard to tell his location with the corruption filling the air.

Claws streaked toward her face. Mae ducked, came up underneath a giant demon's swinging arm, and pierced the base of his skull with Hellreaver. The weapon hummed ferociously as he guzzled the black liquid pouring down his blades.

Mae yanked him out and made a face while she deflected a magic attack and another demon's fist.

What? Hellreaver said defensively when he sensed her stare.

"That was kinda gross."

Movement flickered to her left. She shot up and narrowly missed another barrage of spell bombs. Brimstone grabbed hold of the sorcerers and witches with his jaws and hurled them unceremoniously into a pile of disused machinery.

A shout reached her. "Mae! Look out!"

She whirled around, heart pounding. Nikolai had appeared from the stairs to the south. Her breath locked in her throat when she saw the figures with him.

What the—!

Cognizance resonated through her from Brimstone. The fox seemed to recognize the cloaked, skeletal being with the crimson pupils and giant scythe streaking silently above the crowd of Dark Council members and demons.

That is the true form of Alicia Calvarro.

"What?!" Mae mumbled.

She is Thod, the Queen of the Soul Reapers and a close ally of the Goddess Astarte.

"*You are mine, Barquiel!*" the reaper roared, empty sockets flaring as she scowled at something past Mae's shoulder.

Mae twisted, alarmed. The pressure inside the building plummeted, making her ears throb and her teeth ache.

Rose emerged from a pool of shadows at the north end of the floor.

The demon inhabiting her body met Mae's uneasy stare, smiled, and cast a globe of pure-black lightning directly above her.

Mae's stomach lurched.

It was where the locker room was located on the fourth story.

"*No!*" she roared, her wrath making the air tremble.

The demon's spell bomb wavered for a fraction of a second under her magic before it detonated against the ceiling.

It was all the time Mae needed. Power bloomed inside her. She raised her hands and flexed her fingers, reinforcing the barrier she had erected just as the floor of the locker room collapsed.

Ryu and Ye-Seul appeared inside a crimson, see-through bubble floating in mid-air. Her sister blinked slowly. Her mouth fell open when she saw the battlefield below, the color draining from her face.

Relief made Mae dizzy. She moved the protective globe rapidly across the floor and up.

"Er, Mae?!" Ryu shouted as she and Ye-Seul drifted toward the breach in the roof of the factory, her panicked voice traveling faintly through the shield.

"You'll be safe up there!" Mae waited until they were out of harm's way before advancing toward Barquiel, her brow furrowing with anger. "Now, how about you and I have a little—"

The hairs rose on her flesh. She rocked to a halt, an eerie premonition flitting through her subconscious. Horror froze her body when she recognized the feeling dancing through her mind. Her gaze locked on Brimstone and Hellreaver a second before the binding ritual brought them to their knees.

FEAR GRIPPED NIKOLAI'S HEART IN ICY CLUTCHES AS HE watched Mae, Brimstone, and Hellreaver drop to the ground, the three of them surrounded by an enormous column of black magic. The fox's giant form wavered before shrinking back to his smaller shape.

A circle had appeared on the floor beneath them, the complex arrangement of lines and runes throbbing with evil energy as it entrapped them.

Oscar emerged from the shadows next to Barquiel, the final incantation of the spell falling from his lips. A vicious smile stretched his mouth.

"Shit!" Calvarro landed beside Nikolai, the reaper queen assuming her human form once more.

Dickson rocked to a halt beside them, his blade dripping with demon blood and a scowl on his face. Vlad appeared at the far end of the chamber, Violet, Miles, and their familiars at his side. They regrouped in the middle of the floor and soon found themselves surrounded by their enemy, their defense barely keeping them at bay.

Nikolai scanned the section of sky visible through the roof as he swooped beneath a demon's claws. Relief made him dizzy.

Ryu and Ye-Seul were safe in the bubble of Mae's making.

Thank God!

"She's isolated them with magic that won't waver even if she were to lose consciousness," Vlad said in a hard voice.

Calvarro pursed her lips. "That's pretty incredible."

Nikolai's resolved hardened. He knew what he had to do.

"Shield us!" he ordered Violet and Miles.

A muscle jumped in Violet's cheek. "You're going to undo the binding ritual like you did at the cemetery?"

"Something like that."

Miles frowned, his worried gaze shifting to the ensnared Witch Queen and her companions. "Don't you need to be next to Mae to do it?"

"No. Not for this."

The cousins glanced at each other curiously before erecting a barrier around them. Dickson stabbed his sword into the edge of their shield, the power inside his blade lending strength to the shimmering wall. The Dark Council's spell bombs landed harmlessly against the barricade, as did the attacks of the demons who wished to claw out their hearts. The New York coven emerged from the lower floors and engaged the enemy, the *Black Devils* keeping *Oniks* busy elsewhere in the building.

Nikolai's pulse thrummed as he lowered himself to one knee. He pressed his hands to the floor and brought forth his magic, his jaw aching with tension.

There was no time to draw the runes he'd come up with to counter his father's spell. He would have to follow his instincts and pray that they were right.

Vlad swore. "*Mae!*"

The incubus banged his hands against the wall protecting them, enraged. Nikolai followed his crimson gaze. His heart stuttered.

Rose stood inside the black magic circle. Her hands had punched through Mae's chest and belly. Crimson stained her clawed fingers as she twisted them.

Mae raised her face to the sky and roared, red lines spreading across her flesh as her magic tried to break free. Brimstone bellowed and Hellreaver shrieked where they remained frozen beside her, their rage shivering scarlet around them.

"Submit!" the devil growled.

Mae's head slowly tilted down. Sweat beaded her forehead as she glowered at the demon. *Never!*

"Hurry!" Vlad glared at Nikolai over his shoulder. "What are you waiting for, dammit?!"

"Let me out," Calvarro said coldly. "I'm going to buy you both some time."

The Queen of Soul Reapers shifted into her true form.

Violet and Miles gasped. It was their first time seeing the skeletal figure.

Vlad stared. "I'll clear a path for you."

The reaper nodded. Dickson sliced a temporary breach in the shield. She stepped through it, the incubus and his familiar at her side.

Nikolai took a shuddering breath and closed his eyes, shutting out the torturous image of Mae in the grip of the Sorcerer King's spell. The world faded around him as he focused, Alastair's powers a bright light that melded with his soul.

Magic shot out through his fingers, white lines that sliced through the metal beneath them and darted straight down the steel framework into the ground.

It took him almost a minute to find a ley line under New York. He followed the branch to its source, grasped the pulsing core of power at its heart, and guided it straight back into the building.

CHAPTER FORTY-FIVE

MAE'S HEART THUDDED PAINFULLY IN THE GRASP OF THE demon who held it.

Barquiel's claws scraped futilely against the organ, frustration glinting in his red pupils. However much he tried to pierce Mae's heart, something fought back.

Crimson flashed at the edge of Mae's vision.

She turned her head a fraction.

Magic danced violently on Vlad's black-diamond blades as he carved through the wall of Dark Council acolytes and demons separating him from the binding circle, his face soaked with the blood of the fallen. Calvarro helped, her weapon singing through the air in polished swings that always found their target.

The devil scowled when the soul reaper queen reached the column of black magic and cut through the barrier with her curved blade. He ripped his hand from Mae's belly and grasped the scythe's handle before it could strike his neck, his grip made slick by blood.

Oscar roared and stabbed his sword into Calvarro.

Metal clinked against bone underneath the reaper's cloak.

Calvarro narrowed her orbits. "I'm a skeleton, you fool!"

She kicked Oscar violently in the chest.

Mae's vision flickered as the sorcerer went sailing across the chamber and crashed into a demon. The battle her suppressed magic was waging against Barquiel and the Sorcerer King was starting to take its toll on her body.

Hang on, my bond! Hellreaver shouted, his tone full of agony.

Brimstone's paw pressed against her leg. He'd managed to shift an inch toward her. His magic seeped into her flesh, warming her cold veins.

Whiteness exploded beneath them. Mae gasped, heat filling her in a powerful flash that rocked her senses.

This is—!

Her gaze found Nikolai, her head moving freely for the first time in minutes. His eyes flared with blinding brilliance where he crouched on the floor, brow knitted in a scowl and pulses of dazzling magic passing through his hands and his familiar to reach the binding circle.

The Sorcerer King's spell fractured under the white-magic attack.

Mae ripped Rose's hand from her chest, grabbed Hellreaver as he shot up into her palm, and stabbed the curved blade toward the demon's belly.

Rock-like scales bloomed on Rose's skin, blocking the weapon's attack.

Hellreaver bared his teeth, metal vibrating with rage. Crimson exploded around Brimstone, the fox's body quivering with violent magic as he augmented Mae and Hellreaver's powers.

The blade pierced the demon.

Barquiel froze, pupils flaring with shock. The reaper's scythe broke free from his hold and carved a deep gash across his chest, Mae and Hellreaver's magic having weakened the black plates. The demon looked down jerkily at his wounds, disbelief rounding his eyes. He scowled, lifted his face to the sky, and roared in fury.

Black lightning detonated around him.

Mae and Calvarro jumped free from the tainted bubble that shielded the demon. Hellish energy started to build up inside the building

"That explosion will rip the city apart!" the reaper warned.

"Shit!" Mae turned to Vlad and Nikolai, her heart slamming against her ribs. "Get everyone out of here!"

They stared at her, confused.

Mae gritted her teeth. *Dammit! I don't have time to explain!*

"Brim!"

Yes?

"We need to move everybody out of this building! Now!"

Brimstone's eyes flashed with fire when he caught her intent. Heat flared inside her, her soul brightening with overwhelming magic once more. Mae opened her mouth and barked out the spell birthed from her consciousness.

"Levitate!"

Startled cries erupted around them as everyone who was alive or wounded found themselves inside a bubble of crimson magic. Vlad and Nikolai shouted angrily when they realized her intent, muffled thuds sounding where they banged on the barrier holding them prisoner. Tarang spun helplessly where he floated beside them, Alastair flying around the tiger.

Mae ignored their protests and swiftly guided the spheres to a safe distance outside the factory.

"What do you intend to do?" Calvarro asked, her red gaze still locked on the enraged demon before them.

The reaper was the only one who had escaped her magic.

Mae ground her teeth. "Watch!"

She shot up through the hole in the ceiling Barquiel had created, Brimstone on her shoulder and Hellreaver in her grip. Calvarro followed her as she flew out of the factory.

They rocked to a halt some hundred feet above the abandoned building.

"Mae?!" Ryu shouted from where she and Ye-Seul still hovered inside a bubble of magic to their right. "What's going on?" She pointed at Calvarro. *"And what the heck is that beside you?!"*

Mae looked over at them. Ye-Seul had woken up and was watching her with a serene expression.

The older woman smiled gently. "It's going be okay, Mae."

Mae's heart clenched. She nodded and took a shaky breath. Magic flared inside her, heat blossoming from her soul and filling her veins. She reached for it and invoked the spell.

"Eclipse."

The black orb that burst into life above her was more controlled than the one she'd unleashed the night of the attack on Grandview General. It resisted for a moment before expanding at the rate she willed upon it, the currents' gravitational pull sparing the people she wished to protect.

The factory started to disintegrate beneath them, rusted metal warping and fracturing. Chunks of machinery and walls rose, some as large as cars. They sped up as they ascended into the swirling vortex and disappeared with faint whooshes.

Barquiel became visible far below, the demon still in the grip of his rage, his power making the air throb with violence. The explosion he wished to unleash had halted some dozen feet from him, momentum frozen by Mae's spell. He roared as he was dragged inexorably toward the black hole. Oscar cursed beneath him, the sorcerer losing his hold on the metal pipe he'd been clinging to.

"No!" Calvarro barked.

She dove, scythe glinting under the starlight.

Mae's eyes widened.

A portal had appeared next to Barquiel. The demon reached out, yanked Oscar toward him, and darted into the scarlet-tinged doorway, his hateful eyes on Mae and Calvarro as he vanished. The portal closed behind them.

The rest of the factory was sucked into the vortex, metal screeching and concrete crumbling until there was nothing left but dirt and a gaping void where its foundation had once been.

Mae ended the spell, blood pounding heavily in her ears.

A deafening lull fell on the pier.

Brimstone leapt into her arms as she drifted to the ground, his head butting her chest with affection and relief. Mae hugged him and Hellreaver tightly.

"I am so glad you are mine," she whispered tremulously.

As are we, Hellreaver hummed.

Brimstone's eyes flashed crimson. *Yes.*

The spheres she'd created to protect the others disintegrated when they touched down a moment later, releasing everyone except their foe. To Mae's surprise, the *Black Devils* seemed to take what had just happened in their stride. They started carting away the surviving *Oniks* members, their guarded gazes flitting to Mae from time to time. The New York coven regrouped and did the same to the fallen Dark Council sorcerers and witches, as well as the humans possessed by demons.

Mae studied them with an anxious frown.

I hope we can save the ones who got taken over against their will.

Calvarro alighted beside her. "There is a way."

Mae turned to the reaper, unsurprised she'd read her mind.

Calvarro shrank back to her human form, scythe transforming into a medallion of the same shape that hung from her neck. She tucked it inside her shirt.

"It is hard, but not impossible to return those humans to normal. It requires powerful white magic."

They looked over to where Nikolai, Vlad, and the others were hurrying toward them.

"*His* white magic," Calvarro confirmed as Mae stared at Nikolai. The reaper queen met her gaze, her brow furrowing. "This battle may be over, but the war isn't."

"I know." Mae clenched her jaw. "And I'll be ready, next time."

Calvarro appraised her for a moment. A faint smile curved her mouth. "You are your father's daughter."

Mae's belly fluttered. "You know Azazel?!"

"Of course." Calvarro shrugged. "He is the most skilled magic wielder in all the Heavens and in Hell." She faltered. "I must admit, I have not seen him for eons. Rumor is he has lost his mind to grief and is wandering aimlessly in the deepest parts of Hell."

Mae fisted her hands, pain a heavy weight in her chest for the father she had yet to meet.

"Are you okay?" Nikolai asked anxiously as he joined them.

"Yeah."

The injuries to her body were already healing, another thing that hardly surprised her.

"That was quite a show." Vlad squinted. "Except for

the part where you trapped us." The incubus's face relaxed into a slow, sexy smile. He rubbed his chin, crimson flashing in his pupils. "Although, I gotta say, I quite liked being restrained by you."

Heat flooded Mae's cheeks. Nikolai scowled.

Dickson studied Mae's closing wounds curiously. "It seems Azazel's blood has gifted you with the powers of the angels."

Mae looked at him blankly. "What do you mean?" She made a face. "And also, what's with the sword and that golden light?"

Dickson dragged the sharp edge of his blade across his wrist.

"What the—?" Nikolai gasped. "Are you crazy?!"

The bleeding stopped and the cut sealed itself as they watched.

Mae's pulse quickened.

Dickson's sword retracted into a switchblade. He tucked it into a sheath at his ankle.

"Who the heck are you?" Mae mumbled.

"I'm an Immortal."

The only ones who didn't look in the least bit shocked by Dickson's statement were Calvarro, Violet, and Miles.

He is of the bloodline of Uriel.

Mae looked down at Brimstone. "Uriel? As in, the archangel?!"

Yes. Brimstone made a face. *Though, technically, that title belongs to Michael.*

That archangel is a cretin, Hellreaver declared firmly. *At least Uriel has pizzazz.*

Brimstone sniffed. *I still think Azazel is the best out of the lot of them.*

True, Hellreaver concurred. *Our master has skills* and *looks.*

A distant banging reached their ears. They looked up.

"Can someone please get us the hell out of here?!" Ryu yelled from the floating sphere high above.

CHAPTER FORTY-SIX

Mae entered the kitchen and rocked to a halt.

Yoo-Mi was making tea at the counter. "Want some?"

Mae grimaced. *That woman has eyes in the back of her head.*

Brimstone spoke. *She sure does.*

"Yes, thank you," Mae murmured.

She padded barefoot into the room, Brimstone at her side.

Ye-Seul had been discharged from Grandview General sometime around midnight. To Mae's relief, the CT scan had shown no evidence of skull fractures and the neurosurgeon who'd seen her had declared her fit as a fiddle bar a mild concussion. Mae decided to spend the night at the family home, partly to talk to Yoo-Mi, but mainly to be with the people she loved the most in this world.

Yoo-Mi placed a cup of green tea in front of Mae as she sat at the table. "I made *Hoeddeok* for breakfast."

Mae eyed the trays of cinnamon, honey, and peanut filled pancakes keeping warm in the oven. *Hoeddeok* was her and Ryu's favorite.

Yoo-Mi looked down at Brimstone. "I bet you'd like some meat?"

Brimstone huffed, jaws splitting in a grin as he swept the floor with his bushy tail. Mae's mother had insisted on meeting the familiar and Hellreaver once she learned of their existence. To Mae's everlasting surprise, Yoo-Mi had taken everything she'd told her in her stride, from the attack on Grandview General to Ryu and Ye-Seul's rescue. The fact that Mae was the reincarnation of the child of a witch and a demon never fazed her.

"You're my daughter and always will be," she'd said quietly to Mae last night. "So, no more secrets, okay?"

Mae had nodded tremulously, her vision blurring and her heart light with relief. "No more secrets."

They'd hugged for a long time, Mae's tears soaking into Yoo-Mi's shoulder. The way her mother had trembled had told her she wasn't as unaffected as she was pretending to be.

Yoo-Mi went over to the refrigerator, took some fresh beef steaks out, and laid them on a couple of plates on the table.

"Up you come," she told the fox.

Brimstone glanced warily at Mae before leaping onto the chair beside her. He nibbled delicately on his steak, careful not to make a mess of the tablecloth.

Yoo-Mi eyed Hellreaver. "The second plate is for you."

The medallion hummed hesitantly before transforming and dropping gently to the table. He hoovered his meat up in a single gulp, swallowed happily, and fell silent, as meek as a mouse.

"Wow," Mae told Yoo-Mi. "You gotta teach me how to do that."

Brimstone and Hellreaver looked at her innocently.

Yoo-Mi chewed her lip. "You should get a tenant for that spare room. You're gonna need the extra rent to feed these two."

Mae was about to protest when a voice came behind her.

"Well, this sure warms the heart," someone drawled.

Mae spun around in the chair.

Vlad smiled at her from the doorway.

She ignored the alluring way his shirt stretched across his chest and turned to Yoo-Mi. "He spent the night?!"

Yoo-Mi flushed. "Well, he asked so prettily. I put him in the spare room with the other guy."

Mae narrowed her eyes at Vlad. "Did you use your incubus powers on my mom?"

Vlad's smile widened. Nikolai appeared behind him, Violet and Miles in his wake.

"What's going on?" Miles said sleepily.

Mae gaped at Yoo-Mi. "*Everyone* stayed?!"

Her mother's mouth flattened to a thin line. "They are your friends, Mae," she grumbled. "You should welcome them into our home with grace."

"Yeah, Mae," Ryu said breezily as she entered the kitchen. "They are your *friends*."

She glanced at Vlad and Nikolai and waggled her eyebrows at Mae.

"Have you got a tic?" Yoo-Mi asked suspiciously.

Violet bit her lip.

Breakfast was a noisy affair, Ye-Seul joining them halfway through. Mae was pleased to see her grandmother looking her normal self, having apparently fully recovered from yesterday's traumatic experience. Tarang was banished to the living room with the other familiars when his sweeping tail broke Yoo-Mi's favorite teapot. Vlad called someone and had pastries from the best Italian bakery in town delivered to their door by a pair of dangerous-looking men in suits and sunglasses.

It was almost noon by the time Mae leaned back in her chair and rubbed her full belly.

"I am stuffed," she groaned.

Vlad studied her with a thoughtful air. "You sure have a good appetite." His eyes gleamed. "I hope that extends to activities outside the kitchen."

Ryu's elbow slipped off the table. She grabbed a napkin and dabbed at the tea she'd spilled down her T-shirt.

"Does *everything* you say have to be sexual?" Nikolai snapped.

Vlad shrugged. "I'm an incubus. It comes with the territory."

Ye-Seul observed the two men shrewdly before leaning conspiratorially toward Mae.

"So, who's got the bigger ding dong?" she said in a stage whisper that was probably heard in Jersey.

Miles choked on his drink. Violet slapped him on the back and rolled her eyes hard. Ryu buttered a croissant with avid concentration.

Nikolai and Vlad's stares pierced Mae. She flushed and glanced at where Yoo-Mi was loading the dishwasher.

"*I don't know!*" Mae whispered furiously. "And FYI, there will be no viewing or handling of any ding dongs, now or in the foreseeable future!"

Vlad arched an eyebrow. "I do love a challenge."

Nikolai frowned at the incubus.

"You should get rid of Bob," Ryu murmured to Mae. "I feel he's gonna be redundant soon."

"Bob is dead."

Ryu stared. "Wow. You fried his batteries?"

"He had an unfortunate accident involving a car."

Mae became aware of Vlad's sharp-witted stare. She bit her lip.

A knock came at the front door.

Mae shot up from her chair. "I'll get it."

The incubus smiled knowingly as she rushed out of the kitchen.

Mae patted her flushed cheeks and crossed the foyer. She looked through the peephole, tensed, and opened the door with a frown. "What do you guys want?"

Calvarro smiled. "Good morning, sunshine."

Dickson arched an eyebrow, his expression hurt. "Can't a friend drop by for a coffee?" The detective looked past Mae and sniffed the air. "Besides, one of my informants told me he spotted a couple of *Black*

Devils dropping off a boxful of *Vetriano's* breakfast pastries at your address. There's a waiting list for those things."

"He has a weakness for their cinnamon roll," Calvarro explained at Mae's blank look.

A Lincoln and three SUVs pulled up behind Dickson and Calvarro's Chevy. Abraham got out and opened the rear door of the town car. Bryony emerged from the vehicle, looking regal in her custom-tailored outfit.

Mae chewed her lip and eyed the curtains twitching along the street. "Shit. This is going to be all over Mrs. Son-Ha's network and Koreatown by nightfall."

Dickson stared. "Who's Mrs. Son-Ha?"

"Just shut up and get inside." Mae motioned to Bryony and Abraham. "You two, in, *now!*"

Everyone crowded inside the hallway.

Yoo-Mi popped her head out of the kitchen. Her eyebrows rose. "Oh. We have extra guests. Should I make more tea?"

"No," Mae said darkly. "They won't be long."

"Tea would be lovely," Bryony said graciously.

Dickson perked up. "I would love a cinnamon roll with mine."

"I'm afraid we're all out of cinnamon rolls. Miles just had the last one."

Dickson deflated.

"But we still have some *Hoeddeok* left," Yoo-Mi proposed.

"It has cinnamon in it," Mae told Dickson.

He brightened. She ushered them into the living

room and bumped into Calvarro when the reaper stopped abruptly.

"What happened in here?"

"What do you—?" Mae started, looking past her.

She stopped and sucked in air.

Tarang and Brimstone froze guiltily where they'd been playfighting on a sofa, cushion filling drifting lazily around them. An equally sheepish Trixie, Millie, and Alastair observed her innocently from where they'd frozen in their mad dash all over the furniture, knocking over knick-knacks and family photos.

The only one who was behaving was Hellreaver, who lay on the coffee table. A snore rumbled from the weapon.

"Why you little—!" Mae turned to Abraham, her jaw tight. "Help me fix this place before my mom gets here!"

The aide bristled. "You want me to use my magic to—"

"I swear to God, I will hex you if you don't!" Mae snapped.

By the time Yoo-Mi brought in a tray of drinks and pastries, the living room was back to normal.

She paused and looked at Mae. "Are you okay? You look a bit flushed."

Mae blew a strand of stray hair off her face. "I'm fine."

Nikolai, Vlad, and the Nolan cousins wandered in.

Yoo-Mi paused on her way out of the room. She frowned, adjusted a picture frame on the sideboard, and headed back to the kitchen.

Mae waited until she was out of hearing before turning on her uninvited guests. "What do you want?"

"Oscar and Barquiel have been sighted in Budapest," Bryony said without preamble. "They are back at the Dark Council headquarters."

A tense hush befell them. Mae frowned.

"We have some news too," Dickson said. "Your tip-off about the pineal gland was dead on the money."

"We sent some samples from the demons we killed last night to our lab in Quantico," Calvarro explained at Mae's puzzled look. "The preliminary results came in an hour ago. They found some kind of hormone inside them. They haven't been able to identify what it is yet."

Nikolai's eyebrows drew together. He rubbed his jaw. "That must be what makes possessed humans like Antonovich and Sobol so powerful."

Vlad dipped his head curtly. "Perfect for an army."

"Now that *Oniks* is out of the picture, are you intending to stick around?" Dickson asked Vlad.

Mae's stomach lurched. She hadn't even considered that Vlad would walk out of her life after solving the problem he'd approached them for.

The incubus met her stiff gaze. "Yes. I'm going to stick around. After all, Mae is my queen too."

His meaning was not lost on the room. Heat flooded her cheeks.

Nikolai looked like he was contemplating murder.

Bryony cleared her throat discreetly and observed Calvarro and Dickson. "Isn't it about time you told us what you're doing in New York?"

Dickson rubbed the back of his head and sighed ruefully. "I work for the Immortal Societies. I'm their liaison with the Special Affairs Bureau."

Mae raised an eyebrow. "What's that?"

"It's a branch of the U.S. government that deals with Immortals and magic users." Dickson met Bryony's gaze steadily. "We think one of our people is helping the Sorcerer King and the Dark Council."

Bryony's lips flattened to a thin line.

"Helping?" Nikolai repeated. "Helping how?"

"By melding science, alchemy, and demonic power into something else. Something more devastating than anything we've seen before."

Mae's scalp prickled at the Immortal's words.

"*Oniks* was just a steppingstone for the Dark Council," Calvarro said. "The army the Sorcerer King is looking to build will be made of more than just insignificant criminals." She glanced apologetically at Vlad. "No offense."

"None taken," the incubus drawled.

Bryony frowned at Dickson. "And your sword? Violet tells me it contains divine energy. Was it forged by the man I'm thinking of? The idiot with the rabbit?"

Dickson winced. "Yes. It's a new prototype."

"What idiot with the rabbit?" Mae said blankly.

"I'm sure your paths will cross one day soon," Bryony replied evasively. She turned to Calvarro, her expression sharpening. "And what of your role in all of this?" She glanced at Abraham. "My aide tells me you are some kind of—" she waved a vague hand, "soul reaper."

"She's not just any soul reaper," Dickson said. "She's their queen."

Bryony's jaw tightened. Abraham paled.

"Barquiel killed Sruk, the King of the Soul Reapers," Calvarro said slowly. "When Astarte told me of her adventures with Michael and Samyaza's spawn and the divine beasts allied with those children, it gave me hope that Barquiel could actually be hiding on Earth, as I had found no whiff of the foul fiend during my search of Hell. When we discovered that demons were going missing from the Underworld, the alliance Astarte heads assigned me the task of finding out why. They feared it was Satanael's machinations at first, but it seems they were wrong." The reaper's eyes flared crimson. "My mission has brought me face to face with the one who murdered my husband, and I, for one, am glad of this."

Bryony stayed silent for a moment.

She lowered her brows at Nikolai. "The binding ritual your father taught Oscar. How did you break it last night? From what I've heard, you didn't use any magic circles."

A muscle jumped in Nikolai's jawline. He glanced at Mae and Vlad.

The incubus shrugged. "They're gonna find out sooner or later."

Mae nodded.

Nikolai blew out a sigh and ran a hand through his hair. "I can use ley lines."

His bombshell statement echoed in a shocked silence.

"What?!" Abraham mumbled.

"Is that, like, a *super* skill or something?" Dickson hissed to Calvarro out the corner of his mouth.

"A bit." The reaper appraised the sorcerer with fresh eyes. "It's been centuries since anyone has been able to tap into them on Earth."

Bryony stared unblinkingly at Nikolai. "Is that how you performed—?"

"*The Aura of the Moon?*" He dipped his chin. "Yes."

"If word of this gets out, not only will the Dark Council chase you to the ends of this Earth to get their hands on you, every other magic council will want your blood too," Bryony said stiffly.

Mae's pulse quickened. "You mean, they'd want to kill Nikolai?"

"No," Bryony said somberly. "They'd want to put a leash on him."

Nikolai clenched his teeth.

Mae narrowed her eyes. "Are ley lines that powerful?"

"Ley lines contain the magic steeped into the very

Earth," Bryony explained. "They are the biggest source of power you can imagine."

An expression that almost looked like pity flashed in her eyes as she regarded Nikolai.

Realization dawned. Mae met Nikolai's gaze, anger surging through her blood. "That's why they want to capture you and not kill you! Your father must know of your potential."

"It would explain why he kept your mother and you close for all those years, despite your inability to wield black magic," Bryony pondered.

The horrified look that darkened Nikolai's eyes had Mae reaching for his hand. "Don't. You can't blame yourself for your mother's death. It was Oscar and the Sorcerer King who killed her, not you."

Nikolai's fingers trembled under her touch.

"Thank you," he mumbled.

CHAPTER FORTY-EIGHT

A STILTED HUSH FILLED THE ROOM.

"What do we do now?" Mae finally said.

"We wait." A tired sigh left Bryony. "I'm sure the other councils will be in touch with me imminently. We need to come up with a plan as to how to deal with the Sorcerer King now that our Queen has been resurrected."

Everyone looked at Mae, Bryony's face almost funereal.

Mae pursed her lips. "As long as they don't poke and prod me, I'll talk to them."

Bryony beamed, her exhaustion seemingly vanishing like mist.

Mae furrowed her brow. *She got me, dammit.*

A man with a mop of brown hair and blue eyes appeared in the doorway.

"My team and I are in position," he told Bryony. "We've secured the properties adjoining this one as well as the house across the road."

Mae blinked slowly. "Huh?"

"Oh." Bryony's expression turned guilty. "I should have asked you first, but I thought you'd approve. In view of what happened to your sister and your grandmother yesterday, I decided to assign a security team to guard your family twenty-four-seven. We bought out your neighbors." She indicated the man with the brown hair. "This is Noah Tegner. He's my nephew and a powerful sorcerer. He'll be your protection team lead for the foreseeable future."

Noah dipped his chin respectfully at Mae.

Mae's head spun. She dimly recalled seeing moving vans on the street when they'd come home last night.

Noah grimaced when he saw her expression. "I'm sorry, I hope you weren't close to your neighbors."

"Not particularly." Mae chewed her lip. It seemed the New York coven were determined to do whatever it took to make her happy. And she could not deny her relief at knowing her family would be protected from now on. "My mom and my grandma did like to play Mahjong with the old couple across the road."

Noah pressed his earpiece. "Anyone know how to play Mahjong?" There was a pause. "Good. Ask Joe to buy some Mahjong sets. We start training tonight."

Everyone left a while later, Dickson taking some leftover *Hoeddeok* home. It was late by the time Mae returned to her apartment with Brimstone and Hellreaver. She closed the door, dropped her keys in the tray on the console table, and shrugged out of her jacket. The silence felt loud when she stopped in the middle of the living room.

With the current situation resolved and the Dark Council regrouping in Europe, there was no need for the others to stay over anymore.

"Has it always been this quiet?" she mumbled.

A knock came at the entrance. Mae stiffened.

Brimstone spoke. *It is not an enemy.*

She retraced her steps to the hallway and opened the front door warily.

Nikolai stood on the landing, a rucksack on his shoulder and an enigmatic expression on his face. "Your mom said you needed a tenant."

He walked past her without giving her a chance to utter a word. Alastair greeted Brimstone and Hellreaver with a flutter of his wings.

Mae frowned and slowly closed the door. "I don't do tenants."

Nikolai stopped and dropped his bag on the floor. "Why don't we try it for a couple of months?" His gaze found Brimstone and Hellreaver. "I hear a pound of ribeye steak is going for almost twenty-five dollars these days."

Mae pursed her lips. She headed over to the refrigerator, grabbed a bottle of beer, and lobbed another one at Nikolai. "I thought Bryony was gonna offer you a place to stay, what with you helping the New York coven and all."

Bryony's solution to Nikolai's problem of what he should do now that he had parted ways with his father and the Dark Council had been to offer him an advisory position in her coven while awaiting further discussions with the other councils. The fact that he was the only sorcerer they knew of who could use ley lines meant the job came with a generous salary and perks.

Nikolai sighed and rubbed the back of his neck awkwardly. "She did offer me an apartment. And a car."

Mae stared. "So, why are you here?"

"They were too—" Nikolai grimaced and waved a vague hand, "modern and glamorous."

Mae clamped down on the smile tugging at her lips. "So, you're saying you like old things?"

Nikolai scowled and folded his arms across his chest. "There was a glass fountain in the lobby of the building. That's just an accident waiting to happen."

"One month."

He blinked rapidly. "What?"

Mae put out her hand. "Let's try it for one month."

Nikolai hesitated before shaking hands. Mae ignored the way his touch scorched her skin and showed him where he could put his things. They finished their beers and turned in not long after.

Despite the exhaustion she still felt after yesterday's battle, sleep eluded her. Mae finally sighed, got out of bed, and pulled up the sash window overlooking the fire escape. Brimstone opened a lazy eye.

"It's okay," she murmured. "Go to sleep."

The fox snuggled deeper into the spot he'd claimed at the foot of the bed.

Mae climbed out and headed to the roof garden, the metal steps cool beneath her bare feet. She leaned against the railing at the top and gazed out over New

York. An orange haze hung over Manhattan, the colorful high-rises blotting out the horizon.

Mae looked up at the distant stars and closed her eyes. She hadn't told anyone about what she'd felt when she'd stabbed Barquiel with Hellreaver. About the faint life force she'd detected deep within the demon. At first, she'd thought it was her imagination running wild in the heat of battle. But the more she re-examined the moment, the more convinced she became that what she'd sensed was not a lie.

There was something of Rose left deep within the monster who now possessed her body.

Soft footsteps sounded behind Mae. She opened her eyes and turned, already guessing who her late night visitor was. Vlad crossed the narrow garden toward her, his face cast in shadows and his white suit gleaming ghostly pale in the gloom.

Mae looked past him curiously. "Where's Tarang?"

"Probably the same place the fox is. At the bottom of my bed."

He stopped in front of her, so close they were almost touching.

Mae tilted her head and shivered. The incubus's body heat swirled around her, as seductive as the expression in his red eyes.

"Why are you here?" she whispered.

"To do this."

Vlad gently cradled her face in his hands and pressed his lips to hers.

It was a kiss she never knew she needed. One that was hot and dangerous and sweet. It was as different to the one she'd shared with Nikolai as night was from day and it left her torn.

Vlad's gaze bore into hers when he lifted his mouth off hers. "I will make a better consort than him."

He turned and vanished into the night, leaving her heart vacillating between a light that would burn her and a darkness that would consume her whole.

THE END

Mae, Brimstone, and Hellreaver's adventures continue in Rites of Passage.

ACKNOWLEDGMENTS

To my friends and family. I couldn't do this without you.

To you, my readers. Thank you for reading The Darkest Night. If you enjoyed my book, please consider leaving a review on Goodreads or on the store where you purchased it. Reviews help readers like you find my books and I truly appreciate your honest opinions about my stories.

Make sure to sign up to my store newsletter for special deals on my books and new release alerts. Or you can sign up to my author newsletter to get upcoming release notifications, sneak peeks, and giveaways.

BOOKS BY A.D. STARRLING

Seventeen Novels

Hunted

Warrior

Empire

Legacy

Origins

Destiny

Seventeen Short Stories

First Death

Dancing Blades

The Meeting

The Warrior Monk

The Hunger

The Bank Job

Legion

Blood and Bones

Fire and Earth

Awakening

Forsaken

Hallowed Ground

Heir

Legion

Witch Queen

The Darkest Night

Rites of Passage

Of Flames and Crows

Midnight Witch

A Fury of Shadows

Witch Queen

Division Eight

Mission:Black

Mission: Armor

Mission:Anaconda

Miscellaneous

Void - A Sci-fi Horror Short Story

The Other Side of the Wall - A Horror Short Story

ABOUT A.D. STARRLING

Visit Shop AD Starrling and buy all of AD's ebooks, paperbacks, hardbacks, audiobooks, and exclusive special edition print books direct.

Want to know about AD Starrling's upcoming releases? Sign up to her author newsletter for new release alerts, sneak peeks, giveaways, and more.

Follow AD Starrling on Amazon.

Join AD's reader group on Facebook
The Seventeen Club.

Check out this link to find out more about A.D. Starrling
Linktr.ee/AD_Starrling.